PROTECTING

Her

Book One

The Murphy
Brothers

DANICA FLYNN

PROTECTING HER

THE MURPHY BROTHERS
BOOK ONE

DANICA FLYNN

PROTECTING HER

ebook ISBN: 978-1-957494-13-5
Print ISBN: 978-1-957494-14-2
Alternate Paperback: 978-1-957494-19-7

Cover Photography: VitalikRadko/DepositPhotos
Cover Design: Emily's World Of Design
Editor: Charlie Knight

For everyone who needs a little light and a happily ever after in these dark times.

PLAYLIST

"Your Ex-Lover is Dead" By Stars

"Mine Forever" By Lord Huron

"Skinny Love" By Bon Iver

"I CHOOSE YOU" By Adam Melchor

"His Girl Friday" By The Academy Is...

"Your Guardian Angel" By The Red Jumpsuit Apparatus

"Stay Awhile" By She & Him

"Silver Lining" By Rilo Kiley

"Ocean Eyes" By Billie Eilish

"I Didn't See it Coming" By Belle and Sebastian

"Pretending" by HIM

"Safe and Sound" By The Sounds

"Cover Me in Roses" By Holden Laurence

"I Wish I Was the Moon" By Neko Case

"We Found Each Other in the Dark" By City and Color

"Fade Into You" By Mazzy Star

AUTHOR'S NOTE

This book includes a heroine who has suffered with infertility and who has had miscarriages in the past. These are talked about at length in this book. She is also a widow so this book heavily deals with grief.

CHAPTER ONE

KILLIAN

HALLOWEEN

I loved weddings. Not because I was a hopeless romantic or some shit. But because it was the perfect place to find a meaningless hookup I never had to talk to again. Just the way I liked it.

I took a pull off my beer and scanned the converted barn reception area. Half the single women here either wanted to stab me or were related to me. That was the curse of both being a Murphy and hailing from a small town.

Truth be told, I was only invited because the bride, Lila, was my boss at the pub, and her sister was married to my oldest brother, Brian. In a small town like Drakesville, Pennsylvania, that meant you were family. Sorta.

"Stop," Brian berated me as he bounced his baby Callum in his arms.

I lifted my hands up in surrender. I hadn't done anything to make him mad at me. Yet. "What?"

"Stop trolling for women. I think you've slept with every available woman in town."

I winced. Harsh, but he wasn't exactly wrong.

Some might say I had a reputation for loving them and leaving them. I'd say I liked to have a good time, not a long time. Nothing wrong with that. All the women I took to my bed knew the rules. Killian Murphy was good for a few nights, but don't expect anything more. Ever.

"Bro, when are you gonna grow up and settle down?" Brian asked.

I scoffed. "The fifth of never."

He rolled his eyes.

This was a constant battle with me and my boring ol' married brother. I reminded him constantly that just because he was a dad, it didn't mean he was *our* dad. My younger brothers and I already had one of those.

I took another sip of my beer and glanced around the room again. This barn setup was classy. Not the Halloween freak show I thought it would be when Lila gave me the invite to her Halloween wedding. Plus, all the free MacGregor Brothers Brewing Company beer was a nice touch. Not a shock since Lila's new husband co-owned the brewery.

Brian's wife Kelsey walked over to us, with my little nieces hanging off the hem of her dress. I grinned as Cora bounced over to me and chattered away about being the flower girl. She was so stinking cute, and she knew it.

"Uncle Killian?" she asked.

"Yeah, peanut?"

Her eyebrows knitted together. "When you get married, can I be the flower girl?"

Brian hid his laugh with a cough, but Kelsey didn't bother hiding her reaction. She laughed her head off.

Asshole.

I shot her a glare.

"Maybe one day," I told my niece coyly and ruffled her coppery hair.

Kelsey and Brian traded off the kids because the baby was getting fussy and needed to be fed.

Kelsey's mouth dropped open when she glanced toward the entrance. "Oh. Wow. Siobhan made it. I'm surprised."

I jerked my head in the direction she was looking and spied Siobhan O'Connor walking inside the barn. She wore a slinky black dress that accented her slender figure, her perfect rack perky as ever with that plunging neckline. A pair of black 'fuck me' heels on her feet accentuated her long legs, making her tall frame look ethereal.

Yeah, I've noticed Siobhan before. Who hasn't?

Countless times, I've watched from behind the bar at the pub and lost all sense of speech when she bent over to clear off her tables. It was hard not to imagine what else I'd like to bend her over. Or how those legs would feel wrapped around my back.

I never went there with her because I didn't fuck with married women. I wasn't that big of an asshole.

But... that wasn't a problem anymore now that her husband had passed away.

"Good for her," Brian said. "She needs to get out of the house since Doug's death."

The devil on my shoulder whispered in my ear. Siobhan still wasn't over her husband, which meant she wouldn't be looking for anything serious. But she might be looking for someone to help shake off those cobwebs so she could get back on the market.

Target acquired.

I set my beer down and watched Siobhan glide over toward the bar.

"I'll be back," I said to my family.

"Killian Murphy, don't you dare," Kelsey scolded.

I blew her off and got up, striding over to where Siobhan stood reading the handwritten beer menu.

"Hey, Siobhan."

She jumped and put her hand over her chest. "Killian. You scared me half to death."

"Buy you a drink to make up for it?" I offered and gestured to the bartender. He rolled his eyes and grabbed me another 611 Ale.

"You want to buy me a free beer?" A hint of amusement was in her voice, and the corner of her lush mouth turned up into a smile.

She had such a pretty smile, one none of us had seen since her husband's untimely passing last winter.

I gave her a cocky grin. "It's the thought that counts."

She peered at the menu and chewed on her plump bottom lip. I shifted my pants when I imagined the ruby color of her lipstick painting my cock.

Easy boy.

"Can I get The Drake Pumpkin Ale?" she asked the bartender. "I love pumpkin beer."

The bartender grabbed her beer, popping the top before handing her the bottle.

Siobhan nodded her thanks and then turned back to me. Her dark eyebrow raised up when she noticed me staring. "How was the ceremony?"

I shrugged. I had only half-paid attention to it; the reception was more my jam.

She took a gulp of her beer. "I wasn't gonna come."

"Why not?"

She sighed. "It's been hard losing Doug. But it's time."

"Time for what?"

She picked at the label on her beer. "To move on. Stop feeling sorry for myself. Maybe get drunk on the dance floor."

I gave her a wolfish grin. "I can help with that."

She peered at me, studying me for a second, and then she took another large gulp of her beer. "Ask me to dance, Killian."

I sarcastically bowed and held my hand out to her. She laughed, the sound melodic to my ears, and it made the grin on my face grow larger.

"Ms. O'Connor, will you do me the honor of a dance?" I asked in a terrible, fake British accent.

She laughed but took my offered hand.

Oh, I was definitely gonna have fun with her tonight.

I spun her on the dance floor, our bodies pressing together tight. Her hands slid up my dress shirt, sending waves of electricity down my torso. When we locked eyes, there was a heat in her gaze I hadn't expected. Maybe Siobhan was more willing for a night of no-strings than I realized.

"What you thinking, darling?" I purred.

Her eyes glinted with mischief. "I'm wondering if all the rumors are true."

"Hmm. And which ones are those?"

Big lie. I knew my reputation in this town.

"If you're as good in bed as everyone says you are."

A cocky grin tugged against my lips. "Oh, I'm sure I can help you find out."

She gave me a sultry look. "You wanna get out of here?"

"I thought you'd never ask."

I didn't know where I began and she ended. She wrapped her legs around my waist, and I kissed her while I kicked my front door shut behind us. She gripped my hair and opened her mouth to me, letting me take the lead as I slid my tongue inside her greedy little mouth. Oh, I couldn't wait to slide something else inside it.

I pulled away for a moment to stare into her azure eyes.

"Killian," she moaned, as if she was in pain.

The horny animal inside me screamed at me to fuck her against my front door. Screw the walk up to my bedroom, and take her right here and now like she wanted. "What's wrong, darling?"

"I need you to fuck me."

A devilish smile curled up on my lips. "Yeah, you do."

"Now, please."

My inner caveman could wait a few minutes to get what he wanted.

I walked us upstairs toward my bedroom, and once inside, I deposited her at the foot of my bed. I threw off my suit jacket and quickly undid my tie while she leaned back on my bed. Her plush lips parted as she watched me take off my dress shirt.

My body wasn't cut from manual labor like my brother Ronan, nor did I have a husky physique like my brothers Brian or Finn, but it was somewhere in the middle. It had never been a source of complaint from the women I brought to my bed. Probably because they were too busy coming to worry about pointless shit like that.

Before I got to my belt, she pounced. Or rather, she slid

to her knees, shoving my pants and boxer briefs down my legs.

"Fuck me," I groaned when she wrapped her hand around my cock.

She grinned up at me. "Oh, I intend to."

I watched with heated eyes as she licked around the head of my cock before taking it inside her mouth. I couldn't help the guttural moan that came out of me. I reached down and pushed her hair out of her face, bunching it up on top of her head. Watching my dick sliding in and out of her pretty little mouth was a gorgeous sight that I couldn't help but thrust my hips.

I had to think of hockey stats so I didn't come down her throat when she gagged on it. "You can take it."

She nodded, looking up at me through those long eyelashes.

"I bet your pussy will feel just as good, huh?"

She nodded again, taking me as far back as she could, and I bit my lip, trying to hold it all in. If I wasn't balls deep inside her soon, I was going to explode.

I slid a thumb on her bottom lip and gently removed my cock from her mouth.

"Sorry. I'm out of practice," she said.

Out of practice? The fuck? Didn't seem like it to me.

"Up," I ordered.

She did as I commanded, and I spun her around. I brushed her hair off her shoulder and bent to kiss her neck. I fingered the zipper at the top of her dress. "Let's get you out of this."

"Please."

I slid the zipper down, and the material of her dress fell to my floor. She wore a pair of no-nonsense cotton undies and a matching bra. Not sexy see-through lingerie, like I had been expecting, but the simplicity of it turned me on. Like she didn't care who saw it.

She turned around and looked me deep in the eyes while she unhooked her bra and slid her panties down her legs.

"Killian," she whispered.

"Get on the bed."

She did as I asked, and fuck me was she a gorgeous sight naked and waiting for me. I kicked off my pants and boxers and crawled into the bed with her. I stretched out next to her, plunging my hands into her hair when I took her mouth again.

She was so pliable beneath me, pressing up against me as we kissed. I trailed my lips down her mouth, her neck, and then toward the valley of her breasts. She let out a tiny moan when I took one breast into my mouth, swirling my tongue around her nipple. I repeated the motion on the other one and made my way down her body.

"You don't have to," she said when I spread her legs, my face inches from her pussy.

"Yeah, I do. Relax, darling."

On my first lick, she couldn't help the moan she released, and that egged me on. I pressed a hand down against her stomach, holding her to the bed while I ate her to my heart's desire. She squirmed around like she didn't want me to find the spot deep inside her. But then I did, sucking on her clit until she came apart, crying out so loud she probably woke my neighbors.

I lifted my head from between her legs and wiped at my beard. Damn, she tasted good.

She pulled me up toward her and met me in another kiss. She reached down and wrapped a hand around my cock, guiding me toward her entrance.

"Wait," I said, knowing there was something we were forgetting, but my sex-addled brain couldn't focus on what.

"No," she panted. "Need you now. Please."

I should have listened to the voice of reason in the back of my mind. There was definitely something I wasn't thinking about. Something really important. But with her pleading voice and her rubbing the head of my cock on her clit, my brain malfunctioned, and I gave her what she wanted.

We groaned in unison as I entered her.

"You feel good," I said against her neck.

She wrapped her legs around my back and dug her nails into my skin, urging me to press on. Her pussy squeezing me tight told me I wouldn't last that long.

"Please, Killian," she begged.

I cupped her face. "What you need, darling?"

"You. I need you. To fuck me. Hard."

"Then you better come for me."

She nodded, and we moved together in unison, her arching up to meet my every thrust as I took her like the animal I was. I pressed my thumb against her clit, and she came undone once more.

She dug her nails into my back harder as her orgasm coursed through her. "Oh God."

"You don't have to call me God," I teased, but she was too blitzed out to yell at me for the cheesy joke.

I rolled my hips against hers, taking what I needed from her. Our bodies slammed together until I roared out my own release, my cum coming in ropes inside her.

Seconds later, I rolled off her, and the room filled with the sounds of our panting breath.

She spoke first. "God, I really needed that."

I grinned. "Me too."

I leaned over and kissed her. She seemed taken aback at first, but then she clung to me, letting me take her mouth again like she was mine.

Our hands roamed until she straddled my thighs, and my cock poked her again. "Ready for round two?"

She didn't even answer me. She silently took my cock and guided it toward her entrance. She took control, pressing her hands against my chest, and I liked it. I was used to being in charge in the bedroom, but it was nice when I got to lay back and watch a woman take what she wanted from me.

Siobhan O'Connor was not what I expected, but I was going to love every minute of the rest of our night together.

CHAPTER TWO

SIOBHAN

MID-DECEMBER

God, I was exhausted.

That could have been because I was working my third double in a row, trying to make ends meet as I sorted through the mess of my finances after my husband died. IVF was expensive, but Doug told me he was taking care of it. When I learned how deep in debt we were, his heart attack didn't seem like so much of a surprise anymore. The strain of it all had been dragging me down.

Or I could be so mentally drained from my parents' visit last month at Thanksgiving. My mom drove me batty about working through Christmas and the possibility of moving to Florida with them after I sold the house. No thanks. I loved my seasons in Pennsylvania. Besides, I didn't want to move back in with Mommy and Daddy and have them fix my problems. Once I sold the house and paid off some of our debts, I'd figure it out.

The other reason I was exhausted was because I skipped lunch. Didn't have a choice with how busy the pub was. Not sure why it was so packed in here today. Maybe because Christmas was next week and everyone was out and about shopping.

My stomach could barely handle food right now, anyway. I was hoping it was just a stomach bug I picked up from working with the public. I hadn't been feeling well for weeks but assumed it was stress. I had to admit, waking up to nausea and vomiting for the past week was alarming me. I hoped it wasn't food poisoning or something worse because I couldn't afford a day off from either of my jobs.

"You all right?" A deep voice asked me as I stood behind the bar, trying to remember what I was doing.

Table four needed refills, table five were impatiently waiting on their food, and table six... shit... what did they need?

"Siobhan?" the voice called again.

"Hmm?"

I wanted to cringe when I realized who the voice belonged to. I wished it was literally anyone else. His brother Brian even. Anyone but Killian fricking Murphy.

Here's the thing: I had a great time with Killian on Halloween. He was amazing in bed, and so giving; he made sure I was satisfied before himself. But I never had a one-night stand before. After he fell asleep, the awkwardness crept in, and I snuck out of his house in the wee hours of the morning without saying goodbye. If he was offended, he didn't say. He probably preferred it and had another woman in his bed the next night.

Killian's reputation was well known, after all.

"Siobhan?" he asked again.

I shook my head. "Yeah, I'm fine. Just busy."

He rubbed a hand through his beard and stared at me for a second. "You sure?"

I nodded and looked down at the notepad in my hands, but when I walked away, I got dizzy. My head pounded, probably from too much caffeine and not enough food. I needed to eat, but I had too many tables that needed something from me to get a few minutes to myself. Food would have to wait until the dinner rush was over.

"Darling, you sure you're okay?" Killian asked again.

But I wasn't okay because that was the moment everything went black.

"She'll be okay?" A voice pulled me from the depths.

"That's what we're gonna find out," a second voice replied.

I blinked and stared up at a strange middle-aged man who had me on a stretcher and was studying me.

"Don't move. Let him check you out," the first voice—it was Killian—told me.

"Killian?" I croaked out. "What happened?"

"You passed out."

I blinked and realized I was in an ambulance, and the strange man was a paramedic. What? I had passed out? Why was Killian with me?

"Huh?" I asked.

"Can you tell me your name?" The paramedic asked me.

"Siobhan O'Connor."

He ran through some basic questions, probably checking that I didn't have a concussion. I didn't think I did, but I felt so tired.

"I need to get back to work," I said.

Killian shook his head. "No dice, darling. Brian and Lila said to make sure you get checked out. That's my job."

"What about my tables?"

"Sarah's got ya covered."

"You can go," I told him.

"Nope. I'm going with you to the hospital to make sure you're okay." The tone of his voice was stern, and his face set in a hard line.

Why was he being so stubborn? I had to assume Lila or Brian told him he had to go with me. I couldn't imagine why else he'd stick around. Or why one of them didn't come instead.

Killian squeezed my hand. "You're gonna be fine."

"Oh... o-okay?"

I felt dizzy, like I had whiplash.

Our small town didn't have its own hospital, so we drove to the emergency room in the next town over. After getting checked in, there was a long wait to talk to anyone. I kept telling Killian to go home or back to the pub, but he was as stubborn as a mule. And I was far too tired to argue.

Once I got admitted, I told the staff it was okay for Killian to come back with me. But I wished I told him to go away instead. We sat waiting as they took my blood work and ran other tests that I didn't think were necessary. I was overworked and tired and probably needed to eat something. That was all.

"Why are you here?" I asked Killian.

I felt like we had been waiting for these tests to come back for hours. The silence between us had been so awkward that I had to fill the gap somehow.

"I wasn't gonna leave you," he said flatly.

"I'm fine."

"You looked sick at the pub."

I cocked my head at him. He had noticed that? Before our night together, I never thought he'd looked at me twice. Rumor was he and Sarah used to sleep together. He never even flirted with me before our boss' wedding.

After what felt like forever, a doctor finally came back to tell us what was going on. I was mentally calculating what this visit was going to cost me. I couldn't afford it. Not with all the debt Doug left me.

"Hi, Siobhan," the doctor greeted me and looked at my chart. "So everything's fine."

Could have told him that. I was lightheaded from running around the pub and not eating.

"Make sure you're eating, though. The baby needs it."

"Okay. So I'm..." I paused mid-sentence as his last words hit me like a freight train.

Baby?

And then I wanted to cry. After years of trying and three miscarriages, of course, I'd get pregnant after my husband died. Because that was how fate dealt the cards to me.

Killian cleared his throat, and I felt all my blood drain from my face, remembering that he was still there. "So... she's okay? They're okay?"

"Mom and baby are doing great. She just needs to take care of herself."

"Um..." I stuttered out.

Baby. I was having a baby...

WITH KILLIAN FREAKING MURPHY!

WHAT.THE.FUCK.

The doctor looked between the two of us, and his eyebrows shot up, realizing what was happening.

I didn't need to ask for an ultrasound to find out how far

15

along I was because I already knew exactly when I got pregnant. The worst part? The baby's father wasn't my late husband's. Not by a long shot, because that was impossible when Doug died almost a year ago. The crease in Killian's brow and the way he rubbed the back of his neck told me he had already put it together, too.

Deep down, I already knew, but I had brushed it off as stress or being too busy to properly take care of myself. Then guilt stuck in my gut like a boulder that I jeopardized this baby's survival by not finding out sooner.

"Sorry to be the one to give you the news," the doctor said with a sympathetic smile.

"It's great news, thanks," Killian spoke up.

I stared at him.

It was great news? I was pregnant with his baby, and he was telling the doctor it was great news. Killian, the man who loved them and left them and never wanted to be tied down, was pretending like all of this was fine when it was absolutely not.

"So I can go?" I asked, trying to ignore the man beside me.

"Yes, we're gonna discharge you. Make sure you're eating, okay?"

I nodded.

When he walked away, I jumped up and grabbed my things. I signed out as quickly as I could, ignoring the towering figure following close behind me. I stopped at the entrance of the hospital when I realized Killian had brought me here in an ambulance. Shit, I couldn't afford a rideshare back to town. Or that ambulance trip. Although, I had a feeling Lila would foot that bill. She was that type of boss. Knowing her, she insisted on the ambulance in the first place.

Killian put his hand on the small of my back. "Come on, darling, I got us a ride."

"Um, you didn't have to do that."

He shook his head. "Don't worry about it. Is your car at the pub?"

"Can you take me home?"

He nodded at a Honda Civic that pulled up to the curb. He opened the door for me, and I climbed into the backseat. Much to my disappointment, he slid in after me. I gave the driver my address, and he drove off, engulfing us in a tense silence.

I didn't know what to say. Doug and I had wanted this for so long. I wanted this baby, of course; it was everything I had ever dreamed of. But a baby would tie Killian to me, and he didn't want that. The fact he wasn't saying anything reminded me of that and sent dread spreading through me.

"Are you moving?" His question cut through my thoughts as the car pulled up to the three-story home I once shared with my late husband. Killian nodded at the for sale sign on the lawn with the big SOLD banner slapped over it.

"House is too big for only me," I lied.

I didn't say another word to him, afraid the tears would start falling if I did. As soon as the car came to a stop, I jumped out of it and slammed the door behind me, effectively shutting Killian out. I didn't look back as I walked up my driveway and entered the house.

Once inside, with the door locked, I took a peek out of the curtain. The car idled for a few seconds but then slowly pulled out and drove away. I breathed a sigh of relief. There was no way I wanted to talk to Killian about our situation. I already knew he didn't want anything to do with a baby. Or me.

Walking further inside, the dark and quiet of the house

enveloped me. Even if I had wanted to keep this house, maybe my lie to Killian wasn't that untrue. It *was* too big of a house for one person.

I slid a hand down my stomach. "Don't worry, little bean. Mommy'll figure this out."

I went upstairs into my bedroom and walked into the en suite bath. I opened up the vanity drawer and pulled out a pregnancy test. When you tried for as long as I did, you stocked up on tests.

Muscle memory took over as I opened the package and did what it said. I didn't need to read the instructions anymore since I had taken so many of these over the years. How many times have I done this and prayed for a positive result? Now I was asking any deity that would listen to give me a different result. I tapped my foot against the bathroom tile and closed my eyes as anxiety built up inside my chest. When the time was up, I looked at the test and sighed at the word 'pregnant' glaring back at me. I was hoping maybe the hospital made a mistake.

But I knew they didn't. It wasn't until after I spent the night with Killian that I realized we forgot to use a condom. I hadn't thought much of it when we were together since I stopped using those a long time ago. He probably thought I was on the pill. I said nothing because I wasn't sure I could get pregnant again. I knew that was dangerous, and I went to get tested a couple weeks ago, so no issues there.

I stared down at the pregnancy test. I had false positives before. Back then, they had been the hope I clung to, but now I was wishing for a negative result. I took three more tests to be one hundred percent certain.

All of them were positive.

I snapped a picture of the tests and opened my phone to text my bestie, Freya.

ME: SOS.

I included the picture.

FREYA: OMG! WAIITTT! That's so exciting congrats.

ME: It's not Doug's.

FREYA: WHAT! Girl, come over!

I shook my head at her. God. What a mess. I wanted to climb into my bed and cry myself to sleep, but I needed to talk to someone about this. So I went to Freya's. She only lived a couple of blocks away, so I walked over.

I knocked on her door and heard her Dalmatian barking her head off at the sound. When Freya opened the door, she was holding onto Poppy's collar, trying to restrain her from jumping up on me. Normally, I wouldn't care and give Poppy all the pets, but not now.

Instead, I burst into tears.

Freya pushed Poppy down and hugged me, letting me cry on her shoulder.

"Girl, come in," she said after I pulled away. She turned to her dog, who had calmed down once she saw it was me. "Poppy, be a good girl. It's just Siobhan."

I knelt down to give her some pets. "Hey, Poppy."

Poppy was very excitable, trying to nose her way between my thighs. Why did dogs always want to smell your crotch?

"Poppy, knock it off," Freya said sternly, and Poppy whined but did as she was told.

Freya led us into her living room, and I slumped down on the couch.

"Um, you can take your coat off, you know," she said.

I shrugged out of it. "This is such a mess."

Freya was in for the night, wearing a pair of sweats and her honey-blonde hair tied up in a messy bun. The TV was blaring, and an unfinished glass of wine was on the coffee table.

"Explain everything," she prompted.

I grimaced, and she squealed when I told her about my night with Killian. The gossip about him being good in bed? Accurate. But that was all he was good for. Everyone knew Killian wasn't the guy who stuck around. That was why I slept with him in the first place. I needed to shake off the jitters of getting back into the dating scene. I hadn't imagined the first guy I'd slept with after my husband's death would knock me up.

If only I slept with one of his other brothers instead. His baby brother Lachlan was cute, but I was pretty sure he harbored a crush on my boss at the coffee shop. He seemed nice, though, shy and quiet, unlike the rest of the Murphy clan. Finn was cute, too. If you were into guys who really leaned into their Irish heritage. Ronan had that gruff but attractive blue-collar air about him. All of them would have been a much better choice than the freaking town bicycle.

"But it's a miracle, Shevy!" Freya cheered, trying to stay positive so I wouldn't melt into another puddle of tears.

I rested my hands against my stomach. "I've wanted this for so long. Just... not like this."

She gave me a sympathetic smile. "What did Killian say?"

"Nothing."

She nodded. "Okay... he might still be processing it. But if he wants nothing to do with the baby, forget him. You got me and Poppy, okay?"

Poppy barked at her name.

I frowned. "Freya, I'm scared."

"Of what?"

"What if I lose this one, too?"

She waved a hand at me. "First of all, stop it. Those miscarriages weren't your fault. I hate that Doug said they were."

I sighed.

Freya became 'Team Screw Doug' after my last miscarriage when he asked me what I had done wrong to cause it. Nothing. I did everything the books told me to do. I listened to my doctors, I watched what I ate, quit caffeine, and still lost the baby. The one I had prayed, wished, and hoped for.

That last miscarriage broke my marriage. We hadn't had sex in months before his death, but even if we had, there was no way this could have been his baby. Because he had died last January shortly after that miscarriage. It had been a cruel blow to my already shattered mental state.

Freya reached out and grabbed my hand. "Shev, I love you, okay? I'll be here for you if Killian's not. This baby will be so loved. You know, my dad keeps trying to set me up with all his firefighters because he's still holding out hope I'll change my mind about not wanting kids. He'll be Pop-Pop to your kid while your parents are in Florida. You have us, always."

"I know."

She hugged me. "I love you, and I'm gonna love this baby so hard. You got me, okay?"

I squeezed her back, glad at least I had my bestie to lean on.

CHAPTER THREE

KILLIAN

I walked into my childhood home, looking for my dad, but found my mom in the kitchen making dinner.

"Hi, honey," she greeted me with a big smile.

"Dad around?"

Mom cocked her head at me. "What's going on?"

Mom could always tell when something was wrong. Since I found out Siobhan was pregnant a couple of days ago, I'd been in a fog. No, not in a fog—terrified. The idea of me being a father made me break out in hives. I was so far out of my depth and couldn't wrap my head around the fact that Siobhan was pregnant with my baby.

A long time ago, I wanted nothing more than to have kids one day. But that was before my ex ripped my heart out of my chest and stomped on it with her stiletto heels. Now, all I wanted to do was figure out where Siobhan and I went from here. Too bad the woman in question appeared to be avoiding me.

"Need to talk to Dad about something," I told my mom.

She cocked a ginger-colored eyebrow at me. "Killian Robert Murphy, you better tell me what's going on this instant."

I cringed. Not the full name.

Mary Pat Murphy was not a lady to be trifled with. She was a five-foot-two redheaded spitfire, and we all knew not to fuck with her.

I sighed. "Mom, it's... I need to talk to Dad."

"Talk to me about what?" Dad's voice asked.

I turned and saw him walk into the kitchen. I was forever grateful my coloring favored my dad's rich dark hair, unlike my brothers Brian and Finn, who got the Murphy's red hair. Growing up a ginger kid wasn't fun. Dad stood tall at six-foot-four, a height he passed on to all of us. Well, except for Lachlan. We teased him mercilessly about there being a 'mix-up in the factory.' No wonder he moved to the city and never looked back.

"Well?" Mom asked after I remained silent for a tick.

"Keep in mind, I'm thirty-five and not sixteen."

Dad's face scrunched up, and Mom blinked back at me, still processing my words.

"I don't understand," Mom said.

"I got someone pregnant," I muttered.

"Oh!" Mom said and clapped her hands excitedly. "Oh, Killian, that's wonderful news!"

"It is?" Dad asked. His forehead wrinkled as he took me in, no doubt recognizing the anxiety written across my face.

"Of course," Mom told him. "Another grandchild. Killian, why didn't you tell us you were seeing someone? You have to bring her over for family dinner..."

I tuned her out as she rambled on. Yeah...how to explain to my parents I fucked up and got someone pregnant because my horny brain forgot to wrap it up? Mom wouldn't be happy when I told her I was having a baby with a stranger. Especially one who wanted nothing to do with me.

"Killian?" Dad's voice cut through my tornado of thoughts.

"We're not together," I blurted. "She's... Ah, fuck..."

"Killian Robert Murphy!"

"Sorry."

"Help me in the garage," Dad said. He turned to my mom. "Hun, I got this."

My parents shared a look, a silent conversation held between them until Mom nodded in agreement.

Dad gave her a reassuring look and then walked out of the room. I stared back at the empty spot he had just occupied, unsure of my next move.

"Go help your father and let him talk some sense into you."

I nodded and made my way out of the room and toward the garage.

In the garage, Dad had the hood of his car popped, clearly in the middle of an oil change. Dad had been a mechanic my whole life, and he chose to do the work himself rather than hire someone for his own cars. Even if it meant bringing his work home with him.

After doing research on how much it cost to have kids, I didn't know how my parents managed with five kids as a mechanic and a nurse. I vaguely remembered hearing the hushed whispers of my parents fretting over money when I was really little. When I got older, I realized how much my parents barely scraped by. I didn't want that for my kid.

I slumped down in the chair behind Dad's workbench, trying to find the words. He said nothing as he worked.

Colin Murphy wasn't a man of many words; he waited until you were ready.

"How did you know you were ready to be a father?" I finally asked.

He snorted. "Don't think I ever was."

"Dad! That's not helpful."

He raised an eyebrow. "What's the problem? You're not skirting your responsibilities."

"I didn't say that. I'm just not sure I want to be a father."

"Well, too bad. You're having a kid."

I rubbed the back of my neck.

"Listen, kid, you know Brian wasn't planned, right?"

I laughed. "Mom looks like she's about to pop in your wedding pictures. We all know."

"Right. Was I prepared to be a father? Hell no! Christ, didn't even feel that way when Lachlan was born."

"Dad, Lach's the baby. You should have been ready by then."

"Nope. You're never prepared, but you figure it out and roll with it. So that's what you're gonna do, okay? You're gonna step up and provide for your kid. Who's the mother?"

"Siobhan O'Connor."

Dad gave a quick nod in understanding. "Her folks moved down South, and she doesn't have any other family around. So you better be there for her."

"I never said I wouldn't. But I'm not sure what I'm supposed to do."

Dad slammed the hood closed. "Like, I said, you be there for her. Go be an adult and talk to her. You're definitely not together?"

I shook my head. "Definitely not. It was a one-time thing."

He nodded. "Okay. I'll calm your mother down because

Lord knows she's already got the wedding planner book out."

We rolled our eyes together. That sounded like her.

"Talk to Siobhan. Tell her you're not a deadbeat because we raised you better than that, okay?"

"Dad, I know."

He glared at me. "Then what the fuck are you talking to me for? Go talk to her. Damn, kid, move her into your house if you have to."

I made a face. "Why would I do that?"

He made an annoyed noise in the back of his throat. "So you can step up and take care of her. Show her she's a part of this family now. She's gonna need someone to lean on."

"But she won't talk to me."

Dad pinned me with an annoyed look. "Then get off your ass and go find her."

I blinked back at him.

"Now, Killian!"

I jumped up. "Okay, okay."

Dad was right. I needed to step up. Even if I felt like spiders were crawling under my skin and a thousand what-if questions fired off from my brain.

What if I was a shit dad? What if my kid hated me because I wasn't with their mother? What if Siobhan didn't want me involved? That was the question that stuck in my craw the most.

My reputation preceded me. The whole town knew I didn't do serious, but that didn't mean I'd leave Siobhan to have the baby on her own. Because it was my baby too, and I'd be damned if I wasn't going to have a say.

I slipped out of the house and called Brian.

"What?" he snapped.

"Hello to you, too."

"Unless you're calling to pick up a shift, I don't wanna hear it."

"What's wrong?" I asked as I got into my truck and started the engine.

I wasn't on the schedule at the pub tonight, so I wasn't planning on going in, but if I had a baby on the way, I needed to pick up more shifts. I'd already asked my brother Ronan if he had any big jobs he needed help with at his landscaping company. Babies were expensive, and I needed to squirrel away as much as I could.

Huh. It appeared I was already doing what Dad told me to do.

"Siobhan called out sick, so I got Sarah on the bar. Lila's about ready to take tables. Can you come in?"

I could use the money, but Siobhan calling out gave me the opportunity to finally talk to the woman who was carrying my child.

"Yeah, no. I was looking for Shevy anyway."

"Why?"

"I'll tell you later."

Before he could pepper me with more questions, I hung up on him and pulled out of my parents' driveway. I vaguely remembered that Siobhan lived on the nicer side of town where a lot of the bigger Tudor style houses resided. I found her house easily enough because I remembered the street, and the 'For Sale' sign on the yard was a dead give-away. I parked out on the street and cut the engine.

Was this stupid? I didn't even know what I was going to say to her. I hadn't seen her since that night I took her to the hospital. She kept calling out or switching her shifts at the pub, and I wondered if that was intentional. But she needed to know where I stood. That my reputation didn't mean I was leaving her to have this baby on her own. I might not believe in love or a happily ever after anymore, but I was gonna take care of my kid. No matter what.

I took a deep breath and got out of my truck, then walked up her drive and knocked on the door.

A few seconds later, she opened the door, and her mouth dropped open when she saw me. "Killian...hi."

"Hi," I said back, my shock at our news still rendering me speechless.

She put a hand up to her mouth, and then held up a finger for me to wait with her other hand. She looked like she was going to say something else, but then I watched in horror as she sprinted as fast as she could up her stairs.

I scratched my temple, feeling like an asshole standing at her door, but I didn't want to let myself in uninvited.

A couple of minutes went by before she came downstairs. "Sorry," she offered, but she still looked green. Something inside my chest clawed at me to take away that pain for her. "Did Brian send you? I'm really sorry. This morning sickness is no joke. I had to call out. Again."

"I thought that was only in the morning?"

She let out a sarcastic laugh. "You would think. Tell Brian I'm sorry."

"I'm not here for Brian. I came to talk to you."

"Oh."

"About the baby."

She frowned. "Oh."

"Can I come in?"

"Okay, but it's messy."

By messy, she meant full of moving boxes. She looked like she was in the middle of packing up her house. I didn't like that she did all that by herself. Who was helping her?

She gestured to her couch. "Do you want something to drink?"

I reluctantly took a seat. "Come sit with me. Let's talk."

She nodded solemnly and sat down next to me.

I rubbed my beard, trying to will the words out of me.

"You don't have to be involved," she blurted out, her voice curt.

I snapped my head up. "What?"

She fiddled with the frayed ends of her hoodie. "Killian, I know what you're like."

"What am I like?" I snapped.

She inched away from me, and I felt like a dick for raising my voice at her. "Everyone knows you're there for a good time, not a long time, and that's perfectly fine. I want this baby. But..."

"But what?"

She sighed. "This isn't my first pregnancy."

I stared at her blankly, mentally urging her to explain.

She looked down at her feet. "I've had three miscarriages. Doug and I tried for so long. I don't want... There's a chance—"

"No," I interrupted. "Nothing's gonna happen to you and the baby. I promise you."

"You can't promise that!"

"The fuck I can't. Siobhan, I know we didn't plan for this, but I'm here for you and the baby—whatever you need. You're not doing this alone."

She fiddled with the ends of her hoodie again, not bothering to look me in the eye. "Okay..."

I looked around the living room with the half-packed boxes. "When are you moving out?"

She sighed. "It's complicated. I haven't found an apartment yet. My best friend Freya said I can move in with her, but I have some time before settlement, and I don't want to impose on her. So far, I've been too sick to look at apartments, and I'd love to stay in—"

"Move in with me," I blurted out.

The words were out of my mouth before my brain could process them, surprising even myself.

Well, maybe it wasn't that much of a surprise since Dad had said to move her into my house if I had to. Seeing the state of her half packed up home told me everything I needed to know. Siobhan didn't have anyone to help her and this was how I stepped up and provided for my unborn child. How I proved to her that I was with her in all of this.

Plus, the paternal side of me screamed that the mother of my child wasn't moving out of town where I couldn't keep both of them safe. Fuck that. I wasn't letting her stress about housing on top of being pregnant.

I pointed to her moving boxes. "First, I'm gonna get my asshole brothers to help with all this, and then you move in with me. Until the baby comes. That way, you don't have to worry about rent or looking for a place while you're pregnant."

She shook her head. "No way."

I grabbed her hand. "Siobhan, let me do this."

She pulled away. "I'm glad you want to be involved. That's great...but not like that. We're not together."

I held up my hands. "You know I'm not relationship material. But it's my kid, too, and I'd feel better knowing you're safe. Think about it, okay?"

She chewed on her lip. "Give me time, okay? This is a lot to process."

I stood up. "In the meantime, what can I do?"

"You don't have to do anything. I'm fine."

"Did you eat?"

She clenched her teeth together, her annoyance with

my question evident across her face. "No. I can't keep anything down."

"But the doctor said you have to make sure you're eating."

She rolled her eyes. "If you micromanage me, I'm gonna scream."

I gritted my teeth. "Let me help."

She pointed toward the pile in the corner. "Start there if you're so pressed about it."

For the next hour, I helped her pack up boxes while she rested on the couch.

I went into the kitchen to find the packing tape, but when I saw the grainy image on her fridge, I froze. Everything came crashing down on me at seeing the image of our baby on the sonogram.

Holy fuck, I was going to be a dad.

Was it ideal to have a baby with a stranger? No. Was I prepared for this? Absolutely the fuck not. But I had to be strong for her. Something primal roared to the surface when I saw that image.

I took the photo off the fridge and walked into the living room. Siobhan sat on the couch daintily nibbling on saltines.

"Did you go to the doctor already?" I asked and pointed at the photo.

She nodded. "Like I said, I didn't think you wanted to be involved. It's not like we're together."

Ouch.

Not like her words weren't true, but the harshness in her voice felt unfair. I wasn't husband or boyfriend material, but that didn't mean I wouldn't be there for them.

"Can I go to the next appointment?" I asked.

"Okay..."

"I want to be there."

"Okay."

"Siobhan."

She looked up at me, and the tears in her eyes startled me. "Killian, you don't have to do all this. I know you're only doing it because you think you have to. I'm fine on my own. We'd be fine without you."

I set the sonogram down on her coffee table and knelt down in front of her. I cupped her face and wiped away her tears. "This baby's a surprise, sure, but it's my baby, too."

"Okay."

"Call me before the next appointment?"

She nodded, but I had a feeling she wouldn't tell me. This was going to be way more complicated than I thought. Siobhan might be more stubborn than I was, and that was saying something.

CHAPTER FOUR

SIOBHAN

"*H*e did what?" Freya squealed at me.

I rubbed my temples as I sat on my bestie's couch after my shift at the coffee shop. "Yeah."

"Killian Murphy? *The* Killian Murphy asked you to move in with him?"

I nodded.

"Wow."

"Not like that, Freya."

Freya was reading into this too much. Killian only offered that yesterday because he thought he had to. Given the choice, he'd want nothing to do with me.

She cocked her head at me. "Then what's it like?"

"He thinks he has to."

She rolled her eyes. "Well, duh. He's trying to step up and be a father. I'm impressed."

"Really?"

She bobbed her head up and down excitedly, and then she jerked her head up at the sound of Poppy's bark from outside. She went to her back door to let the dog inside and I reared back at her frustrated scream. Seconds later, she rushed back into the room with panic in her eyes.

I jumped up. "What's wrong?"

"Poppy dug up the fence. AGAIN!" she shrieked. "Sit down, preggo. I gotta chase her down the street."

I sat back on her couch. "She's probably in Mrs. Edwards' garden."

"Don't remind me." She threw on her winter coat and stormed out the door.

I lay my hand on my stomach and peered at the lesson plans Freya had been working on before I came over. Once upon a time, Freya and I were both teachers at the school across the street, but I learned quickly that teaching wasn't for me.

That's how I ended up at the pub. I had worked there as a hostess back in high school and worked my way up to server when I came home during my summer breaks from college. I had loved it and going back to it was better than suffering in teaching when I hated every second of it. Sure, some people were jerks, but I loved my job. I only took up a second job at the coffee shop when Doug and I started IVF treatments. He always reassured me everything would be okay, and we'd have the family we always dreamed of, but hindsight made me wish I had asked more questions.

Freya's lesson plans had me thinking about the future. In a couple of years, my baby would sit in her classroom learning sight words and how to share. But fear climbed up inside me, reminding me of all the times I brought a pregnancy this far only for my dreams to come crashing down.

That was one of the other reasons I didn't want Killian to get involved. It was better if he stayed away, instead of upending his life for this baby we didn't plan for. If he got attached and I lost the baby, I wasn't sure how he'd handle it. Not sure how I would. I wanted this baby so badly, even if it was with a stranger, but I wasn't sure I could go through the agony of another loss. It wasn't something he'd ever understand.

I jumped at the sound of Freya flinging open her front door and Poppy's nails clacking against the hardwood floor. The Dalmatian trotted into the living room and put her head on my leg. I pet her and gave her some scratches behind the ear.

"Are you a troublemaker?" I asked.

"YES!" Freya answered. Her face was flushed from the cold as she shed her coat and hung it up. "Such a bad girl."

Poppy howled back at her.

A grin spread across my face. "Yeah, but we love her. Where was she?"

"Mrs. Edwards yard next door. You know what's weird?"

"What's that?"

Freya sat on the couch next to me. "You know how she hates men?"

I snorted. Poppy didn't hate all men, she loved Freya's dad. But Freya's dates? Not so much. Not like she dated anyone long enough for them to make an impression.

"Ronan Murphy was putting up Mrs. Edwards Christmas lights and Poppy was lying on the ground beneath him like she was in puppy heaven."

I felt my eyebrow raise. Definitely not like Poppy. "Really?"

Her eyes sparkled like when she got a bad idea. "He's kinda hot, too."

"Freya, please don't sleep with one of Killian's brothers. It's bad enough I'll have to be tied to him forever."

She pursed her lips, but before she could say anything, I felt my phone vibrate in my purse. I pulled it out and saw an SOS text from Brian Murphy. God, could I ever escape this family? Since it was Brian I knew it was about work.

> BRIAN: Hey, any chance you could pick up a shift tonight? I know it's your day off, but I'm in a bind.

I was exhausted and I felt like shit, but I needed the money. The house didn't go to settlement for a little while, but I needed to find a new place, and that meant I needed money. Especially with a baby on the way.

> ME: When do you need me there?

> BRIAN: YOU ARE AMAZING. ASAP.

I sighed. That meant I had to quickly run home to change and rush out to the pub.

"What's wrong?" Freya asked.

"Brian needs me to pick up a shift."

She frowned. "Tell him no. You shouldn't overwork yourself."

"Freya, I need the money."

She pursed her lips. "Okay... I'm gonna make a suggestion and promise not to get mad at me, okay?"

I squinted at her.

"Move in with Killian."

I stared at her, my brain not fully processing her words. Because she couldn't be suggesting what I thought she was.

She held up her hand before I could voice my rebuttal. "Hear me out. You need money for the baby, and Killian wants to step up and provide, so let him. Move in with him while you're pregnant, so you don't have to worry about rent. I can help you look for a place in the meantime."

"Freya," I sighed.

"It'll give you a chance to get to know each other better. Strictly platonically, but if he's willing to help you, you gotta let him."

I ran my hand through my hair. "I don't think that's a good idea."

"Why not?"

"I don't want him to think I'm expecting us to play house and be together."

"I said platonically. As roommates. It will help you co-parent. Think about it, okay?"

I was too tired to argue with her and gave her a curt nod.

I didn't want to think about it at all, because moving in with Killian sounded like a recipe for disaster. Some of her points were valid. If I moved in with him it was a cost savings, but I didn't want him to get any ideas about it being anything other than a co-parent situation.

"Promise me?" my bestie asked.

I rolled my eyes. "Fine you pain in the ass."

She gave me a bright smile. "You love me!"

I pulled her into a hug. "I do, but I gotta go."

"Seriously, if you move in with him, you don't have to work yourself into an early grave. You need to think about the baby."

I was thinking about the baby; it was why I agreed to pick up the shift. I gave Poppy some more scratches, and she howled at me when I got up. I waved goodbye to Freya and headed out.

On my walk home, my thoughts swirled in my head as I considered Freya's points about moving in with my baby daddy. But then the dark thoughts reared their ugly head.

Reminding me of all the times I had been here before. Of all the tears and pain when I suffered a pregnancy loss. But fate couldn't be that cruel, right?

I rushed around getting dressed when I got home and then drove over to Sullivan's Irish Pub. I loved working at the pub. After Lila took over, changed the name, and revamped the marketing, it felt like things were thriving. It helped that her husband co-owned the brewery in town and we did a lot of joint marketing with them.

That was the one thing I missed now that I was pregnant. I could really use a beer, but I would never risk jeopardizing the little bean. I loved them too much already, and I had to be careful about this pregnancy. I wasn't drinking coffee anymore, even though it was safe to do that in limited quantities. Although that was much debated among pregnant people. I'd rather err on the side of caution.

When I walked into the pub, it was during the full force dinner rush. Freya and I had planned for dinner together, but we were still debating where to go when Brian asked me to come in. Not like it mattered, because I still couldn't keep anything down. The pub being busy would keep me preoccupied.

I went behind the bar to clock in, ignoring the eyes of a particular bearded bartender.

"I thought you weren't on the schedule tonight," Killian said.

"Brian called me. Do you have a problem with that?" I snapped, and then I cringed. Okay, maybe I was hangry. Or these pregnancy hormones were making me a bitch.

Killian studied me for a moment. "Have you eaten today?"

"Yes," I lied. If two saltine crackers counted, because I

threw up the avocado toast I tried to have at the coffee shop on my lunch break.

I said a silent prayer in thanks when Brian walked over to the bar, interrupting us. "Table four's sat. Table five needs their dinner order taken."

"On it," I told him and spun on my heel.

The next couple of hours were a mad dash to make sure all my customers were happy. I loved the thrill of a dinner rush because it made a shift go by quicker. Was it stressful? Hell yes, but I thrived on the pressure. And Killian wasn't bugging me while he was busy at the bar and I was running back and forth from table to table.

I was inputting an order at the bar when someone set a bowl of barley and vegetable soup in front of me. Then, a cup of ginger tea appeared next to it.

I shot Killian a sideways glance but finished my order before questioning him. "What's this?"

"You need to eat something," he said matter-of-factly. He wiped down the bar with the boredom of a bartender who thrived on keeping his hands busy.

"I'm fine. Thank you very much," I said to him, even though it was a lie.

He crossed his arms over his chest. "You think I didn't notice you sprint to the bathroom five minutes ago?"

"I had to pee."

Not a lie, but I also thought I was gonna throw up. There was nothing in my stomach, though.

I peered at the soup, wondering why that was the first meal he thought of.

Killian picked at his nail. "I read soups could be helpful when you're dealing with morning sickness. And ginger tea. I wasn't sure if you could drink ginger beer, but herbal teas are fine."

I stared at him.

He read about morning sickness? Did that mean he was reading the baby books?

He sighed. "God, I don't want you to fucking pass out again and have something happen to the baby."

Tears pricked my eyes at his thoughtfulness. Of him doing the research and thinking about my well-being. I tried to press it all down, but the sob bubbled up from me, all my emotions spinning out of control.

"Christ," Killian muttered. "Why are you crying?"

"Because you're being nice," I sobbed out.

"I'm not that big of an asshole that me being nice makes you cry!"

"But you don't have to be nice," I blubbered on.

I was aware I was making a scene, but I didn't care. Killian had a pained look on his face that I only saw through the slivers of my blurry tears. I felt his hand on the small of my back as he guided me into the service aisle and toward the office.

He sat me down at Brian's desk and set the soup and tea in front of me. "Please eat something and stop crying."

"I can't! It's the fucking hormones, you asshole."

He rubbed a hand through his beard, frustration eking out of him. "Siobhan...I'm not trying to be an asshole, okay? You have to eat."

I wiped my eyes. "Why do you care?"

"Oh, my fucking God," he growled. "Eat your goddamn soup."

"I'm just gonna throw it up again!"

He reached a hand out and brushed my hair behind my ear, and a small part of me melted at his gentle touch. It reminded again of how tender this man could be when he wanted to. "Do it for the baby, not me, okay? I'm trying to help you. You've been running ragged all night. Christ, I'm pissed at Brian for calling you and not Sarah. I told him you're pregnant and don't need the extra stress."

Fear tightened around my chest. "You what?"

His brow furrowed. "I told him you're pregnant."

"Killian, it's too early."

His eyes softened. "I told you, nothing's gonna happen to the baby."

"You don't know that."

Instead of arguing with me, he shoved the soup spoon at me. "Then eat something and make sure it doesn't."

I glared at him but dunked the spoon into the soup and took a bite. I aggressively ate as he stood there watching me like a creep.

"Don't you have to manage the bar?" I asked sarcastically. His hovering was grating on my last nerve.

He shook his head. "Nope. Asked Brian to handle it for now since we have a lull. The doctor at the emergency room said you need to make sure you're eating."

"I know that," I said bitterly, shoving another spoonful of soup into my mouth.

I didn't love our vegetable barley soup, but I wouldn't have eaten the stew since it had Guinness in it. I wasn't taking any chances with this pregnancy, even if the alcohol content was low.

"I know you like the stew, but it has beer in it, and I'm not doing anything to harm the little bean," Killian told me.

I dropped my spoon into the bowl at his words. How had he been thinking the same exact thing about the stew? And then he called the baby 'Bean' too?

His brow knitted together. "What's wrong?"

I peered up at him, my eyes shiny again with tears. "You what?"

"Brian said it would be fine, but I'm not taking chances with little bean," he said and gave me a sheepish smile. "Is it weird to call the baby that?"

"That's what I call them," I whispered.

"Okay, so we're on the same page there."

I nodded and continued to eat slowly so I didn't hurl again. I took a sip of the ginger tea, too. "I'm sorry."

"For what?"

"For being a bitch."

He shook his head. "It's the baby. I'm one of five. I've seen my mom go off at all of us for no reason before. I get it."

"Okay...thank you. But you don't have to take care of me."

He narrowed his eyes at me. "Are you kidding me? Of course I do."

I pressed a hand to my stomach. "I know you don't want this baby, but I want them so badly. I prayed for so long for God or Fate or the Universe to give me a baby. But you don't have to upend your bachelor life."

"Goddammit, Siobhan," he growled. "I may not have planned for this, but it doesn't mean I'm not gonna be here for both of you. Let me fucking take care of you. This is my baby too, and I'm not going anywhere."

"Okay..."

"Eat your soup. I have to make sure Brian doesn't get overwhelmed," he said and walked off in a huff.

I stared at the empty spot where he had been standing. My emotions were all over the place, but this Killian, the one who was kind and protective, was not one I was familiar with. There was something tugging at my heartstrings, but I pushed the feeling away. We were not going down that road.

CHAPTER FIVE

KILLIAN

I cringed every time I saw Siobhan struggle with bringing out food to her tables. I wanted to take all the burden off her. Her emotions were out of control tonight, but I knew she wasn't eating. I could tell by the exhaustion in her eyes, and that bothered me.

"Dude, you gotta give her room to breathe," Brian said as he counted the drawer next to me behind the bar.

We were closing in a few minutes, waiting for Siobhan's last table to finish up, but they were lingering.

I grumbled at him.

Brian shook his head. "Props to you for stepping up, though. I'm surprised."

I glared. "What the fuck does that mean?"

Brian had always been a pain in my ass. As the oldest, he was practically a second dad half the time, and it was very much not wanted by me and my younger brothers. He was always on my ass about something. It was annoying as hell.

He didn't look up from counting money. "You've made it perfectly clear you don't want to be tied down is all I'm saying. It surprised me that you stepped up and wanted to help her."

"It's my fucking baby, too," I snarled.

"Watch that overprotective shit because she looks like she wants to punch you in the dick."

I sighed. That was definitely true. I was being a micromanager, but I saw the fatigue on her face and how she kept snapping at people. After I made her eat and take her break, she seemed in better spirits.

"Give her the space she needs, okay? Her emotions are all out of whack. Trust me, I know. Kelsey wants to murder me when she's pregnant."

I raised an eyebrow at him. My brother doted on his wife, so it surprised me to hear him say that. It wasn't a lie, though. When Kelsey was pregnant with Callum, she threw a book at my head because I asked her how she was one day.

"I can't wait to get my vasectomy," he said. "I love my kids, but we don't need a whole crew."

I nodded. Christ, how had Mom and Dad handled five? I was sweating bullets at the prospect of one.

He clapped me on the shoulder. "Proud of you, though, for stepping up. Maybe you can make a husband out of a hoe."

"Asshole!"

He laughed as he walked away to take the cash into the safe.

I had no desire to be anyone's husband. Or even boyfriend. Having a kid with Siobhan didn't mean I was asking her to marry me or some shit. I only asked her to move in with me because when she cried in front of me about all her past miscarriages, this protective nature inside me screamed at me to take her pain away. That didn't mean I wanted us to be together.

Siobhan walked over to the bar and rang a credit card through the other till that Brian hadn't cashed out yet. "Almost done. Finally," she breathed out and then walked back over to her table. I watched them complete the transaction, and then the last table finally left.

Our busser came over to help her clear off the table and close down her section. The other servers had cleared off their tables and were rolling silverware, waiting until they could leave. I had finished my work a while ago, but Brian never let us leave until everything was done.

I grabbed a rag and went over to Siobhan's section, wiping down her other tables and putting the chairs on top of the others so we could vacuum and get out of here on time.

"Oh, you didn't have to do that," she said.

"I got it."

I helped her finish until Brian said we could all go home.

"I'll walk you to your car," I told her.

"It's literally in the parking lot."

"Don't care. I'm still walking you."

She rolled her eyes, but we went into the back to grab our coats. She shoved mine at me, and I set it down to help her into her own. She begrudgingly let me, and I shrugged on my coat before she raced out of here without me. I called out to my brother that we were leaving and led Siobhan outside into the parking lot. I opened her car door for her, waiting for her to get inside.

"Why did you pick up the last-minute shift?" I asked her. The question had been on my mind all night.

She sighed. "My husband left me with a lot of debt;

that's why I sold the house. With the baby coming, I need the money and to find a new apartment. And…God everything's expensive. I want to cry. I do. Every night, I cry because I can't believe he left me with mountains of debts."

"Then move in with me like I offered."

She ground her teeth. "You don't have to lose who you are because we're having an unplanned pregnancy. I'm not forcing you to be with me."

I held up my hands. "Whoa. I'm not talking about that. I'm talking about moving in with me so you don't have to worry about money. I'll take care of everything."

"I don't want you to, though."

I gnashed my teeth. "Siobhan, I swear to God."

"You swear to God, what?"

I tried not to ground my teeth down harder. "Shove aside your pride for one fucking minute and realize I'm trying to do the right thing. By you and Bean. I know this wasn't how you expected things to go, but let me help you. You're not in this alone."

"I said you don't have to be involved."

"But I want to be."

"Shev, stop being so damn stubborn and let me help."

"Fine!" she snapped and then shut her car door, leaving my next sentence to die on my lips.

I watched her speed out of the parking lot, not sure if that meant 'fine, leave me the fuck alone, asshole' or 'fine, I'll let you take care of me.'

Well, if she was gonna be difficult, two could play that game.

I walked home, mulling over my plan. She was gonna be pissed, but it was the only way to get her to stop being stubborn. If I hadn't shoved food in her face and forced her to take a break, she wouldn't have eaten tonight. Sometimes, you had to take matters into your own hands.

My house wasn't as big as hers. It was a modest twin home, but Siobhan would have her own room, plus the nursery when the baby was born. Ronan had helped me remodel the kitchen last year, so I was definitely roping him into baby-proofing my house, too.

When I walked inside, I sat on my couch and let my plan unravel in my brain. I pulled out my phone and sent an SOS to the group chat with my brothers. They'd know what that meant.

"Why are we here?" Finn asked, rubbing a hand through his unruly red hair.

"Because you assholes owe me a favor," I said.

They reluctantly followed me as I walked up to Siobhan's front door. If I told them before we got here what we were doing, they might try to talk me out of it. Brian had already tried when he pressed me about what I was thinking.

"But you didn't explain anything," Finn argued.

I shot him a glare.

"What gives, bro?" Ronan asked.

"Where's Lachlan?" I asked.

"Traffic!" called out my youngest brother, jogging up the driveway to join us.

"Move back home," Brian teased.

We all gave Lachlan shit for complaining about his commute from the city when he was in town half the time anyway.

"Your fault for living in the city. We don't have a lot of time," I said and rang Siobhan's doorbell.

"But what are we doing here?" Finn asked again, shooting me an annoyed look.

I threw him the bird and waited for Siobhan to answer her door. She was gonna be pissed when I ambushed her into moving today. Hence, roping in all four of my brothers.

"Tell them," Brian urged.

I turned back to my other brothers. "We're moving Siobhan into my house."

"Siobhan O'Connor?" Lachlan asked.

"Yeah."

"Why?" Finn asked.

"Because..."

"What the hell is this?" Siobhan's annoyed voice cut into the conversation.

Her dark hair was piled high on her head, and she looked comfy in a pair of old leggings and a sweatshirt. I turned around and saw her with her arms over her chest and her foot tapping against the ground impatiently. If she was a cartoon, she'd have steam coming out of her ears.

I hiked a thumb over my shoulder. "These assholes are here to help."

"Help with what?" she asked.

"Your move," I said and muscled my way into her house. It didn't look like she did much since the day I came over and helped her pack up.

I gestured for my brothers to come inside and pointed out where they should get to work and start loading up their cars.

"KILLIAN!" Siobhan screeched.

"What's wrong?"

"What the fuck is going on?"

My brothers pretended not to notice the obvious tension in the room. I walked over to her and gently guided her toward her couch. "You sit and rest. We'll take care of everything."

"Why are you here?"

"We're moving you in today. Relax—that's why I got my brothers here. Tell them what to do."

She gritted her teeth and stood up. "Can I speak to you in private?"

My asshole brothers made 'ooohhh' noises, and the glare I sent them didn't stop them. Dicks.

I followed Siobhan into her kitchen. Her pale face was beet red, and she curled and uncurled her fists when she rounded on me with an icy look in her eyes. "I'm only going to ask this one more time. What the fuck are you doing?"

"We're moving you into my place."

"Killian," she spat out, "I'm not moving in with you."

I rolled my eyes. "Well, since you yelled 'fine' at me and slammed your car door in my face, I had to figure it out myself."

"You're such a micromanaging asshat!"

"Well, someone has to make sure you're taking care of the baby."

She reared back at that. "Do you hear yourself? I've been here before. I..."

Before she could finish her thought, she ran from the room.

The sounds of her getting sick in the powder room had me searching her cabinet for a glass. I grabbed the water filter from her fridge, poured her a glass, and stood outside the powder room, waiting for her. My brothers looked on from the living room floor, by now piecing together why we were here.

The door swung open, and Siobhan walked out, still steaming mad, but she took my offered glass and stomped upstairs.

"Explain everything," Ronan said.

I sighed. "Siobhan's moving in with me because she sold the house and needs a place to stay."

"And?" Finn coaxed me to continue.

"And you're smart, asshole. You figure it out," I shot back.

"She's pregnant?" Lachlan asked.

I nodded.

"With your baby?" Lachlan asked.

"Yes, asswipe, with my baby."

He ran a hand through his hair. "Okay, that's... Good on you, Killian. Never thought you had it in you to grow up."

I glared at him. What the fuck did that mean? Why did everyone keep on saying that?

"I didn't know you were dating," Finn said as he taped up a box.

"They're not," Brian answered for me.

That got three sets of raised eyebrows from my younger brothers.

I rubbed my beard. "Look, she needs a place to stay, and I'm taking care of my kid. End of story. Now get to work, you dicks."

"Maybe you should talk to her," Lachlan offered. "She seemed upset."

I rolled my eyes. Of course, she was upset. I sprang this on her, and she was pregnant. But she could be pissed at me all she wanted. We both knew deep down this was the best solution.

I ignored my brothers and went into her kitchen to make heads or tails of what she wanted to take and keep. Today was gonna be a long day, and my baby mama might kill me at the end of it.

CHAPTER SIX

SIOBHAN

I lay on my bed staring at my phone and trying to will Freya to respond to my SOS text. She had another date today, so I doubt she saw it yet.

I rested my hand on my stomach, trying to calm my nerves, but only for the sake of the baby because I was absolutely furious at Killian. Who did he think he was barging into my house and forcing me to move in with him? I refused to go downstairs and help him and his brothers, who clearly had been roped into this without understanding the situation. Poor guys.

A light knock sounded on my door, and then it creaked open. I narrowed my eyes at Freya's blonde head peeking in. She waited for me to tell her to get out before opening the door wider and stepping inside. She held a plate in her hand and walked over toward me.

"First, I got your SOS text and came over as soon as I could. Second, Killian wanted to make sure you ate something."

I pulled a pillow over my head and screamed into it.

Freya laughed. I heard her set the plate on my night-stand, and then she sat on the other side of me.

"It's sweet," she said.

I pulled the pillow off my head. "He's being a micro-managing asshat."

A laugh bubbled up out of Freya, and I gave her the stink eye.

"You're probably hangry, so eat already."

I grumbled but sat up against my headboard while Freya got up and opened my closet door. I took a bite of the grilled cheese sandwich and had to hold back the moan. I was so damn hungry, and tired, and angry.

Okay... Freya had a point. The baby was forcing my emotions all over the place. This one was going to test me because my other pregnancies hadn't been this bad.

"I thought you had a date," I said.

She pulled clothes from my closet and threw them on the bed. "He was a douche. I think my dad set us up on purpose."

"For what?"

"So I'd never in my life want to date a firefighter."

Hmm, didn't know about that one. Freya's dad wanted her to settle down with a nice firefighter, but Freya had a penchant for assholes. Or she got scared whenever someone got too close. There had been a couple of guys who were really sweet on her in the past and who were good for her, but her abandonment issues always forced her to push them away. I hated that for her, but that was her own trauma to work through.

"I'm glad you agreed to take Killian up on his offer," she said. "It'll help you figure things out for when the baby gets here."

I shoved my sandwich into my face so I didn't snap at my best friend. I hadn't exactly said yes to Killian. In what world did slamming my car door in his face equal a yes?

Freya threw more clothes on the bed and arched an eyebrow at me. "You said yes, right?"

I grimaced. "Not exactly. He's being an overbearing asshole."

"Explain."

I told her about last night at work, and instead of cheering me on about him being annoying, her face lit up. "Aw, he wants to take care of you. Let him."

I rolled my eyes but finished my sandwich while she got my clothes together. I had cleaned out and donated a bunch when I put the house on the market, but I still had so much stuff to go through.

I was sipping on my tea when Kelsey Murphy walked into the room. "Hey, Kels."

"Hey. How are you feeling?" she asked, as she rocked the baby sleeping against her chest.

I shrugged.

"Brian called me for reinforcements. You don't want the boys going through your unmentionables. They're nosy," she said with a grin.

I raised an eyebrow. I'd learned that pretty quickly.

Freya came out of my closet, and I gestured to her. "Do you know my friend Freya?"

Freya gave Kelsey a big smile. "Of course. I had Cora in my class. How is she?"

"Stubborn!" Kelsey said with a laugh. "You're gonna have Callie soon, and I'm sorry. I'll buy you lots of wine, from one teacher to another."

Freya laughed. "Cora's too smart for her own good, but a good kid. I can't wait to have the others. And this one is..."

"Oh, Callum. He's my little angel." She turned to me. "I'm here to help, so put me to work."

Freya was already on it, tasking Kelsey with a section of my bedroom. I finished my tea and disappeared downstairs to clean up my dirty dishes.

My house was a bustle of activity. There was another redheaded woman packing boxes with Killian's brother Finn in my living room. I didn't recognize her at first until she lifted her head, and I realized it was Eilish O'Doul.

Freya and I had been casual acquaintances with her in high school. I sympathized with her on no one remembering how to pronounce her name either. Although hers was way harder than Siobhan. We joked her full name was 'Eilish, no, it's pronounced AY-lish, O'Doul.' She and Finn were attached at the hip, so it made sense he'd roped her into helping today.

I gave her a small smile and headed for my kitchen. That's where I found Killian with his nieces running circles around him, their father nowhere in sight. The way he listened intently as his niece talked his ear off sent flutters to my heart. Almost as if I was getting a look into the future with him. Not *my* future with him, but a premonition of the type of father he'd be.

He lifted the little one in his arms and stood up while the older of the two grabbed onto his leg. "Come on, munchkins. Let's go find Mom-Mom and Pop-Pop."

"But we want to help!" the older girl whined.

I felt a smile tug at my lips, but then Killian glanced up and saw me standing in the doorway. "Hey. You feel better?"

I nodded and headed for the sink.

"I got it," he said.

"It looks like you have two stage-five clingers, so no you don't," I teased.

I washed my dishes by hand, then I put them in the dish drain. I pretended I didn't feel Killian's eyes boring into me when I opened the cabinet above my head and surveyed what we still needed to pack.

"Uncle Killian, are you getting married?" the older girl asked.

I froze at her question. How were we going to explain this to her?

"Cora, listen, munchkin. Siobhan's my friend, and she needs a place to stay, so she's moving in with me," Killian explained.

She scrunched up her little face. "But Daddy said you're having a baby."

"That's true," Killian conceded.

I crossed the room and knelt down in front of her. "Sometimes, grown-ups have a baby but don't get married. Okay, sweetheart?"

Her little brow furrowed. This must have been so hard for kids to understand, but I wasn't sure how to say, 'sorry, kiddo, your uncle fucked me, and now we have an oops baby, and he's moving me into his house.' How did we explain the weirdness of our situation?

"But Mommy said—"

"Cora! Callie!" a deep voice called from the other room.

"Pop-Pop!" they both cheered and scampered away.

Killian stood up and sighed in relief.

"How are we gonna explain it to them?" I asked.

He rubbed his beard. "I don't know. Sorry, I didn't know Bri and Kels were bringing the kids. My parents are coming to collect them so they'll be out of our hair."

I nodded and spun back around, pulling out dishes from

the cabinets and placing them on the counter. I figured Killian had stuff, but I could always keep my boxes at Freya's until I found my own place. It would make it easier when I moved again.

"You don't need all that. I've got dishes," he said.

"I will after I find a new place."

"Okay, but let me do it."

"I'm just pregnant, Killian. I'm capable of doing this myself."

I swear I heard him growl under his breath like he was some wild animal. He was being a commanding asshole, and I fought the urge to clock him.

Okay...that might be the hormones talking. I hadn't expected to have the entire Murphy family up in my business today, and the mention of his parents put me on high alert. I hadn't told my parents about the baby yet, and here Killian's entire family was stomping through my house.

It was too early for everyone to know about the baby, and I was scared about losing this one, too. So much that I wasn't sure I wanted to tell my parents yet. Word got out fast in a small town like Drakesville, but with my parents living down South, I could keep it from them a bit longer.

"I'm pissed at you," I admitted.

"What else is new?" he muttered, probably hoping I didn't hear him.

I glared at him, and his face reddened at getting caught.

"My parents don't fucking know, Killian. And you barged in today guns blazing with your family in tow. How are you gonna explain it to your parents when I miscarry?"

"Is everything okay in here?" came a feminine voice from behind me.

A petite redheaded woman stood in the doorway of my kitchen. From the way she arched her eyebrow at Killian, I immediately saw the family resemblance. And then I burst into tears because I was being a raging bitch, and this was his mother's first impression of me.

Fan-fucking-tastic.

"Hey, Mom," Killian greeted. "This is Siobhan. Siobhan, my mom Mary Pat."

"Oh, honey. Do you need a mom hug?" she asked me, completely ignoring her son.

"Yes," I blubbered out and wiped at my eyes. Today was an emotional rollercoaster, and I hated how I was acting. My composure—and possibly my sanity—were unraveling.

The tiny woman grabbed me into a hug, and it was exactly what I needed. Her soft body squeezing me tight was the comfort I had been missing while my own mom was a thousand miles away.

"I'm sorry. This is the worst way to meet me," I told her after she pulled away.

She laughed. "This is what those Murphy kids do to you. I've been through it. Now, go lie down, and we'll take care of everything."

"But—"

"Rest, honey. My boys got this."

Mary Pat was right. In a matter of hours, the Murphy brothers had all my stuff carted off to Killian's house on the other side of town. He had a cute little twin home near the town square that I only vaguely remembered from our night together.

After Mary Pat told me to go lie down, I didn't. I went upstairs and packed up my bedroom with Freya and

Kelsey's help. Still, it surprised me we got all of this done today.

"Here?" Freya asked me, holding up my jewelry box as I lay on the bed in Killian's guest room.

I groaned. "I don't care."

She laughed. "Okay, you need to eat something, but I have to bounce soon."

"Why?"

"Date."

I sat up. "Did you double book yourself today?"

She shot me a devilish smile. "Yup."

"Freya, how are you juggling all these men?"

She gave me a wicked grin. "No big. I knew the coffee date was gonna be a bust, but this one's taking me to dinner, and I wanna get laid."

I shook my head at her. One day, my bestie would settle down, but it was definitely not anytime soon.

"Hey, do you know if Ronan's single?" she asked.

"No clue. But I already told you that you can't date one of Killian's brothers."

She rolled her eyes at me, but she'd better not try to sleep with Ronan. I really didn't need to deal with this family more than I had to.

I got off the bed and walked Freya downstairs. Killian had kicked his brothers out about an hour ago since he had a shift at the pub, and I welcomed the silence. I was so not prepared for my baby to be a Murphy.

Freya gave me a hug on the porch. "Everything's gonna be fine."

"What if this is a mistake?"

She shook her head. "It's not. He's helping you. Now you can cut back on your hours because you don't need to work yourself to the bone. This is good. Killian's stepping up."

I frowned. "I still haven't told my parents."

"You should get on that."

"I didn't even want Killian to tell his family yet. I'm so scared I'll lose this baby."

She hugged me again. "Thinking about the what-ifs is gonna stress you out, and that's not good for the baby. You have to relax. But call your mom. They might not live here anymore, but you know how Drakesville is."

Yes, that was exactly the problem. I loved living in this small town, but people talked, and it got annoying. Once word got out about me and Killian, it would be all anyone could talk about. I was not looking forward to the whispers and stares about me.

I let go of Freya and watched her walk down to her car. The upside to moving here was that Killian's house was smack dab in the middle of town and a perfect walking distance from both of my jobs. It was going to make opening up the coffee shop tomorrow not as bad.

I walked inside the house and went up to the guest room. I lay on the bed, my hand on my stomach as I rehearsed what I was going to say to my mom. God, I was thirty. Why was I so scared to tell her this?

I took out my phone and dialed her number. She answered on the second ring.

"Hey, sweetie. How are you?"

I sighed. "Okay."

"You don't sound good. Everything okay?"

What a loaded question. Not really.

"I have to tell you something."

"What's up?"

"I'm pregnant."

There was a moment of pause. "Oh, sweetie, that's amazing news. I know it's hard without Doug but—"

"It's not Doug's!" I blurted out and silently cursed myself.

"I know that, but I didn't know you were dating again. When we were in for Thanksgiving, you didn't say anything."

"It's complicated. We're not together."

"Okay...but he wants to be involved?"

"Too much," I grumbled.

She laughed. "Okay, that's good. Who is it? Do I know him?"

"Killian Murphy. He's annoying. He forced me to move in with him while I look for an apartment. And he keeps bothering me every time I don't eat. The morning sickness for this pregnancy's awful. I can't keep anything down, and I'm so tired."

Mom was silent for several seconds, processing my rant. "Oh, sweetie. I know that's a lot. Are you sure you don't want to move down here? Your father and I can help take care of you."

No. I had no desire to move to Florida; I hated Florida. My pale-white Irish skin couldn't handle the heat. I barely survived the humid summers in PA.

"No. I like my life here."

"Okay, it was just a suggestion. Killian's Mary Pat's son. He comes from a good family."

I grumbled.

"Let that man step up and be the father, okay?"

"He's annoying me. He barged in with his four obnoxious brothers and moved me in today."

She laughed. "He sounds like he's just what you need after Doug."

I frowned. "Mom, it's not like that. We're only co-parenting."

"Mmmhmm."

I rolled my eyes, glad she couldn't see me. Mom always jumped to these conclusions.

"It's not like that. He thinks he has to," I protested. I needed to make it clear to her that there wouldn't be any wedding bells in the future.

"Then let him. He had a part to play in this, too."

I clenched my teeth, holding back the harsh words I really wanted to say. "Fine."

"Is this why you weren't feeling good when we visited?"

"Probably. I just found out, and I'm mad he already told his family. I'm scared about another miscarriage."

"Oh, Siobhan. You can't worry about that. Just make sure you take care of yourself. And tell Mary Pat to give you a big mom hug for me, okay? I wish I was there to give one to you. Why don't you come visit for Christmas?"

"I have to work."

A lie. We were closed on Christmas Day, but I volunteered to work the Christmas Eve closing shift. No one liked to work on the holiday, but I was trying to take every shift I could. Brian didn't care because I was one of the most well-liked servers at the pub. I wondered, now that his brother had gotten me pregnant, if he was going to cut my hours at Killian's request. I had to nip that in the bud.

"You sure you can't get off?" Mom pressed me. "I hate that you don't have any family with you around the holidays. You could come in on Christmas day."

I held in my groan. The idea of working all night at the pub and then having to get up early to get on a flight on one of the busiest days of travel didn't appeal to me. "Don't worry about me. I've got Freya and her dad. I'm not completely alone."

Plus, it seemed like Mary Pat had already welcomed me into the Murphy family. She was really nice and would be a great grandmother to my baby.

"Okay, sweetie. Your father and I just worry."

"I know, Mom."

"Hang in there, sweetie. And don't worry so much. You've wanted this baby for so long. It doesn't matter to us if you're with the father or not. Your baby will be surrounded by love. I know Mary Pat will do that, too."

I nodded, even though she couldn't see me, and then I changed the subject and let her tell me what she and my dad had been up to. I felt a weight off my shoulders now that my parents knew, but that ever-present fear still gnawed at me.

CHAPTER SEVEN

KILLIAN

a shrill ringing woke me from a deep sleep. I slapped at my phone and rolled over, but the noise wouldn't stop. I slid one eye open and grabbed my phone, but it wasn't my alarm. I squinted at the time; it was five in the morning. After a night of closing down the pub and not getting home until a couple of hours ago, I had no desire to be awake.

What the fuck was that noise?

I rolled out of bed and opened my bedroom door. Across the hall, the door to the guest room was closed. Like it had been when I came in last night after closing. I had crept in as quietly as possible so I didn't wake Siobhan.

Why the fuck was she waking up this early? I couldn't see her as an early bird when she closed the pub as much as I did. But I was low on sleep and her alarm was fucking annoying.

I pounded on the door. "Siobhan? Can you turn that off?"

Silence answered me, and as I turned to head back into my room, I spied the light underneath the closed bathroom door. Then I heard Siobhan getting sick.

Oh.

I walked down the hall and knocked on the door. "Hey, you okay?"

The toilet flushed, and the water ran for a couple of seconds, and then she opened the door. She wore a tank top and tiny shorts that did nothing to hide her figure. She wasn't showing the pregnancy yet, but I saw it in her face. The exhaustion and sickness evident there crushed me.

"Fine. Why are you up?" she asked.

"Your alarm?"

Her eyes went wide. "Oh, shit. Sorry."

She ran into her room, and the noise subsided. I walked back down the hall and leaned against the door frame of the guest room. She looked over at me, her eyes tracing down my body. I forgot I was only wearing a pair of boxers, and I tried to not be a cocky asshole about her checking me out.

"Siobhan?"

"Huh?" she asked. Her head snapped up when she realized she was caught staring.

"What are you doing up?"

"Oh. I have work."

I stared at her. What was she talking about?

"At the coffee shop. I have to open today," she explained.

"I thought we discussed you don't need to pay rent."

"I still need the money," she said and crossed her arms over her chest. Now it was my turn to stare. Her breasts were practically spilling out of her tank top. Why she was wearing such skimpy clothes in the dead of winter was beyond me.

"Killian!" she snapped.

I brought my eyes up to hers, and there was a fire in those blue orbs. Busted.

"Stop staring at my chest!"

"Woman, I'm half asleep," I grumbled.

"Then go back to sleep and leave me alone."

I sighed. Oh, she was super pissed at me for sure.

Brian gave me hell last night when he realized she wasn't exactly on board with living together. But Dad basically told me to do that. I wasn't gonna leave my baby mama in a tough financial situation. Not when I had the perfect solution.

"I'll make coffee. Do you want to eat something before you go?" I asked.

She stared at me for a split second. "No. Go back to bed. I'm fine. Just morning sickness. Your stupid spawn wants me to suffer."

I cringed. "Darling, I'm sorry. What can I do?"

"Nothing. Leave me alone, Killian. Please, for the love of God."

I put my hands up and backed away slowly. "Okay, okay."

I walked into my room and shut the door behind me. The selfish part of me wanted to go back to sleep, but the paternal part hated seeing her suffer. So, I got dressed and went downstairs, put on a pot of coffee, and made eggs and toast. I wasn't sure she was going to eat it, but I wanted to put in the effort.

I was pouring creamer in my coffee at my kitchen island when she came downstairs wearing a black Drakesville Drip t-shirt and a pair of jeans.

She wrinkled her nose at the smell. "Coffee smells horrid to me."

"How are you gonna handle going to work then?" I asked.

I took a sip of my coffee and pushed a cup over to her. I didn't know how she took it, so I left it black.

She shook her head. "No, thanks. I can't risk it."

"Risk what?"

"The baby. I can't take any chance I'll lose them. Not like the others."

I set my coffee down, came around behind the island, and moved over to her. I cupped her face. "Siobhan, you can have one cup of coffee."

She shook her head indignantly. "You don't understand. I've prayed for this baby. To any deity who'd listen. I can't do anything to jeopardize this. I want Bean to survive longer than their siblings."

I put a hand on her stomach. "Darling, I'm sorry. I'll do everything I can to make sure that doesn't happen. What can I do?"

She jerked away from me, causing me to frown as my hand hung in the air where she had just stood. "You can stop touching me."

"Are you sure you don't want to eat something? Can I make you tea?"

She tilted her head to the side and blinked at me for a few seconds. "Who are you, and what have you done with the Killian Murphy I know?"

"I'm trying to do right by you, okay? Let me."

She clenched her jaw and pulled away from me. She made her way over to the hall closet to grab her coat. "I can't eat yet. I gotta get to work."

And with that, she walked out the door, still very much pissed at me.

I slid onto one of the bar stools at my kitchen island and

drank my coffee, eating my breakfast while hers went cold. I didn't want to be awake this early, but there was no way I was going back to sleep.

After I ate, I went upstairs and grabbed my phone, shooting off a text to my brother Ronan.

> ME: Hey, man, you got any extra jobs I could help with?

Ronan's landscape business had been doing well, and he always needed more guys working with him. I had picked up a couple of jobs with him when the pub wasn't doing so well.

> RONAN: Not really. Winter's tough. Why?

> ME: Umm baby on the way?

> RONAN: Meet me on Walnut Street.

My muscles were screaming as I helped Ronan put his equipment back into his work truck. He was a liar. Helping him with Christmas light installments had been a lot of work. No wonder he was cut from all the manual labor. Closing the pub later was gonna be torture, and I definitely needed a shower before heading there.

"You at the pub tonight?" Ronan asked.

"Yup."

"Okay. You want to talk about the shitshow that was yesterday?"

"What do you mean?"

He raised an eyebrow. "She was pissed at you. Why'd

you move her in? You're not the type who wants to play house."

I sighed. "Dad practically told me to."

"Okay, but you didn't have to listen to him, numb nuts."

I shoved him away. "Man, fuck you."

He laughed but gave me a serious look. "Seriously, what gives?"

"Her husband left her with a lot of debt. She's struggling, and I don't want my baby to suffer because of her stress. Plus, she told me she's been pregnant before."

Ronan's face got serious. "Okay, wait...you didn't convince her to have this baby, right? If she wanted an abortion, that's her choice."

I shook my head. "Hell no! That should be a pregnant person's decision. She wants this baby, but she's had three miscarriages before. She's scared, and I don't know, man..." I raked a hand through my hair. "I want to take care of them, ya know?"

Ronan nodded solemnly. He and his ex went through multiple miscarriages early in his marriage. That was before he found her in bed with someone else.

"Okay," he began, obviously choosing his words carefully. "You need to let her be. The miscarriages crushed Chrissy. It's why I sunk everything into the business and what led her into the arms of another man."

I grumbled. I had a lot of choice words for what Chrissy did, but Ronan didn't want to hear it anymore. He blamed himself for their marriage crumbling, but he wasn't the one who was unfaithful.

"I don't have a lot of work right now—it's my slow season," Ronan said with a grimace. "But once we get that first big snow, I'll need some extra hands. And I think it's great you want to be there for her. But..."

"But what?" I gritted out.

He ran a hand down his trim beard. "You sure there's nothing there between you and Siobhan?"

"Absolutely not."

He gave me a suspicious look. "Okay. I'll call you later. Not much until after Christmas, though."

"Alright. I gotta get to the pub anyway."

I waved to him and got into my truck. I drove home, parking in my driveway, annoyed that Siobhan's car was parked on the street. There was room in the driveway, and she didn't have to drive to either of her jobs. One of the biggest factors in buying my house was its walking distance to the pub.

I took a quick shower and threw on a Sullivan's Irish Pub t-shirt and a pair of jeans. The servers usually had to wear uniform pants, but I didn't care. Lila gave me shit about not following the rules, but she still let me get away with it.

Siobhan wasn't home, so I locked up behind me and walked over to the pub. I gave her keys yesterday before my shift so she could come and go as she pleased. I couldn't remember if she was working at the pub tonight.

Walking into the pub, I stepped into chaos. It was the dinner rush and only Brian was behind that bar, which didn't seem right. Silas was supposed to work with me tonight.

"Bout time you got here," Brian said as I clocked in at the register behind the bar.

"I'm five minutes early. Where's Silas?"

"Quit."

"Seriously? No notice?"

He nodded. "Yup. I'd pull Sarah to the bar, but we need her on the floor."

Probably best Sarah and I weren't behind the bar together. We used to bang, and even though she ended it, she had been avoiding me at all costs. It wasn't my fault she thought we could have something more than a casual hookup. I'd made it clear I wasn't relationship material.

"You gotta stop sleeping with the wait staff," Brian said.

I brushed him off. "She knew the deal. They all do. Not my fault they catch feelings."

He opened his mouth, but then one of our locals sat at the bar in front of me.

"Hey, Mr. Davies. What can I get you?" I asked.

"Old Man Sullivan."

"You got it."

I grabbed a glass from underneath the bar and poured the Irish Red beer from the tap. I lost my concentration when I saw Siobhan walk out onto the floor. She gave a tight smile to her table as she delivered their food. That was her fake customer service smile.

"BRO!" Brian's voice screeched in my ear.

I pulled myself out of it and noticed the beer I was pouring had overflowed. I shook my head and poured some down the drain. I wiped off the glass before handing the beer to Mr. Davies.

He gave me a wry smile before handing me his card. "Pretty girl got you distracted, Killian?"

"Something like that. You want to keep a tab open?"

He nodded, and I kept his credit card on the register. A couple more customers came up, and I served their drinks, trying to busy myself with work instead of worrying about Siobhan. How she was flitting about from table to table when she was up at the asscrack of dawn was beyond me.

The pub was busy tonight, but I didn't mind because it made the night go by quicker. As the night wound down, the clientele filtered out. I busied myself with cleaning up and flirting with the smoking hot redhead at the bar who kept ordering Manhattans and giving me 'the look.' Not sure who she was. I think I'd remember if I took her to bed. Ehh. Maybe not. Sometimes, I didn't ask their names.

"When do you get off, handsome?" she asked, giving me a wink at her double meaning.

"Not for a while," I said with a sly smile. "What else can I get you?"

"I can think of something I can't get here."

I smirked at her. I knew what that meant, and hell, I needed the release. I hadn't had sex since...

Fuck. Siobhan.

I couldn't take this chick back to my place. We might not be together, but Siobhan didn't want to hear me fuck someone else. I could go to this lady's place, but leaving Siobhan alone in my house while I went off to bang other women didn't sit right with me. My sex life would need to take a backseat until the baby was here. I had a duty to take care of Siobhan and Bean first. Besides, the women would always be there later.

"Maybe another time," I said.

She pouted. "Too bad. You can close my tab then."

I rang up her bill and handed it to her. She left shortly after signing her bill, and when I took it back, I noticed she left her phone number on the receipt.

"Why didn't you take her up on that offer?" Siobhan asked from behind me.

I nearly jumped three feet at her voice. She had a hand on her stomach and was bouncing on her feet, clearly tired from being on them all day.

"Not interested," I lied.

She squinted at me. "Don't say no on account of me. We're just roommates."

Then she turned away as swiftly as she'd come.

I didn't see her for the rest of my shift. Not until we were closing up, and even then, she walked away like she was in a mad dash.

I ran after her. "Siobhan!"

She kept walking, her head low.

I felt out of breath by the time I caught up with her. "Can you at least let me walk you home?"

"For what?"

"Um, because it's three o'clock in the morning?"

"I'm fine. The only person stalking me is you."

I sighed. This fucking woman. I thought no one could outdo Mary Pat Murphy's passive aggression, but a pregnant stranger was beating her out.

"Did it bother you I was talking to that woman?" I asked.

She shook her head, pulling her coat around her as we walked the couple of blocks to my house. "You're free to see whoever you want. I don't care."

The ice in her voice told me that was a lie.

"Siobhan—"

"I don't care, Killian. You can do whatever you want. I'm so tired. I have to open the shop again tomorrow, and I want to get into bed and sleep."

"You're opening the coffee shop again?"

We got onto my street, and she walked up the porch steps with me behind her. I jumped in front of her, unlocking the door and letting her inside. She kicked off her shoes and shed her coat while I locked up.

I took off my coat and hung it in the hall closet while

she trudged further inside. I was right behind her because this conversation wasn't over.

"Are you seriously going to get a couple of hours of sleep and go to the coffee shop tomorrow?"

"Killian, this is my life," she said flatly, annoyance laced in her tone.

I gnashed my teeth. "This is why I wanted you to move in. I'm going to help you so you don't have to work this hard."

"I'm used to it. It's fine." She looked exhausted, and I felt that, but I didn't want her working herself to death.

"Siobhan—"

"Goodnight, Killian," she said and raced up the steps, the sound of the guest room door slamming behind her.

How the fuck was I having a baby with the most stubborn woman on the planet?

CHAPTER EIGHT

SIOBHAN

I used to love the smell of coffee brewing first thing in the morning; it was why I always volunteered for the opening shift at the coffee shop. I loved getting up early and opening before everyone started their day. But now, it made me want to puke.

"You okay?" my boss, Willow, asked me.

I swallowed. "Uh-huh."

She peered at me, interrupting her latte art. The tiny brunette exuded that whole artist aesthetic, and she put that all into her business—from the décor, which featured her own paintings and other local artists, to the way she painstakingly created latte designs.

I finished my task and handed the to-go coffee container to one of our regulars. "Here you go."

"Thanks," he said, making a show of adding money to our tip jar, and then he was out the door.

"You know he only comes in because he has a crush on you," I told Willow.

She shook her head. "No, he doesn't. I have literally never talked to him in my life." She slid over the latte. "Here."

I peered down at the intricate snowflake design in the cup. She was getting good at those designs. I could do the simple ones she taught me, but I wasn't as talented as her.

"No coffee, remember?"

She frowned. "I looked that up, and it sounds like bullshit."

I sighed. "They say it's okay in moderation, but I can't take a chance."

She reached out and squeezed my hand. "What did your doctor say?"

"To stop stressing."

I had another appointment after the holidays, but that hadn't stopped me from calling my doctor multiple times. The nurses were likely screening my calls now.

Willow pursed her lips. "Okay...I want to talk to you about something, and I don't want you to get mad."

"What's up?"

"I think it's in your best interest to switch up the schedule."

I stared back at her. "But I love opening."

A wrinkle appeared on Willow's forehead, a sign she was thinking hard about her next sentence. People thought Willow was flighty because she had been a trust fund kid, but she was cautious and thoughtful. She wasn't one to speak before she thought. It was what made her a great business owner.

"Siobhan, you're one of my best employees, but you're so sleep deprived you're messing up too many orders. It's not personal, just business."

She had a point there. I screwed up two different drink

orders this morning, and that wasn't like me. I had to admit, this pregnancy was taking a lot out of me. I was so tired and sick all the time. Killian was nice enough to let me move in with him, and I could squirrel away my money, but my thoughts were constantly on the mountains of debts Doug left me.

"I need the money," I whispered, looking down at the counter, unable to meet her eyes.

"I'm not firing you. Gosh, nothing of the sort. I'm willing to work around your schedule at the pub. I'm just worried about you."

"Okay," I muttered.

Another reason I liked the open shift was because it didn't interfere with my shifts at the pub. But I had to admit I was exhausted. Not getting home until three a.m. every night, getting a few hours of sleep, and then opening the coffee shop was wearing me down. It didn't help that the morning sickness was still in full force.

As if on cue, a wave of nausea hit me, and I rushed to the bathroom.

After suffering through it for a few minutes, I trudged over to the sink to wash my hands. I splashed water over my face and peered at my reflection in the mirror.

Willow was right. I was driving myself into an early grave trying to work so much while this pregnancy was running my life. Might not be a bad plan to switch something up.

I walked out of the bathroom and found a line of people waiting while Willow took their orders.

Ack! I felt like a jerk for leaving her hanging like that.

I jumped on the second register while she made their drinks. We worked in tandem to serve our customers as quickly as we could. I made small talk about the snow coming down and whether we would close early or not. The morning rush went by quickly as the snow pelted the sidewalk.

Working the morning shift was nice because I usually got off around lunchtime and could go home to nap before my closing shift at the pub. Luckily, I didn't work at the pub tonight and had a much-needed night off.

I stared out the window, where thick clumps of snow fell to the pavement. I hoped it didn't get so bad that walking home would be dangerous.

"Can I offer you a suggestion?" Willow asked.

"Hmm?"

"For the morning sickness."

I gave her a pained look. I had tried those morning sickness bands, and they didn't work. Even the morning sickness lozenges did nothing but put a foul taste in my mouth. But I'd try anything at this point.

"It's unconventional, and I wasn't sure what you'd think," she said.

I gave her a confused look

She sprinted off to the office and returned with a tiny cloth bag in her hand. "My friend sells healing crystals. She recommended the clear quartz for all around healing."

She offered the bag to me, and I opened it, pouring out the contents into my hand. Inside was a wire-wrapped clear crystal. There was a notecard explaining what it meant. It touched me that Willow thought about me, but I wasn't so sure this would work. The necklace was pretty, though.

"I'm not sure I believe they have healing powers, but her crystal jewelry's awesome," Willow explained. "I'm thinking about asking if I can sell them in the shop."

I put the crystal around my neck and pocketed the bag

it came in. "I'll try anything. Do you think her stuff would sell here? People come here for coffee, not jewelry."

She chewed on her lip. "True. Although...I'd love to one day expand to a bookstore coffee shop combo."

"Hey! Isn't the storefront next door for rent? I remember seeing a sign in the window when I walked up today."

She frowned. "I was considering moving the roastery there, but someone nabbed it already."

"One day, Will. Let's focus on making the coffee shop a success, then expansion." I gestured to her beautiful decorations. I loved the aesthetic of the Drakesville Drip from the moment I stepped foot in here a few years ago. It was cozy, yet funky. "You do such a good job."

She dipped her head down, not willing to take my compliment. "I wish people took me seriously."

I laughed. "That's because you hire your friends who no-call no-show."

"I fired Kira."

"Really?"

"Yup. She's pissed at me, but I'm not paying people to hangout. This is my business."

I beamed like a proud mom at her impassioned speech. Willow worked hard to open this business, and she wanted it to succeed. I admired her for that.

Because of the snow, it was a slow day at the shop, which meant we practiced latte art and Willow worked on social media scheduling while I cleaned and re-cleaned the counters. I hated when work crawled to a snail's pace. It made the seconds tick by like we were frozen in molasses. I only had an hour left, and it felt like the clock stood still.

The chime on the door rang, forcing me to glance up and find Killian standing in the doorway. He brushed the snow from his hair as he walked inside. Underneath his beard, his skin was flushed red from the cold.

"What do you want?" I asked. Then I cringed when I realized how bitchy that sounded when I meant what did he want to order.

He ignored my rudeness. "When's your shift over? It's coming down out there. I'll come pick you up."

"You don't have to. I'm fine."

"Ronan sent me to shovel the walk anyway. I don't want you to slip and something happen to Bean."

Willow looked up from her computer and peered at Killian. "He has a point."

"Fine," I bit out.

He marched out of the door, and I felt my jaw get slack as I watched him through the window shoveling the snow on the walk. There was something beautiful about watching as he worked. Killian was of average build, not physically fit like his brother Ronan, but something about the way he took charge to take care of me and the baby had me remembering how we created Bean in the first place.

Willow's voice snapped me out of my daydream. "I thought you said nothing was going on with you and Killian."

"Huh?"

She arched an eyebrow at me. "Shev, is there something between you?"

I shook my head. "No, he's..."

Hot. He was hot. So sue me, I noticed my baby daddy was one of the hottest guys in town. Probably why he could have any woman he wanted. And usually did.

She tilted her head to see what I was staring at. "Oh, yeah, he's got a nice butt. I can appreciate the view."

Heat rose on my cheeks. Killian did have a nice butt,

but I wasn't supposed to notice that. Maybe that was my hormones. That usually didn't happen until the second trimester, but every pregnancy was different.

I tore myself away from the view and went back to meticulously wiping down every surface.

"We should close early," Willow thought out loud.

"Do you want me to call the next shift?"

"I'm not sure yet. That means a loss of profit."

And a loss of wages.

No one else came in as the minutes ticked along slowly for the rest of my shift. Killian walked back inside, brushing the snow out of his dark hair, and for the first time, I noticed the stress on him. His shoulders slumped as if a boulder was weighing him down and the circles under his eyes told me perhaps he wasn't sleeping either. A part of me felt guilty that I was the reason for that. Which was why I hadn't wanted to force him to be involved in the first place. The prospect of this unplanned baby had turned his world upside down and wreaked havoc on his well being. That made my already queasy stomach turn sour.

"You want a coffee?" I asked.

He nodded.

"On the house!" Willow called from the kitchen.

Killian pulled out his wallet and shoved some cash into the tip jar anyway.

"What can I get you?" I asked him.

"Latte."

Huh, I'd pegged him for a black coffee kind of guy. I punched in his order. "Will, I need you to do the comp!"

I went behind the bar and started making the espresso. I poured the shot in while I frothed the milk and carefully added the milk into the cup, making an easy design out of the foam.

I slid the cup over to him, and his lips curled up. "Cute."

I grimaced. "I need practice."

Willow came back behind the counter and punched in her authorization code. "Oh, it looks good. You'll get better."

Killian took his latte and parked it at the table in front of the window. I cleaned the espresso machine and restocked while the snow blanketed the world outside.

"You can head out if you want," Willow said. "I made calls to the closing shift. I hate to close, but they're calling for more snow."

"First blizzard of the year!" I exclaimed.

"Better get to the store for all your bread and milk," she joked.

I laughed.

People in our area were dramatic when it came to snow. Even when the forecast was only a couple of inches, the grocery stores would be completely out of the staples. We could laugh about it when it ended up being only a few flurries. Today, though, it was coming down hard.

I nodded at Killian. "He needs a minute."

"I didn't realize he was working for Ronan. Ro's great, but he usually comes himself during winter since he doesn't have a lot of work this time of year."

"I didn't know either."

I had no clue Killian was working with his brother. Perhaps he was working as hard as I was with thoughts of the baby coming. I never asked him to do anything extra just because I was carrying his baby. Moving me into his house had been more than enough. It made the guilt in my stomach churn. But a tiny part of my heart warmed at how he wanted to take care of us. I ignored that part of myself.

"You ready?" Killian asked.

I jumped when I noticed him standing in front of the counter.

"Let me grab my things."

I went into the office where we kept our coats and personal items. I pulled my coat on and slung my purse over my shoulder. When I came out, Killian had his hands in his pockets, waiting for me.

"Be safe out there," I said to Willow.

"I'm not going far," she teased.

I forgot that besides owning the shop, she lived in the tiny apartment above it. I always forgot people lived up there and they weren't just for show.

I waved to her while Killian held open the door for me and we walked outside. He surprised me when he grabbed my hand, but I realized it was because of the slippery walkway. He had just shoveled it out, but it was already getting covered again. I put my hood up as the snow pelted me in the face. I couldn't wait to get home and climb into my bed.

Not home. Or even my bed. To his house where I was a guest until the baby came.

Killian guided me toward his pickup and helped me inside. He shut the door for me and then ran around to the driver's side. He turned the engine on and slowly eked out of his parking space.

"You don't have to go that slow," I said. He was driving like a grandma.

"The roads are icy."

I rolled my eyes.

We sat in silence on the short ride to his house. He didn't let me get out of the truck. Instead, he came around and helped me out and then guided me to the front porch. It was a sweet gesture, but it got on my nerves that he was treating me like I was fragile.

I wrenched open the front door and shook the snow off my coat. Stomping out of my shoes, I slipped them off and put my coat in the closet.

"Are you at the pub tonight?" Killian asked.

"Nope. Night off. I'm going to shower and take a nap."

"I gotta head back out to help with the snow. I'll see you later."

And as quick as he came, he was gone. There was a part of me that was disappointed, but I was too tired to think of what that meant.

CHAPTER NINE

KILLIAN

*M*y body was screaming Uncle. I had no idea how Ronan handled doing all of this snow removal on his own. Manual labor was no fucking joke.

It was still coming down, but Brian had already called and told me not to bother coming into the pub tonight. That sucked, but if no one showed up, it was a waste of time. Who was going to trek out in this blizzard for me to pour them a beer? Well, a lot of people, actually, but not enough to make it worth my while.

I wiped the sweat from my brow and shoveled the walk in front of my house. I didn't care how tired I was. I wouldn't risk Siobhan falling and something happening to the baby. When she told me she couldn't take any risks, it set something in stone for me. No matter what, I'd do everything to protect and keep them safe. Even risk my own body.

"Killian, that you?" my next-door neighbor, Mr. Riley, called out from his porch.

I waved to him. "Yup. You need your drive shoveled?"

"You've been running around town with that brother of yours all morning. You need a break."

I gestured to the sky above me. "There's no stopping it."

"Be careful."

"I am careful."

He shook his head and walked back inside. Mr. Riley was alright. He was my parents' age and had lived in his house forever. Not unusual for a town like Drakesville. I'm sure he had his fair share of judgments about me from sharing a wall with me all these years. He never said a word, though, God love him.

I sighed and took up my shovel again. After I finished my driveway, I shoveled out Mr. Riley's. It took me a while, but once I was done, I took my shovel into my shed out back and came inside.

I trudged up the steps and walked toward the bathroom, stripping down immediately and turning the water all the way to hot. The steamy water cascaded down my weary bones, and for once, I was glad I was going to miss a shift at the pub. My body ached so much from all the hard labor that I welcomed the break from the pub. I shampooed my hair, trying to get the sweat out of it, and scrubbed down my body, already feeling the soreness I'd wake up with tomorrow. I conditioned my beard and washed my face last.

I turned off the faucet and stepped out of the shower, grabbing a towel from the rack and wrapping it around my body. Once in my bedroom, I shut the door behind me and rummaged in my drawer for a t-shirt and a pair of sweats.

I went in search of Siobhan and found her in my living room, gingerly eating a pack of saltines while she watched some reality TV show.

"Is that all you ate today?" I asked.

She jumped at my voice, and I cringed that I'd startled her.

She grimaced. "Nothing's working, and I'm so hungry."

"What can I do?" I asked sincerely. Watching her suffer made me feel helpless, especially given the fact she didn't want my help.

She shook her head. "Nothing."

"Are you sure?"

She frowned.

"When do we go to the doctor next? Let's talk to her about this."

"I've already called a million times. I'm early in this, so they think it'll pass."

I nodded. That's what Kelsey and my mom said, too. I hoped they were right because Siobhan looked down-right miserable.

"Well...I'm going to make something for dinner. How about I make some extra?" I offered.

"You don't have to," she muttered, her gaze returning to the TV.

I didn't bother arguing with her and walked into my kitchen.

I was starving. I had shoved a granola bar in my mouth this morning when Ronan called me, and Mom fed us plenty when we shoveled out the driveway for her, but all the back-breaking work burned a ton of calories.

I peered into my fridge, realizing I had meant to go grocery shopping this weekend but did double shifts at the pub and was too tired to do it. But I had eggs, and maybe Siobhan would eat that.

I took out the egg carton and cracked some into a bowl. I whisked them together and poured the egg mixture into a pan on the stove.

My phone vibrated in my pocket while I waited for the eggs to cook. I took it out and saw a text from an unknown number.

> UNKNOWN: Hey, stranger. Wanna have some fun during the holidays?

I stared down at my phone. I had no fucking clue who this was, and I wasn't bringing any hookups into the house when Siobhan was living here. Sure I could go to them, but it made me feel like a dick leaving Siobhan to suffer while I banged my way around town.

Another text popped up.

> UNKNOWN: It's Molly, if you forgot, hot stuff.

Ohhh.

Molly was a great girl, fun in the sack, but a stage five clinger. Then she moved to New York for a job, and I was off the hook. Hell no. I had to nip this in the bud. Even if I seriously needed to get laid. No way was I getting horizontal with her again.

> ME: Sorry. Too busy with family stuff this year.

Not exactly a lie but not exactly the truth, either. A little white lie never hurt anyone.

I set my phone on the counter and stirred the eggs. I grabbed the bread, popped slices into my toaster, then got the cheese from the fridge. The eggs firmed up, and I scrambled them until they were just right, sprinkling cheese on top at the last second. As if on cue, the bread popped up from the toaster.

I opened the cabinet above my head and got out two

plates. I plated the eggs and buttered my slices of bread, leaving Siobhan's plain in case she couldn't handle the eggs. One of the articles suggested eggs might help while she was dealing with morning sickness.

I walked back into the living room, and Siobhan turned toward me. She cocked her head, but then I handed her the plate. "Oh! You didn't have to do that."

I slumped down into my armchair. "It didn't take me that long."

She gingerly took a bite of her eggs, and before I knew it, she had ravenously eaten all of it.

I could only stare at her in wonder. "Damn girl."

Her cheeks reddened. "I was really hungry."

"You feel okay, though?"

She shrugged and sat back on the couch. "We'll see. Thank you."

I nodded.

I stared up at the TV, shaking my head at the cheesy dating show she was watching. My phone vibrated again as I took another bite.

> UNKNOWN: [Sad face] Come on, Killian.
> You know we had a good time together.

I sighed and shoved my phone back into my pocket. I wasn't hooking up with someone looking for more, and Molly had big hopes in her eyes. Didn't really have time either, if I was focused on making sure I had enough money for Siobhan and Bean.

Siobhan was busy on her phone, and then she let out a long sigh. Before I could ask what was wrong, she answered it. I tried not to eavesdrop, but it was hard not to catch bits and pieces from her end.

"Hey, Mom... No, I'm home. Well, at Killian's... Yeah,

he came and got me... Yup, we're good... I promise... Okay... Okay...Mom, I can't. Christmas is days away, and tickets are too expensive... No, I have to work anyway... Okay, love you too."

She clicked off her phone and gave me a pained look. "Sorry. My mom's really been laying on the guilt about not seeing me for Christmas."

"Do you usually visit them?"

She shook her head. "Nah, I usually work."

"You can get someone to cover for you."

She fiddled with the crystal pendant around her neck. "I need the money."

I made a noise in the back of my throat. I wanted to argue with her, but my brothers had already told me to stop pushing her so much. Instead, I took our dirty plates into the kitchen and cleaned up.

I stared out the kitchen window, peering at the snow dumping down in my backyard. It was the first big snow of the season. Right now, it looked pure and pretty, but in the morning it would turn to grey slush.

"It's really coming down."

I jumped at the sound of Siobhan's voice behind me. She gave me a sheepish look as she glided over to the cabinet to put away the box of saltines.

I dried my hands off and rubbed my sore shoulder. "Yeah. I hope it's not too bad in the morning."

"As much as it sucks, I love the snow. It makes it look so pretty and Christmasy this time of year. I hope it stays so we have a White Christmas." She peered around my mini-malist house. "So are you anti-Christmas?"

"What do you mean?"

"Where's your holiday spirit?"

I rolled my eyes. "We usually go to my parents', and Mom goes all out. I'm too lazy for that shit."

She stared out the kitchen window at the snow coming down with her hand resting on her belly. "I love Christmas. I want to work hard this year so Bean can have the perfect first one. Hopefully."

She whispered that last part, and it wasn't lost on me the fears she had about the pregnancy.

She turned back to me. "Can I ask you something?"

"Hmm?"

"Have you always worked with Ronan?"

I gave a slow shake of my head. "Need the money."

"Why?"

I stared back at her. "Same reason you do."

Her mouth formed a small 'o.' "You don't have to—"

"Yes, I do."

She looked like she wanted to argue, but instead, she nodded, choosing her battle tonight. I was going to take that as a win.

She slipped out of the kitchen, and I finished cleaning up. When I was done, I found her in the living room again, lying on the couch and flipping through the channels. I sat down in the armchair.

"Are you gonna make me watch your cheesy reality shows?" I teased.

"If you keep annoying me, maybe," she shot back, but she sent a smile my way to tell me she was only joking. "What do you normally watch?"

"Hockey, this time of year."

"Boring!"

I laughed. "Hockey's fun."

"I like the Bulldogs, but I'm definitely a fair weather fan."

"Damn band wagoners," I teased.

"Shut it!"

I grinned at her, and for once, the tension between us faded away. If only for tonight. Having a baby with a relative stranger and moving her into my house was awkward, but it didn't have to be. Siobhan and I could be friends. It was probably better in the long-run that we got along for the sake of our child.

We landed on reruns of CSI, finding we were both fans of police procedurals. Outside, the snow bombarded the ground, and I could only imagine how much work Ronan needed help with tomorrow.

My phone buzzed again.

I pulled it out and groaned at more texts from Molly. This chick didn't take a hint.

Siobhan eyed me. "Someone wants your attention."

I grunted in response and deleted my messages.

"Kill?" she asked.

"Yeah?"

"If you have a lady friend that wants your attention, I won't be offended if you take off."

"No. This one's trouble." I stroked my beard. "Sorry, that makes me sound like an asshole, but she's a stage five clinger."

Siobhan let out a soft chuckle. "Oh."

"Damn, I still sound like a dick."

She shrugged. "Hey, if you're upfront that you're only looking for something casual, that's on them. But if you've got somewhere you'd rather be, don't mind me. If I wasn't living here, I wouldn't expect you to be celibate."

"Not this one."

She pursed her lips, and it seemed like she wanted to

say something else, but she let it go. She lay back on the couch, one hand on her belly as we watched TV together.

After we watched an entire episode in silence, I glanced over and saw her eyes closed. I wanted to head to bed anyway, so I stood up and walked over to her.

I bent to her ear. "Siobhan."

"Hmm?" she muttered, still half asleep.

"Let's get you up to bed."

"No, the dinosaurs," she whispered.

I stared at her. The what? "Huh?"

She closed her eyes again, and not wanting to disturb her because she needed the rest, I picked her up bridal-style and carried her to the guest room. She stirred when I set her down on her bed and pulled back the covers.

"Shush, go back to sleep," I whispered. I slid her underneath the covers and tucked her into them.

Her eyes fluttered open. "Killian?"

"What's wrong?"

"Can you stay?"

"I'm right across the hall."

She shifted into the bed, her eyes half-lidded. "No. Here with me. Please?"

"Why?"

"I want to be held."

A part of me knew she was still asleep and didn't know what she was saying, but the other part of me, my protective side, wanted to hold her and make sure she was safe. The latter won.

I slid into the bed beside her. She lay on her back, and her breathing got steady again. I rested my hand on her stomach and held her protectively.

"Little Bean, I'll do everything I can to keep you and your mama safe. I can promise you that."

It wasn't long before sleep took hold of me, too.

CHAPTER TEN

SIOBHAN

*M*y stomach roiled, but when I tried to get out of bed, I discovered something pinned me down. God, I was gonna puke all over myself if I didn't get to the bathroom right this second.

I opened my eyes and looked down to find a man's arm across my middle. I stared down at the big hand splayed across my stomach as if guarding me and my unborn child. It took me a beat to realize whose hand that was.

"Killian?" I whispered.

It was way too early to be up, even for me, but this baby wanted me to throw up my dinner from last night.

Killian stirred beside me, and I flinched when he nosed across my neck. "Go back to sleep, darling." His voice was thick with sleep, and he pulled me closer, trapping me in his warm embrace.

Why was he in bed with me? And acting like we were a couple?

I wanted to snuggle down into the comfort of his arms,

to let myself give into feeling held like this. But the queasiness in my stomach meant I had to get up now before it was too late.

I struggled to push his arms away from me. "Get off of me, or I'll puke on you."

"Huh?" came his sleepy reply.

His grip on me slackened, and I launched myself out of the bed and down the hall to empty the entire contents of last night's dinner into the toilet.

Fantastic.

I sat on the floor of the bathroom, slouching against the cold tile wall, hoping another wave didn't wash over me. Would this morning sickness ever go away? Since I moved in, I tried not to disturb Killian with all my vomiting, but he didn't have a big house. He likely heard this every single morning.

"Here."

I flinched at the sound of Killian's deep voice. He knelt down beside me, offering me a glass of water. I took it and sipped it slowly. "Thanks."

"You okay?"

I nodded.

"You sure?"

I rolled my eyes at him. Could he lay off for once? "No."

He took a seat next to me on the bathroom floor. "What can I do?"

"Nothing." It was sweet he brought me water and wanted to do something, but there wasn't much he could do. I fingered the crystal around my neck. Maybe my skepticism kept the healing crystal from working. "I really wanted this to work."

"Huh?"

I hadn't meant to say that out loud.

I gestured to my necklace. "My boss gave me this healing crystal. I didn't think it was going to work, but I wanted to believe."

"What else can we try?"

"I have to ride it out."

"What about—"

I held up my hand. "Killian, it's very sweet you want to help, but I've tried everything. I talked to Kelsey, and she said all her pregnancies were like this. It's a Murphy thing."

He grimaced and raked his hand through his beard, guilt evident across his face. I didn't want him to feel bad when it wasn't his fault the baby was tormenting me. I'd suffer for a little, and then hopefully, once I reached the second trimester, I'd be over it.

I placed a hand on my belly. The second trimester was a dream for me. None of my other pregnancies ever went that far. Last year, I lost a baby at nine weeks, but I was holding out hope that didn't happen this time around. I wanted this rainbow baby so badly. I needed Bean to stay healthy inside me. Even if they were making me miserable.

"Hey," Killian whispered, the concern dripping in his voice.

I had to physically shake my thoughts away. "Huh?"

"No more tears," he said. He reached over and wiped the stray tears I hadn't realized were on my face.

"I really want this baby."

"I know, darling."

My chest felt warm every time he called me darling. The confusing feelings inside had to be the baby's love for their father rubbing off on me. My emotions were all over the place; that had to be the case.

I struggled to get up from the floor, and he lent me a hand, pulling me up to stand. He walked me back into my room, and it was sweet that he made sure I had my water and was safely back in bed. But when he walked across the hall, the bed felt cold and empty.

I stared up at the ceiling, my thoughts invading my sleep until my alarm blared to life on the bedside table. I was probably lonely because I was missing my parents, and remembering my miscarriage last Christmas had me on edge. Last winter was a living hell. After losing the baby I thought was my miracle and then my husband a few weeks later, I wasn't sure how I came out of it. This baby was the hope I clung to.

I shut off my alarm and played with the crystal pendant at my neck. It was thoughtful of Willow to give me this, and I would try anything for this morning sickness to let up, but I didn't think it worked.

I lay in bed for a little while longer. I had no desire to get up and go make coffee when the smell made me want to throw up. Again.

Willow might have been right about me cutting back my hours. I'd feel different if not for the fact Killian had been letting me stay here rent-free. Freya told me I should let him take care of me, and he was being such an annoying mother hen that maybe I should.

I heard signs that Killian hadn't gone back to sleep either, and I resigned myself to getting up. I got dressed, tugging down my Drakesville Drip t-shirt over my stomach. My pregnancy wasn't showing yet, but I saw the subtle changes in my body. I wanted all the aches and pains that came with pregnancy. I was desperate for Bean to be my true rainbow baby that I got to hold in my arms at the end.

I opened the door to my bedroom and walked downstairs to find Killian at his kitchen island, sipping on coffee.

"Oh, you're awake," I said.

He nodded. "Gotta dig everyone out. You ready?"

I stared blankly at him. "Huh?"

"I'm doing work in the town square. I'll drive you to the coffee shop."

"Oh, you don't have to."

His jaw ticked, but he said nothing and sipped on his coffee in silence.

I put my hands on my hips. "Killian, I don't need you to drive me to work. Living here's actually made it better for me. You're closer."

"Fine."

"K, bye!"

He was being so grouchy this morning. I'd chalk it up to him not being fully awake yet. I took my coat out of the hall closet and pulled it on. I didn't say anything to him as I left the house. The sidewalk had been shoveled, and the snow-plow was already hard at work. I carefully walked the couple of blocks to the coffee shop.

Willow was behind the counter when I keyed into the front door. We weren't open yet, so I made sure the sign was still flipped to 'closed.' I shook the snow off my boots and waved to her on my way to the office. I hung up my coat and found my black apron, tying it around myself. I was hungry but didn't want to chance it with throwing up again since my stomach was still feeling queasy.

Coming around the counter, I found Willow starting the drip coffee. She gave me a bright smile and nodded at my chest. "Hey, did that work?"

I shook my head. "I wanted it to work so badly, but I threw up again this morning."

"Well, did you charge it?"

I raised an eyebrow. Did I what now? I didn't know how you charged a crystal, but okay.

She laughed. "You have to charge them in the sun or moonlight or something. It was on the instructions."

Yeah, I didn't bother to read that.

"Don't give me that face." Willow started the batch of decaf. "You said you'd try anything."

"Okay, true," I conceded. "Before we open, can we talk about something?"

"What's up?"

"You're right."

She flicked the switch to start the pot and wiped down the countertop. "About what?"

"That I need to lessen my hours."

She chewed on her lip. "I hate that, but I get it."

"Maybe I can go down to two days?"

She gave me a tight smile, trying to not let the stress show on her face. Willow told you what she was thinking with her facial expressions. She couldn't help it. I hated letting her down, but I had to do what was right for the baby.

"I'll figure out the schedule. Don't worry about it," she lied. She walked over to the front door, flipped the sign, and unlocked the door.

You would think the snow on the ground would have led to a slow day, but within a matter of minutes, Willow and I were tag-teaming making lattes and taking orders. It didn't give either of us time to think about how decreasing my hours would affect her business.

Working at both my jobs was exhausting, but being in the early stages of my pregnancy and wanting to puke every two seconds made today absolutely hell. Plus, customers were annoying me by asking why I wasn't going home for Christmas. Like, hello, because I need the money, so buy another beer. I gave them my customer service smile instead. They meant well; I was just crabby and hungry.

The pub was busy tonight. Probably because it was the day before Christmas Eve, and all the college kids were back in town out drinking with their friends. And being f-ing annoying.

Damn, I needed to eat something. I was being a huge bitch for no reason.

I passed the bar on my way toward the kitchen, and I couldn't help but notice the blonde flirting with Killian. An ugly thought popped into my head, and I rushed off before my mouth opened without thinking.

I punched in my orders and dropped off the food ready for my tables. It was a whirlwind out on the floor tonight. Lila was even here tonight, working in the office, while Brian picked up making drinks with his brother.

After dropping off more orders, I rushed back into the kitchen. I ordered a grilled cheese for myself, not sure I had time to eat it or if I could keep it down, but I was craving it. And cheesesteaks.

"Jose! Eighty-six that last order!" I yelled to one of the cooks.

"Why?" he asked.

"It's for me, and I want a cheesesteak instead."

He shot me a flirty smile through the kitchen window. "Oh, you got it, girl. I'll make it real good for you."

I shook my head. Line cooks... They never stopped flirting with the servers, no matter the restaurant.

I sipped on water and rubbed the back of my neck as I waited for my food. My tables were in a good spot. Everyone had their food except for the drunk college students who kept asking for more beers and staring at my chest like I didn't know what they were doing. The more obnoxious of the bunch made a comment about my ass when he thought I was out of earshot.

Sarah sauntered into the service aisle and punched in some orders. "Oh, there you are."

"Were you looking for me?"

"Your table wants to cash out."

"Which one?"

She grimaced. "Fourteen."

I sighed in relief. "Thank God."

She gave me a look of pity. "One of them screeched about my tits like I couldn't hear."

"Apparently, they like my fat ass."

She laughed. "Sorry, girl. At least they'll be gone soon. Can I ask you something?"

I nodded and set my water down on the counter.

"Are you and Killian a thing?"

I blew out a breath. A thing? Not exactly. His family knew about the baby, but I wanted to keep a lid on it. I'd been down this road before, and telling people too soon only led to heartbreak.

I shook my head. "No. Why?"

She squinted at me. "Okay, well, he has been staring death glares at those guys. When he's not staring at your ass."

"Huh?"

She waved me away. "But he always does that."

Um...what? Since when?

She rolled her eyes and pushed her blonde bangs out of her eyes. "Girl, even when I hooked up with him, he had wandering eyes for you."

None of that seemed right. I was sure Killian never looked at me twice before Lila's wedding.

Sarah laughed again. "Oh, Shev. He never made it known because you were married. He might be an asshole, but he's not a home wrecker."

"Uh...okay," was all I managed to get out.

Had Killian been attracted to me this entire time? She couldn't possibly be right.

She moved to the side so I could use the register and print out the bill for my customers. Sarah didn't know what she was talking about. She just saw Killian's eyes on me now because he was an overbearing baby daddy.

I sprinted out of the service aisle before she could say anything else and dropped off the bill for my annoying table. I grabbed refills for a table, and when I came back, the rowdy college students had money out, ready to pay.

I walked over to them with my sickly-sweet server smile. "All set?"

The douchiest of the bunch eyed me up and down. I shifted on the balls of my feet, waiting for any of them to say something.

"You can keep the change," one said with a sinister smirk that made me uncomfortable.

Whatever, creep.

"Thanks," I said, not counting it in front of them because that was rude. I walked behind the bar, seeing the register available, and punched in the cash.

A whole fifty-five cents tip. What a bunch of assholes.

Tears stung my eyes as the drawer opened, and I counted the petty cents. I knew how some people felt about tipping, but man did it suck when you went out of your way to be good at your job only to be insulted.

I had a thick skin and could usually handle it, but not

tonight. I was tired and hungry. And I really missed my parents.

"What's wrong?" Killian's voice pulled me away from my morose thoughts.

I wiped my eyes. "Nothing."

"Siobhan." He searched my eyes, the worry etched across his face.

I set the receipt and the coins down on the counter. "Bad tip. Love it when they say keep the measly change."

"Fourteen?" he asked.

His eyes hardened, and his jaw ticked as he stared across the room at the three rowdy kids. Before I could stop him, he grabbed the change and the receipt and marched over to them.

"What's he doing?" Brian asked.

I was afraid to find out. I couldn't hear from here, but I watched in horror as Killian slammed the coins down on the table. He pointed his finger in one of the kids' faces while the others laughed like it was the best joke he'd ever heard.

I rushed over to them to stop the impending fight. Killian had been known to literally throw a rowdy patron out the pub doors. We didn't need him to cause a scene tonight.

"Killian," I said calmly when I approached the table.

He ignored my presence, his finger still in the kid's face. "You heard me. Keep your shitty change. Are you happy with yourself, making a pregnant person cry?"

"KILLIAN!" I snapped. It was loud enough that I felt all eyes on me. Which was exactly what I didn't want. "Why don't you announce it to the whole fucking town?"

He turned to me. "Siobhan—"

"God fucking damnit, Killian. Stop trying to protect me. I never asked you to do any of this. Butt out of it!"

Now everyone *was* staring at me. People in this town talked, and they totally saw me screaming at Killian with tears streaming down my face.

Killian looked ready to fight my asshole table. He clenched his fists like he might take a swing at one of these kids.

"Office. Now!" Brian's booming voice came from behind me. I'd heard that voice before. That was his 'dad' voice.

I felt a warm hand on my back, and my stomach dropped when I turned around. Lila gave me a small smile. I hung my head and followed her into the office. She sat behind her desk and handed me a tin of cookies.

"My sister-in-law makes the best Christmas cookies, and she made me these ginger snaps. They really helped at the beginning of my pregnancy," she explained, resting her hand on her obviously pregnant belly.

I took a cookie and bit into it. God, I was hungry. I should have grabbed my cheesesteak from Jose. "Am I getting fired?"

She laughed. "God, no. I kicked those assholes out an hour ago, but I got buried in the schedule. One of them pinched my ass and called me a bitch. They're barred from the pub."

I dropped my cookie in my lap. "Wait, are you serious?"

Lila was the sweetest. I couldn't imagine anyone calling her such nasty things.

She wrinkled her nose. "Assholes. But it's my pub, so I can do what I want."

I picked my cookie up and devoured it, then reached for another. These were fantastic. I also might be starving.

"So..." Lila trailed off.

"Hmm?" I mumbled between bites of cookies.

She squinted at me. "You got pregnant at my wedding, huh?"

I sighed. "Yeah. Did Brian tell you?"

She shook her head. "Nope. So are you and Killian..."

"Co-parents. Nothing more. Annoying ass."

The corner of her lip twitched. "Yeah, he is, but he has his good moments."

"I swear he'd put me in a bubble if he could," I muttered. "I'm sure the whole town knows I'm pregnant with his baby now."

"Just the drunks at the pub," his voice cut in.

I whipped my head around at him. He held a plate with my cheesesteak and brought it over to me. I glared at him. I was pissed at him for going all over-protective on me. Those guys were dicks, but it wasn't unusual to get stiffed on a tip. I'd been in this industry long enough to know that.

"Can we talk?" he asked.

"No," I snapped.

I picked up my cheesesteak and took a huge bite. My tastebuds did a little jig at the delicious meat and cheese. I had been craving one all day. I might regret it later, but for now, I'd savor this tasty meal.

I glanced up and saw Lila nod at Killian. "Man the bar, Kill. I gotta talk to Siobhan."

I silently thanked her and ate my fries. He walked off in a huff, and Lila stifled her laughter while I gave him the finger behind his back. Seriously, this man was driving me up a frigging wall.

I finished half of my cheesesteak. "Sorry, that was bitchy of me."

Lila rubbed her stomach. She was much farther along than I was that she actually looked pregnant, where you couldn't tell I was yet. She must have already been pregnant at her wedding. "These hormones make us act irrational. But I wanted to talk to you about the holiday."

"What's up? Are you closing on Christmas Eve now, too?"

She shook her head. "No, but I was looking at the numbers from last year. So we're going to close at midnight instead of two, like normal."

"Okay, works for me."

That was actually smart. Lots of people in town went to midnight mass, so after midnight, the crowd petered out, and we ended up rolling silverware and shining every surface out of boredom. Lila was right to make that call.

"And congrats. Maybe it's not ideal that this baby is with Killian, but I know you've wanted this for so long."

"Thank you," I whispered.

I boxed up the rest of my cheesesteak and stuck it in the staff fridge. I steeled myself and walked out to the floor again. Celtic Kiss played on in the corner of the room. Finn was tearing it up on his fiddle while Eilish belted out lyrics. All eyes were on them, not me.

Sarah and Brian were handling my tables while Killian stood behind the bar, looking bored.

I sidled up beside him and put a hand on my hip. "Killian."

"Huh?"

I waited for him to turn toward me, and the worried look was still etched across his face. "Don't you ever fucking do that again. I never asked you to be my protector. And I damn sure don't need you fighting the drunk assholes who come here. You got me?"

He nodded, but I wasn't entirely sure I got my message across. I didn't care to find out. Instead, I hustled over to one of my tables and got back to work.

CHAPTER ELEVEN

KILLIAN

*F*inn scrubbed a hand across his unshaven jaw and stared me down. "Why the fuck are we at the Christmas farm on Christmas Eve?"

"I need a favor," I explained.

Lachlan squinted at me. "If anything, you owe us a favor."

Ronan nudged me. "Tell them."

Brian gave me the side-eye. "He fucked up."

I shot him a glare.

"With what?" Finn huffed. He and his best friend Eilish knocked back shots after their set at the pub last night, so he was definitely hungover and irritated.

Lachlan tilted his head. "With Siobhan?"

"Yuuuup," Brian elongated the word.

Before I could explain, a leggy blonde rushed over toward us. I gave Ronan a sideways glance when he immediately straightened up at the sight of Freya Reynolds. "Hi.

Sorry, school has been so busy I'm doing last-minute shopping."

"Hey, Freya," Ronan greeted her with a flirty smile.

She shot him with her own seductive grin. "Hey, Ronan. I didn't realize the whole family was coming."

Finn looked between Freya and me. "Okay, can someone clue me in?"

Freya pinned me with a serious look. "Oh, you one hundred percent need to grovel. She's pissed at you."

"What did you do?" Lachlan asked.

"Went after some assholes who didn't tip, tried to fight them, and then shamed them for making a pregnant lady cry. Oh yeah, and then pretty much announced to the whole town that Siobhan's pregnant, and she's not far along enough. She really effing hates you right now," Freya explained.

I felt like I got whiplash from her spitting it all out.

And what did my asshole brothers do? The dicks tipped back their heads and laughed. Well, except Brian, since he was there and already scolded me about my poor choices.

"So why are we at the Christmas tree farm?" Finn asked again.

Freya flashed him a bright smile. "Because Shev needs some holiday cheer. She won't admit it, but she misses her family and..." She looked down at her feet suddenly. "Last year was terrible for her."

I stared at her, but she clamped her mouth shut.

Ohhh. That was probably when Siobhan lost one of her babies. Then her husband died in January. Her mental state made a lot more sense now. Wish she'd have said something sooner.

"So...why did we get dragged into this?" Lachlan asked.

He didn't have his arms crossed over his chest like Finn, but his brow was furrowed.

"I got a guy here," Ronan said. "And you assholes are gonna help your brother fix his shit."

"Man, why the fuck I gotta do that?" Finn snarled and sent me a glare.

Since kids were around, I couldn't flip him the bird, so instead I held up three fingers. Finn knew to 'read between the lines.'

"Because I fucking said so," Brian said, acting like we were his kids. "Mom and Dad are at the house preparing for Christmas Eve dinner, so we're gonna get a tree, and then all of us are helping our dumbass brother decorate for the holiday."

"Why?" Finn asked.

"Because Siobhan's family now, and she needs us," Brian told him. That got Finn to shut up, and Freya gave Brian an approving look. "Help us figure out what she wants, Freya."

She beamed and darted away, forcing us to catch up to her.

I nudged Ronan when his eyes lingered on her ass. He shook me off, but I knew that look. It was about time he got over his ex.

Ronan smirked when his buddy who owned the place noticed us and told us he put something aside for me. I was worried I was going to have to buy a Charlie Brown tree that would make Siobhan mad or, worse, cry again.

Getting a tree the day before Christmas was never a good plan. But then again, it had never been on my agenda. Mom liked to do it up big for Christmas with a massive dinner before midnight mass; it hadn't even been my damn idea to do this. I called Freya because Lila scolded me last night about being an overbearing dick and told me to. I didn't even know Freya, and I had to ask Kelsey for her number. Not sure why this was Freya's suggestion, but if it made Siobhan not want to stab me, I was all for it.

Freya and Lachlan were in the craft shop picking up wreaths and other decor I didn't give a shit about. Lachlan was artsy-fartsy and into that shit; he always rearranged Mom's decorating if something was off center.

"Ready?" Ronan asked me.

I nodded, and we hefted the tree into the bed of my pickup. Finn and Brian helped us strap it down and then we waited around for Lachlan and Freya.

As if on cue, Freya came bouncing out of the shop with my baby brother on her heels. "Okay, all set. I'll see you later."

As swiftly as she came, she was gone. That girl gave me whiplash.

I gave Ronan a side eye again, noticing his longing stare. I nudged him with my shoulder, and he shoved me away.

"It's good you're doing this for Siobhan," Lachlan spoke up. "It's sweet."

"Surprised you even give a shit," Finn murmured.

"Man, what's your problem today?" I snapped at him. I thought he was hungover, but he was being a dick for no reason.

"Eilish's got a new boyfriend," Ronan revealed.

Finn punched Ronan in the arm. "Fuck off. It's not like that."

The rest of us swiveled our heads to stare at him. Yes, the fuck it was like that. Finn and Eilish were like two peas in a pod, but instead of putting on his big boy pants and asking her out, he moped whenever she was in a new relationship. She had the worst taste, too. One of her ex-girl-friends was such a disaster, the girl had been barred from the pub.

Lachlan pushed against my chest, trying to prevent me and Finn from going at it again. "Stop it. Anyway, I need to tell you guys something before I tell Mom and Dad."

"We already know you're bi," Ronan deadpanned.

"Sexuality's fluid, man," Finn argued. "Labels are stupid, anyway."

Lachlan rolled his eyes. Both my younger brothers identified as queer, but Finn didn't like having to define himself to a certain sexuality. Lachlan had always felt differently.

"I'm still bi as fuck, you dicks. And I'm moving home," Lachlan finally announced.

I swore I heard all four of us blink as we stared at Lachlan. At our baby brother who fucked off to the city and swore he'd never leave Fishtown. Our brother who claimed living in a small town was annoying as fuck.

Brian was the first to speak. "The contract went through?"

Lachlan nodded.

I narrowed my eyes at Lachlan. What contract?

"Congrats. Proud of you. The studio will be great," Brian added.

"What studio?" I asked.

"I'm renting the empty storefront next to The Drakesville Drip."

"For what?" I asked.

He rolled his eyes like my question was the stupidest he'd ever heard. "For my photography studio."

Ronan gave him a little playful shrug. "That's great news."

"Mom'll be psyched," Finn added.

"Yeah, I know," Lachlan agreed. "But now I need to find a place to live."

Normally, I'd let him stay with me. I tried to get Ronan to move in with me instead of Mom and Dad when he and Chrissy split, but Ronan said Mom's cooking was better. I was planning on turning my other guest room into the nursery, though, so unless Lachs wanted my couch, he was shit out of luck.

He held up his hand. "I'm not asking to stay with any of you assholes. Especially not you, Killian."

"Well, fuck you then," I joked.

He shook his head. "Wanted you to know because it's gonna be Mom's Christmas gift."

We all laughed at that.

"All right," I announced. "We got work to do."

I smiled as my sister-in-law told her kids they could open one present and then they had to go home.

"Gah!" Callum shrieked at me.

I had half a mind to hand Callum off because he kept pulling on my beard, but he was so stinking cute that I couldn't be mad at him.

After church, my family surprised me by piling into my house instead of Mom and Dad's. I wasn't sure what Siobhan would think when she found the whole Murphy clan here when she got home.

I shifted my nephew in my arms.

Mom smiled at me. "Pretty soon you'll be holding your own baby like that."

I hoped. The way Siobhan was worried about the baby, had dug into my subconscious. Bean wasn't planned, but the thought of losing them wasn't something I wanted to think about. Fatherhood scared the shit out of me, but I had gotten used to the idea that one day, it would be me holding a baby in my arms. After my ex, Liz, betrayed me, I never thought that would be a possibility.

"When does Siobhan get home?" Kelsey asked. She and Lachlan sat between the girls on my floor, helping Callie unwrap her gift while Cora ripped the wrapping on hers to shreds.

"Soon. Brian went to walk her home," I explained.

"Oh!" She gave me a sheepish look. "I didn't realize he was gone."

"How didn't you notice?" Finn asked from the armchair. He sipped on a beer. His sour mood hadn't improved since earlier. "He stomped out of here a couple of minutes ago."

"Mom brain," Kelsey said with a shrug.

I scanned the room. It looked like Santa's workshop had blown up in here. Even Mom said it was a bit much, and she loved the holidays. The decorated Christmas tree stood in the corner of my living room with pretty white lights twinkling away. Garlands hung over the mantle of my fireplace and wrapped around the railing of the staircase. Christmas decor littered my kitchen and dining room. It was a lot, but I hoped it cheered Siobhan up enough that I could apologize for butting into her life.

I couldn't help myself last night. Those guys were douchebags, and Lila told me she banned them from the pub for life. I had permission to literally throw them out on their asses the next time they came in, and I might actually do that. But it was clear Siobhan didn't like anyone fighting her battles, and she had a point about the whole town knowing she was pregnant now. My next door neighbor told me congratulations this morning, so the cat was definitely out of the bag.

I turned at the sound of the front door opening. Siobhan stomped the snow off her feet and pulled the hood of her coat down. It hadn't helped, as flurries sprinkled her dark hair. They fell to the floor as she shook her hair out and shrugged off her coat.

"DADDY!" Cora cried out and ran to my brother.

If there could have been a record scratch on the Christmas music blaring in my house, I'd have heard it in the way Siobhan's eyes got wide as she took it all in.

"Wh...what's going on here?" she finally stuttered out. She scanned the room, her nose wrinkling in thought.

"Surprise!" Freya said with an infectious smile. "I told Killian you needed some Christmas cheer."

Siobhan squinted at her friend. "You helped with this monstrosity?"

I barked out a laugh. I was glad she noticed it was as bad as I thought it was, but I let Lachlan and Freya run the show. I didn't know shit about interior decorating.

Freya gave Siobhan a hug, and they slunk upstairs together. They were back a few seconds later, and I grinned at the Grinch-themed pajamas Siobhan wore. The shirt looked tight across her middle, and I wondered if that was from the baby. I thought it was still too early to see the signs of the life we made together.

"Hi," she greeted everyone. "Sorry. I'm grumpy after a long shift."

Mom waved her off and stood up. "That's okay, dear. Freya told us you're missing your family."

Siobhan nodded, and my mom pulled her into a big hug. Her unease melted away as she relaxed into my mom's arms. Mom's hugs could do that to you.

"You eat yet?" Dad asked.

Brian and I rolled our eyes in unison. Only Dad would ask that.

Siobhan shrugged. "Not really. I'm pretty nauseous."

"Still?" I asked. "Have you tried—"

"Will you stop?" she snapped, sending me a fiery glare. Stubborn Irish woman indeed.

Kelsey laughed her head off. "Oh, girl, you're struggling. I've been there. My coworker makes these amazing ginger snaps. They helped me with my last pregnancy."

Kelsey stood up and led Siobhan into the kitchen. I heard them chatting in there and all seemed well. It was only me that Siobhan hated.

Brian took Callum off my hands and bounced him in his arms. Although Callum just wanted to make a grab for the Christmas ornaments. "We should get out of your hair."

"Why?" I asked.

Lachlan gave me an exasperated look. "Because she looks tired and doesn't want to deal with the whole family here after she got off work."

"It's totally fine," Siobhan's voice cut in. I hadn't noticed she walked back into the living room. She sat down on the couch next to me with a mountain of cookies in her lap. "It's so late, though. I'm sure the kids have to get to sleep before Santa gets here."

"They do," Brian agreed. "Come on, munchkins. Say goodnight to your uncles."

I grinned when I watched the girls attack Lachlan in hugs. They were extra hyper from all the cookies I snuck them when we got home from mass. They went down the line of us all, and then Brian and his family left in a whirlwind.

Finn and Freya took that as their cue to leave next. I watched as Freya hugged Siobhan tight before she left.

"Will you come to dinner at our house tomorrow?" Mom asked Siobhan.

Siobhan frowned. "I don't want to impose on your family gathering."

Mom waved her off. "Nonsense. You're family, Siobhan. You and the baby will always be welcome."

"Shev," I cut in, "she makes enough for an army. And I know you're missing your family."

She cut a glare at me for revealing that.

"Well, that settles it, then," Mom said. "You'll come with Killian tomorrow for dinner."

That wasn't an invitation; it was a command. My mom was good at having that effect on people.

Siobhan gave her a slow nod. "Okay. I'll come."

Mom clapped her hands. "Great! I do a honey-glazed ham on Christmas that the boys never stop begging for."

"It sounds great. Thank you for including me."

"Oh, of course, honey."

Siobhan got up and hugged my mom, thanking her for her kindness. Ronan and Lachlan left with Mom and Dad, and soon, it was just the two of us again.

I sipped on my beer while Siobhan chewed on her cookies. The only sound was of the awful Christmas music. I set my beer down on the coffee table and got up to turn off the stereo, then slumped back down on the couch next to Siobhan. "Cute jammies."

She laughed. "Freya gave them to me. I've been grumpy and not in the Christmas spirit." She gestured to the tree. "Was this her idea?"

I nodded. "Yeah. She said you needed to be cheered up and..."

She tilted her head at me, and I couldn't help but think how cute she looked with her mouth full of cookies. That should be weird, but it wasn't. "You're trying to make up for pissing me off last night."

"Am I forgiven?"

The corner of her mouth twitched. "Maybe."

"Are you tired? It's late."

She shook her head and grabbed the remote, flipping the TV on. "I want to stay up a bit. I'm wired from work and want to watch a Christmas movie. And eat. I'm hungry."

"I'll make you a plate."

Before she could reject it, I walked into the kitchen.

Mom always made shepherd's pie for Christmas Eve, which I thought was gross because I hated food touching, but my brothers loved it, so my opinion didn't matter. I took out the leftover containers and made up a plate for Siobhan. While it spun in the microwave, I placed more cookies on another plate. She seemed to like these ginger snaps. Couldn't blame her—I was pretty sure I ate five of them already.

The microwave beeped, and I took the food out, stirred it, and put it back in for a few more minutes. Finally, it was hot enough that I took the plate out to Siobhan.

She sat on the couch with her feet up on the coffee table and her hand on her stomach. I didn't think she realized how much she did that already.

She smiled at me in thanks as I handed off the food. "Oooh. I love shepherd's pie."

I blanched.

"You don't like it?"

"Pass. Food touches too much for my taste."

She dug into her food and let out a long moan. "Your loss because it's so good."

I shifted, trying to forget the sound of her moans and the memory of our night together. Or how those memories had been haunting my horny dreams. "Yeah. Mom's a good cook."

"My mom wasn't much of a cook," she explained. "But your mom makes the perfect mashed potatoes, and whatever spices she uses in the stew are to die for."

"It's alright."

She elbowed me. "It's not just 'alright.' I can taste the care she puts into everything."

She hoovered in the rest of her meal, and I raised my eyebrow at her damn near licking the plate. My mom was a good cook, sure, but I never saw anyone do that before.

"Oh my God. I was so hungry," she said with a laugh. "The pub was actually super busy tonight, and Miles isn't as quick as you are behind the bar."

That was true. He flirted a lot but not in a way where he was still knocking back drink orders. He needed to learn to multitask.

Siobhan munched on the cookies while we watched A Christmas Story.

"Thank you," she whispered.

"For what?"

She gestured around the room. "I didn't know I needed this and your family... You're right, I miss my parents. And..." She wrung her hands. She turned to me, and her eyes were shiny. "I lost my last baby on Christmas Eve. That's probably why I freaked out on you last night. It's too early to tell everyone, and now the whole town knows."

I sighed. "I'm sorry."

"I know."

"I promise not to do it again."

She shot me a glare. "Are you sure?"

I chuckled. "I'll try."

"Thanks for bringing me the Christmas cheer. I definitely needed it."

I squeezed her hand, and we didn't say anything else as we watched the movie. I wished I could take the worry away from her, but I'd be lying if I said I wasn't worrying too.

CHAPTER TWELVE

SIOBHAN

"*O*kay, you're forgiven," I said after we finished watching A Christmas Story.

It was late, but working at the pub, you got used to weird hours. I had been hungry when I got off and hadn't been expecting Brian to walk me home. Or to find the entire Murphy family crowded into Killian's living room. As overwhelming as it was, it was nice. Despite the fact that that Killian and I weren't together, Mary Pat and Colin made me feel like I belonged in the family. With my parents a thousand miles away, it was exactly what I needed. She was so kind to invite me for dinner tomorrow and made me feel a little better about missing my parents.

Killian's eyes twinkled with amusement. "Is that so?"

"Yeah, I guess. But if you pull something like that again, I'm moving in with Freya."

He held up his hands. "Alright, alright. I hear you loud and clear."

I studied him for a moment. There were dark circles

underneath his eyes, and his normally trimmed beard had grown out. He looked as tired as I was.

I took another bite of the ginger snaps Kelsey brought over. Turned out her coworker was Lila's sister-in-law. That was the problem with living in a small town. Everyone knew everyone, even if you didn't think so. And news got around fast.

Just as I feared, news of my pregnancy had already gotten around town. I had been congratulated multiple times tonight at the pub. Sarah's eyes were saucers when someone said it in front of her. Maybe now she'd get that Killian looked at me the way he did, not because he wanted me, but because he was overprotective.

I put a hand on my still-small stomach.

I flinched when Killian rested his hand on top of mine. He was warm to the touch, whereas I couldn't get the chill out of me.

"I promise nothing's gonna happen," he whispered.

I wanted to scream at him. Doug said those same things to me. The doctors said everything looked normal. And then I went to the bathroom, and everything ended in an instant. They never could tell me why. Chalked it up to 'these things happen.'

But Doug blamed me. He screamed at me, demanding to know what I did to cause another one of our babies to die. He never did that before. I hated to admit this, but before he died, our marriage was crumbling. I found even more proof of that after his death, but I hadn't told a soul that. Not even Freya.

"What's wrong?" Killian asked.

I rubbed my eyes.

"Stop thinking about it, okay?"

I nodded.

He was right, of course he was right, but I couldn't be rational about this. I talked to my mom earlier, and she said the same thing, but the fear had dug its way inside my heart. All the horrible things Doug said to me stuck there, too, whispering to me that all of this could disappear.

I got up and put my dirty dishes away, but I grabbed another cookie from the tin. Killian smirked at me when he saw. "What? I'm hungry!"

He smirked. "I ate a fuckton already."

"They're really good. I didn't realize Kelsey's coworker and Lila's sister-in-law were the same person."

"We live in a small town."

"Sometimes I forget. Other times..."

He sighed. "I know."

I squinted as I tried to imagine the family tree of how we were all connected. "So Lila's married to Declan...and his brother's Nolan. He's the one with the big beard that does the beer at the brewery, right? The big guy, right? And Declan does the business stuff?"

Killian stroked his own beard with a look of admiration. "Yeah, dude has an epic beard."

I wrinkled my nose. "It's too big and bushy. I like a beard, but...neat. Like yours."

I reached a hand out and brushed my fingers across the fur on his face. It might not be as cleaned up as before, but it was as soft to the touch as I remembered. The sensation ignited my libido, making me wonder what it would feel like as it scraped against my jaw again. Or my thighs. The uncontrollable thoughts had my breath hitching in my throat.

"Yeah?" Killian stammered out. His voice was thick and husky, like it had been the night we slept together. It made my lustful thoughts roar even more.

"Yeah," I whispered back, my heartbeat pounding fast in anticipation.

I didn't pull my hand away, and the room got smaller as we stared into each other's eyes. Maybe it was all the holiday cheer. Or a sugar rush from the cookies. But the way his eyes twinkled like the lights on the tree made me want to do something I shouldn't. Something that had been on my mind for a while, but I had restrained myself. Maybe it was time to give into these urges. For just one more night.

"Siobhan, I—"

But everything snapped back into place when I felt the upheaval in my stomach. In a split-second, I wrenched my hand away from his face and sprinted upstairs to the bathroom. I barely made it before I hurled up everything I ate.

Footsteps padded across the carpet in the hall, and I glanced up when Killian stepped into the bathroom. He held a glass of ginger ale out toward me.

I shook my head. "No, that won't help."

That deep crease formed on his brow again. "When's the next doctor appointment again?"

"After New Years."

It would be the standard checking of my weight and blood pressure, but in this appointment, we'd get to hear the heartbeat for the first time. That might explain why I was on edge. I was so afraid there wouldn't be one.

"We're talking to the doctor about this," Killian said firmly.

I sighed. He wasn't budging on that, and I was too tired to argue with him. I just wanted him to leave. Or else I might do something foolish. Like kiss him. We weren't going down that road again.

"I'm gonna get a shower," I announced.

He nodded and quietly closed the bathroom door behind him.

I got up off the bathroom floor and striped my clothes off. I ran a hand down my torso, inspecting my changing body. It barely looked like the baby was there, but I felt them in the way I was sick all the time and how my breasts were tender at a mere touch. That didn't stop me from thinking about a man's hands on them.

I shook my head, trying to physically shake the thoughts away. I turned on the shower head, waited for the water to heat, and then I got in. It felt good against my skin; I should have done this as soon as I got home. But when I walked in and found the Murphys here, I felt obligated to spend time with them. Now I wished I had marched up to the shower and then went to bed without a care in the world. I'd do that to Killian but not his mom. She was too sweet for me to be rude to like that.

I ran my fingers through my hair and rubbed shampoo into it. As I closed my eyes and washed my body, my thoughts went back to the moment in the living room. Of what would have happened had I not thrown up. Would Killian have pressed his hand against the back of my neck and devoured me whole in a kiss? Would I have let him? Would I have gotten on my knees in front of him and taken him down my throat?

I angrily rinsed the shampoo out of my hair and moved on to the conditioner. I shouldn't be having these thoughts. But as I moved onto washing my body, my brain replayed the images of the night we conceived Bean. Of how he ate my pussy without me having to ask, like he hungered for it.

Before I could ask myself what was wrong with me, I touched myself to the memory of it all. I needed to get it out of my brain and forget how I got in this situation because there was no way in hell I was sleeping with Killian again. What had I been thinking earlier?

The water had gone cold by the time I panted out my orgasm. I felt a pressure lift off my shoulders, like all I needed was that release to calm my mind.

I turned off the faucet and wrung out my hair in the shower before stepping out and wrapping a towel around myself. I tip-toed into the guest room where I changed into a pair of new pajamas. I still felt like I smelled of fried food, but maybe that was just my pregnancy senses.

It was around three by the time I brushed out my hair, but since I usually wasn't getting in until this time, I was still wired.

Killian's bedroom door was closed, so I assumed he went to bed as I crept downstairs. It really did look like the North Pole in the house, and it was nice Killian had appeased me. It was a kind gesture, even if Freya had recommended it.

At the thought of my bestie, I found my knitting box in the living room and sat on the couch. Every year, I made her a new pair of gloves because Poppy was always stealing them. I was running late this year and needed to put the finishing touches on it. I'd give them to her tomorrow sometime.

I turned on the TV and grinned at the classic old Grinch movie that came on. I worked my needles and basked in the quiet early Christmas morning.

"Hey, you got your wish."

I jumped at Killian's deep voice. "Holy shit, you scared me!"

I looked up at him and almost swallowed my tongue. Was he trying to get me to jump his bones? Killian wore a hoodie and a pair of grey sweatpants that showed the outline of the exact body part I'd been thinking about in the shower.

"Siobhan?"

"Huh?"

He pulled back the curtain of the window, and that's when I saw the white powder coming down. Not in big ugly chunks but in tiny pretty flakes.

"Oh, wow. A white Christmas."

"Merry Christmas, darling," Killian whispered before bending down and giving me a soft, yet chaste kiss on my temple. And then, as quickly as he'd appeared, he disappeared up the stairs again, leaving me in utter confusion.

I stared outside at the white coating the backyard. As if the scenic view would help me figure out what had happened to my life. There was one thing I knew for sure: I had the hots for my baby daddy, and I had to nip that in the bud before it made this arrangement even more complicated.

I lied. Whatever hots I had for this man died when he became the most insufferable annoyance in the world.

Christmas had come and gone uneventfully. I spent the day with Freya and her dad, and then I had the best dinner at Killian's parents' house where Mary Pat pulled out all the stops. I ended up throwing it all up later that night, but it had been so worth it, and I was grateful she included me in the family, even if I still felt like an outsider. New Year's wasn't that exciting either. I spent it at the pub hustling for tips until the wee hours of the morning.

Now that it was the new year, I had high hopes for the rest of my pregnancy. Today was supposed to be a routine appointment, but Killian had to question Dr. Lee about literally every single thing. I was surprised she wasn't staring daggers at the back of his head as much as I had been. She had the patience of a saint.

"She's had really bad morning sickness. Could it be hyperemesis gravidarum?" he asked.

Huh? He knew what HG was? Was he doing research? And why was he bringing this all up? That was my job.

Dr. Lee gave him a patient smile and then looked over at me. "Do you think it's that bad, Siobhan?"

"No," I lied. It didn't seem as bad as the symptoms of HG. It was only normal pregnancy symptoms. It annoyed me that Killian was butting in about that. "I'm fine," I said to my doctor, but I shot Killian a warning glare.

He clenched his jaw, clearly not wanting to fight me in front of Dr. Lee.

Truth be told, I was going out of my way to be annoyed with him since that moment on Christmas Eve. At literally anything. I had to remind myself that he was an overbearing control freak because I wasn't going to sleep with him again. No matter how hot he was. Or how good he looked when he walked around his house in those grey sweatpants. I had to stop thinking about how his beard would feel against my thighs again...

Something was wrong with me. In all the years I had worked with Killian, I never once looked at him this way. My hormones were messing with my rational brain. That was all.

"Look, I'm not concerned yet," Dr. Lee continued. "In a couple of weeks, it might be a thing of the past."

"He's an overbearing worry wart," I muttered.

It was Killian's turn to pin me with an annoyed look. "I'm worried about you and the baby."

His answer made me feel like a bitch, but he was driving me up a frigging wall.

"Make sure not to stress yourself out, okay?" Dr. Lee said gently.

I nodded. "I'm not. I even cut down my work hours."

Killian's eyes narrowed. "No, you didn't."

"At the coffee shop, I cut down to two days a week, but not at the pub because I make more money there."

He clenched his fist, and I knew what he wanted to say, but he held his tongue in front of the doctor. For once.

"Make sure you're eating healthy and resting, but Siobhan...I feel great about this pregnancy," my doctor admitted. "We'll do everything we can to make sure this one sticks, so take care of yourself. And try to eat even if it makes you sick. I think this will cease in a couple of weeks."

I felt my vision get blurry from tears building up at her kind words. Dr. Lee had been in the hospital with me, holding my hand, after the last miscarriage. After Doug stormed out when he found out I lost yet another baby. My doctor had comforted me, not my husband.

"O-o-okay," I blubbered out. I hated these tears. "I want this baby to survive."

I felt Killian squeeze my hand, and I squeezed back, even though I wanted to punch him for being annoying. Hello, mood swings.

"We'll see you next month when you hit the second trimester. Let Daddy help you. You're not in this alone." She opened up her file and offered a piece of paper to Killian. "Here's the copy you were asking for."

Killian took the piece of paper, and when his expression softened, I realized what she handed to him. He made that same face when he took the sonogram off my fridge and promised me everything would be okay. A part of my heart felt full at his expression.

Dr. Lee gave us both a nod and then walked out of the examination room.

Killian folded up the ultrasound printout and put it in the chest pocket of his shirt. Right against his heart. I wasn't sure why that made my own heart flutter.

Killian turned to me, and his face fell. "What's wrong?"

"Huh?"

He knelt and cupped my face. His calloused thumbs wiped away the tears I didn't know had fallen. "What's with the tears?"

"I don't know!"

"Aw, darling. Everything's gonna be okay."

I wanted to believe him, but I'd been here so many times before. And yet, there was something in Killian's voice that reassured me.

He pulled away and offered me his hand. I took it, and he helped me off the examination table. Then he helped me into my coat, and we left together. I climbed into the passenger seat of his truck, and we drove back to Drakesville in silence.

Killian parked in his driveway, and I got out of the truck, careful not to slip on the snow-coated drive. We walked into the house together, and I watched as Killian took the photo out of his pocket and proudly pinned it onto his fridge.

If I didn't turn on my heel right then and there, I might have done something I'd regret. Like kiss him again. Or something even worse. Like succumbing to my hormones and sleeping with him again. I had to keep him at arm's length, even if that meant being an unnecessary bitch.

CHAPTER THIRTEEN

KILLIAN

FEBRUARY

*G*od, she was so pretty. I couldn't keep my eyes off her, but I knew I should because I wasn't supposed to have the hots for my baby mama. Resisting the temptation that was the beautiful raven-haired woman had been a feat these past couple of months.

The holidays had come and gone, and then January went by in a blink. We had fallen into a steady rhythm of work, sleep, and then back to work. I hadn't even realized we were well into her second trimester until she woke me up this morning with a big breakfast during which she inhaled her damn waffles like a champ.

Over these last few months, I had grown fond of having her in my house, and it was getting harder to keep my distance. After that almost-kiss at Christmas, I reminded myself to keep her at arm's length; I didn't need her confusing my love for the baby with something else. But it didn't mean I couldn't look. Because holy hell was my baby mama fucking hot. Just had to remind myself not to touch. A feat that was getting harder with each day.

Fingers snapped in front of my face, pulling me out of my daze. "KILLIAN!" Sarah screeched at me.

"Huh?"

"DUDE! I needed three beers for table twelve like ten minutes ago. What are you staring at..." Sarah's voice died off when she swiveled her head and watched Siobhan hustling to another table with a bright smile on her face. God, she was practically glowing tonight. "Oh, bud. You got it bad."

"What?"

I grabbed three glasses from under the counter and filled one with the Old Man Sullivan beer. I chuckled at the name every time I saw it. That had been a collaboration with the brewery and was named after Lila's dad. The artwork on the bottles even depicted Sean Sullivan. He thought it was hilarious. Plus, it was an awesome Irish Red.

I set the beer on the serving tray Sarah had slapped on the bar, and then I filled the other glasses with the basic light beer from the big beer corporation we always had on tap. Lila wanted to get more local stuff for the pub and not just from her husband's brewery. She wanted the pub to be a local hub, and I had to admit she'd done wonders for the place since she took over.

Sarah tapped her nails against the bar and gave me a smug look. "Siobhan, Killian. You got it bad for her."

I shook my head. "No, I don't."

"Yes, you do," Brian muttered as he breezed by on his way to the kitchen.

Sarah arched an eyebrow at me. "You never looked at me like that."

"Sar, that was different."

"Why? Because I wasn't your baby mama?"

"Christ, quiet down about that."

"Why?" She grabbed her serving tray off the bar. "The whole town already knows because of you throwing those assholes out around Christmas."

"They assaulted Lila. They're barred," I argued.

Sarah rolled her eyes and sauntered over to her table. For once, I didn't check out her ass, as nice as it was, because Siobhan strolled over to the bar. She smiled at me and punched an order into the register.

"What was Sarah giving you grief about?" she asked.

I wiped down the bar. "Nothing. You're in a good mood."

"I can actually eat, Kill. This baby's not gonna kill me. And everyone's being nice tonight. It's unusual."

"Probably because this asshole glares at anyone who makes a wrong move," Brian said from behind me.

I swiveled around and glared at him. Why was he lurking today? Siobhan put her hands on her hips. "Killian, don't interfere with my customers. I've been dealing with this a long time."

She spun on her heel, heading toward a customer who had flagged her down.

I elbowed Brian. "Dick."

He shrugged. "Sarah's right."

"No, she's not."

"When's the last time you got laid?"

I gave him an annoyed look. "What's that got to do with anything?"

"You haven't looked at another woman since Siobhan moved in with you."

That wasn't true. I totally looked at all the hot women

who came into the bar and shamelessly flirted with me. I just hadn't been taking them up on their offers.

Brian pierced me with a knowing glance. "That's not like you."

Half the reason I didn't take those offers was because I was dog tired from pulling double duty with Ronan and then the pub. It definitely wasn't because I was too enamored with my baby mama and fighting my growing attraction to her every minute of every day. Definitely because I was way too tired putting in extra work.

"Fuck off, man," I muttered.

I was saved when a big group of rowdy college students trudged up to the bar, and I took their orders. Of course, these assholes wanted a round of shots. I got busy behind the bar and stopped watching Siobhan like a hawk.

The college kids dropped mad cash throughout the night, keeping me busy and on my toes. I slung shots and made drinks for the servers, and by the time it slowed down, it was almost time to go home.

With the night coming to a close, I wiped down the bar and found myself searching for Siobhan again. She was running checks back and forth, trying to get her last few customers to leave. I'd be yelling for last call soon, but hopefully they'd be gone by then. There were only a few patrons sitting at the bar, mostly locals.

"Holy shit," Miles breathed from beside me. "Sarah's right."

Why the fuck was everyone up in my shit tonight?

I glared at him. "No, she's not."

He grinned. "Hell yeah, she is. You haven't stopped staring at Siobhan all goddamn night."

I shoved him away. "Fuck off."

"Never thought I'd see the day."

"You haven't, asswipe."

I stormed off into the back to grab the vacuum and start cleaning, hoping everyone would leave me the fuck alone. I wasn't smitten with Siobhan. She was hot and having her in my house and carrying my baby confused my feelings. I needed to get laid. That was it. I'd have to find a hookup soon and then I'd get her out of my system. I was not sleeping with Siobhan again. That was a recipe for disaster, and we both knew it.

"How are you not beat?" I grumbled at Siobhan on our way home.

Home. To my home, but not hers.

"I'm tired," she admitted. "Just...happy."

"No more morning sickness?" I asked as I led her up the porch steps to my house. I pulled my key out of my coat pocket and unlocked the front door.

"Nope. The first day I woke up and didn't want to stab you in your sleep."

"Thank you?"

She laughed as she stepped inside and shed her puffy winter coat. I hung it up for her in the hall closet while I took off my own. Winter this year had been brutal, and I couldn't wait until spring. That also meant more jobs with Ronan and money coming in to help when the baby came.

She stepped inside, and I locked up behind her. I went into the kitchen to grab a beer, but I found Siobhan staring at the ultrasound I pinned to the fridge.

"You okay?" I asked.

She nodded, but she wouldn't look at me. Instead, she put a hand on her stomach.

At the bar, the dim lights hit her at all the right angles so that you could barely tell, but in my kitchen, the signs of the life we created together was more evident. A protective growl wanted to climb up inside me at the sight, but I pushed it down at the worried look on her face.

"Darling?" I whispered.

She turned to me, and alarm hit me at the sight of her shiny eyes. "I've never made it this far before."

Oh. These were happy tears.

"I want Bean to make it."

I put a hand on her stomach next to hers. "They will. I promise."

"You can't—"

I put a finger to her lips. "Stop stressing. We'll be okay."

She nodded.

I pulled away. I wanted to linger with my hand on her belly, but I knew she'd snap at me soon for being too touchy. I had quickly come to understand the pendulum swing that was her moods.

I opened the fridge and pulled out a beer, cracking open a can of Drakesville Lager. "You staying up?"

"I'm gonna get a shower. Three different drunks spilled beer on me tonight."

I didn't remember that happening.

Before I could respond, she spun on her heel and tore off up the stairs. I sipped on my beer and dug my phone out of my pocket. I scrolled through my contacts, looking for a distraction, but the realization dawned on me that none of my previous hookups were a good idea.

Clingy. Hated my guts. Married now. Also married. And another now married. Hated my guts even more. Sarah.

I was about to open one of the dating apps to look for a

hookup when I heard the shower turn off. And then I dropped my phone at the sound of Siobhan yelling for me. I left my phone on the kitchen floor, sprinted toward the steps, and took them two at a time.

I flung open the bathroom door and stopped in my tracks, my mouth nearly hanging open at the gorgeous sight before me. There in my shower with the curtain pulled back, Siobhan rang out her wet hair with the delicious curves of her body on full display. Water dripped down between her generous breasts, and I couldn't stop staring.

My tongue was thick in my mouth, and the blood rushed all the way to one particular body part.

"Wh-what's wrong?" I managed to stutter out.

She gave me a sheepish grin. "I forgot a towel."

"I, um...uhh...okay?"

I was at a loss for words, and I couldn't keep my eyes off her. She was glowing. Or maybe it was because she looked sexy dripping with water.

"Sorry. Can you get me one from the hall? I didn't want to drip all over the floor."

My heartbeat calmed down. She was fine. The baby was fine. She just needed a towel. A towel to cover her gorgeous body that was growing with our child inside. I had to remember she was the mother of my unborn child. She wasn't a quick fuck. We weren't going there again.

"Killian?"

"Right. Towel!"

I marched into the hallway, opened the closet outside the bathroom, and grabbed her a fluffy towel.

Don't think about her naked.

I walked back into the bathroom and handed her the towel. She took it but didn't wrap it around her body, and I didn't leave the bathroom.

"Kill?"

Her voice was husky...like maybe that towel wasn't the only reason she asked me up here.

"Huh?"

She finally wrapped the towel around her body. "Why are you still here?"

I stared at her, and she studied me, but all I could think about was ripping that towel from her body and licking the bead of moisture sliding down between her breasts.

"I.... Fuck it."

I banded my arm around her waist, pulled her against me, leaned down, and took her mouth. She didn't push me away or tell me to go fuck myself. Instead, she let me deepen the kiss until the towel fell, and she clutched onto my t-shirt.

I pulled away only for her to push my t-shirt up my chest and over my head. She ran her hands down my chest and undid my belt. No words were shared between us. We were desperate after that kiss, and I was painfully hard.

I snapped back to reality when she reached inside my jeans and palmed my cock. Holy shit. This was not happening.

I gently pushed her hands away. "Siobhan—"

"Please."

"I... What's happening?"

"Don't care," she muttered and then her lips were on mine again.

Fuck, me neither. I knew I shouldn't, but I was a fucking asshole who needed to get laid. And damn, the sensation of her lips on mine was enough to make me forget all the reasons this was a bad idea.

I angled her head the way I wanted, gripping the back of her neck in a firm grasp. Our kisses were urgent and needy, both of us trying to find relief in the other. I ran my hands down her body, feeling the changes of the baby growing inside her, and I settled on her hips.

She wrenched her head away from my lips, wrapping her arms around my neck and burying her head in the hollow of my throat. "Kill."

"What ya need, darling?"

"To come," she moaned.

Fuck me.

I did say I'd take care of everything for her. Even that.

I lifted her into my arms and walked toward my bedroom. She clung to me for dear life, as if I'd ever drop her and risk anything happening to the baby. I'd never endanger either of them.

I kicked my bedroom door open, not caring that she dripped all over the hallway carpet. I didn't give a fuck. Then I carefully laid her down on the bed and shoved off my jeans and boxers.

"C'mere," she purred. Her eyes darkened with her desire for me. Holy hell, had I never noticed her look at me that way before? All of this was happening so fast, but the way her eyes traveled down my body told me not to care.

I crawled into the bed beside her, and before I could take her mouth again, she pushed me onto my back. She straddled me and bent to take my lips this time. Our kisses were urgent as our hands wandered. She moaned into my mouth when my fingers danced between her thighs and found her clit.

"Oh, God," she moaned into my neck.

"You don't have to call me God," I teased.

I pressed my fingers inside her, groaning inwardly at how tight she felt wrapped around my digits. Couldn't wait to sink my dick inside her again and give her the relief she desperately needed. What we both needed.

"Please," she moaned.

"Please, what?"

"I need you—now."

I didn't stop the motions of my fingers and smirked when she let out another moan. She was gorgeous when she pressed herself into my hand and tipped back her head.

My dick throbbed beneath her, begging for the same pleasure, but her needs came first. I increased the pace of my fingers until she cried out her release. Then I slid my fingers out of her and licked her cum off them, staring her down as I did.

Before I could stop her, she grabbed my cock and slid down on it, torturing us both by slowly joining our bodies. She didn't wait for me to move. She leaned back and rode me, getting her fill of me without a care in the world.

The way our bodies fit together so perfectly mesmerized me. The darkness of my bedroom muted the curves of her body, and I regretted not slapping on the light so I could bask in her gorgeousness.

I slid my hands down her sides and gripped her hips, grinding her down on my dick. "There you go. Take what you need, darling."

"I will," she growled out and pressed her hands onto my chest.

Hell yeah. I loved that way she took control. She wasn't afraid to tell me who was boss in the bedroom. I liked that about our night together. Even more so now as I watched her take what she needed from me.

Neither of us said another word as our bodies rocked together, slowly, like we could be here all night. She drew out her pleasure with every downward stroke, and I thrust up to meet her, giving her the exact care she needed.

When she closed her eyes tight, I took over from the bottom, hitting her deep and letting the beast out. Our pants grew heavy, our bodies merging into one while I gave her one last touch of ecstasy. She bent to me and met my lips again, quieting the sounds of my moans as we came together.

Something inside my heart stirred, but I pressed it down, chalking it up to the endorphins of finally having sex again. Tonight didn't carry any weight. It was just to give her what she needed. What we both needed. Nothing more.

CHAPTER FOURTEEN

SIOBHAN

I reluctantly slid off Killian as I came back down to earth and slumped on my back beside him. My hair was a tangled mess, and the bedsheets were damp from not toweling off, but I didn't care. I had zero cares in the world right now. God, he was as good in bed as I remembered.

"I really needed that," I breathed out.

"Me, too."

I arched an eyebrow at him. I highly doubted that.

Killian flirted with every pretty woman that sat at his bar. They always reciprocated and slid over their number to him before the night was over. Did the green-eyed monster of jealousy rear its ugly head when I saw that? Yes. But I couldn't explain why.

"It's been a while for me," I explained.

"Yeah, me too."

I turned to him. "Really? Probably not as long as me, though."

He rubbed a hand through his beard, and my horny brain was immediately bummed I hadn't felt it rub against my thighs.

What was wrong with me? I took a cold shower as soon as we got back from work because he looked too hot tonight, and I needed to calm down. I was so horned up with thoughts of him that I ended up forgetting my towel.

Then he stared at my body like I was a goddess he wanted to worship. His gaze raked down my form, and my desire had swelled. If he hadn't bent to kiss me, I might have thrown myself at him.

"Right?" I asked after realizing he hadn't answered me.

He shook his head. "I haven't had sex since Halloween."

Huh?

I turned toward him and squinted; my brain hadn't completely processed his words. He couldn't be serious. I saw all the women he flirted with. There was no way he had been keeping it in his pants since we created the baby.

"Why?"

He shrugged. "Not sure."

"Kill, you don't have to be celibate because we live together."

"I know."

The awkward tension between us returned, and I needed to take care of my hair, but I couldn't think of one good reason to leave the comfort of his bed. "Sorry I jumped you, but thanks for this."

"Oh, any time you want to ride this dick, darling, you know where to find me."

I rolled my eyes. There was the Killian I knew.

I slid out of the bed and padded into the hall. We didn't use a condom because I was already pregnant, but I needed to clean myself off. I grabbed a washcloth from the hall closet. After cleaning up, I tossed the washcloth into the hamper and noticed my towel still lay strewn on the floor along with Killian's t-shirt. I threw those in with the discarded washcloth.

I found my leave-in conditioner in a drawer and spread the creamy substance through my strands, working it through my ends. My hair was still a mess, and it would take a bit to work out all the tangles. Even with the special brush I used.

I pulled out said brush and worked it through my strands. My hair was almost dry by the time I got all the knots out. A memory of sitting at my mom's vanity while she brushed through my knotty hair surfaced in my brain. I rested a hand on my stomach. Maybe one day I'd have that same memory with my child.

"What's taking you so long?"

I jumped and dropped my brush in the sink, the clattering sound echoing in the quiet house.

My heartbeat slowed when I caught Killian's image in the mirror's reflection. Mirror him towered above me, but his eyes stared at me like he wasn't done with me yet.

"What do you mean?" I put my brush back into the drawer I used for my toiletries. Again, I was reminded of how this man had changed his entire life for me, and we weren't even together.

"I'm not done with you yet," he growled.

Before I could push him away, my world tipped up toward the ceiling. It took me a moment to grab onto Killian's shoulders as he carried me bridal-style back into his room. Once he had me flat on my back and was beneath my thighs, I forgot all about why it was a bad idea. Especially when his beard brushed against my skin. Future Siobhan could worry about that later.

The next morning, I woke to a cold bed with unfamiliar blankets wrapped around me. I opened my eyes and realized I was in Killian's bedroom. Naked. Because I had sex with him last night.

My baby daddy fucked me silly into the wee hours of the morning until he expelled all my pent-up frustrations from the past several weeks. And then he brought the comforter up over our naked bodies and held onto me as we passed out from the exhaustion of it all.

But now he was gone, and there was a pang in my heart. I knew what Killian was like, but I didn't imagine he'd duck and run from his own bed. I glanced at the clock on his nightstand and gasped out loud. I was supposed to meet Freya at Old York Grille in twenty minutes, but my phone was in my bedroom.

SHIT!

I threw off the covers and darted into my bedroom. I grabbed clothes as quickly as I could. But my jeans were too tight now, and I needed to go maternity clothes shopping, and shit, I was going to be late.

Gah, sleeping with Killian had been a terrible idea. What had I been thinking?

Oh, right, I wasn't. I let my pussy do the thinking, nearly throwing myself at him because the hormones made me want to jump him at every turn. And he let me, because of course he did. He was Killian. He fucked any woman who smiled at him the right way. I wasn't special in his eyes.

And yet... he hadn't slept with anyone since we conceived Bean. I wasn't sure what to make of that revelation.

My feelings swirled around in my head as I threw on a pair of leggings and a sweater dress. My thoughts pierced me while I shoved on my boots and raced downstairs. They nagged me even more when I pulled on my coat and hustled out of the house toward the town square.

I didn't see forever in Killian's eyes when I stared back at them last night. He just wanted to protect me because I was having his baby. He wasn't the guy you married or even dated. I knew all this, but it bugged me that instead of being an adult and talking about what happened last night, he ran away. Maybe avoidance was how he could do all the casual sex.

What an asshole.

I tried to push my feelings away as I approached the entrance of the bougie diner in town. They had weird recipes, but Freya loved it, and I owed her for being a shitty friend during my first trimester.

I felt flush from speed walking over, but Freya didn't seem to notice when she waved to me from the entrance. "Hey!"

"I had sex with Killian," I blurted out.

Oh, shit. I didn't mean to say that.

She raised an eyebrow. "Um. Yeah? Everyone knows that."

I ran a shaky hand down my makeup-less face. I had been in such a rush this morning I hadn't even slapped on some lipstick. God, I was a mess. "No. Last night."

Her eyes went wide. "Wow! Aw, Shev, I knew there was something between you. Why didn't you say something?"

I shook my head. "No... It wasn't... I don't know!"

"Okay, you're explaining everything over brunch today."

I groaned. Why did I even open my big mouth?

Freya laughed and hooked her arm through mine. We walked into the tiny place and waited a while for a table. I didn't want to blurt out my story until we had a little more privacy.

After we were seated and our orders were in, Freya gave me the 'girl spill' look.

I sighed and blurted out the whole story. How Killian and I ended up in his bed last night still baffled me. Obviously, we were horny and needed relief from each other. That was all.

Freya was practically beaming when I replayed the story to her. For someone who was such a commitment-phobe, she sure was a romantic.

"Shev, I'm gonna ask you something, and don't get mad, okay?"

I chewed on my lip. "Okay."

"Do you have feelings for Killian?"

There was the million dollar question. I didn't have an answer because I couldn't trust my feelings. Killian had done so much for me—letting me live in his house, cheering me up at Christmas, and taking care of me every step of the way. It endeared me to him. And he was hot. Like, so freaking hot. But that was obviously my pregnancy hormones talking. I wasn't sure I could trust that. On the flip side, his overprotectiveness made me want to scream.

"I don't know," I admitted.

"Hmm."

I shot her a glare. "Don't 'hmm' me!"

She laughed. "Well, if Killian wants to take care of you, and I mean in every way, you should let him. It doesn't have to mean anything."

I had thought about that, too. Killian would have no qualms about us continuing to sleep together, but my sensitive heart couldn't handle it. Even though last night was to get it out of my system, the hurt when he was gone this morning stung.

I shook my head. "I don't think so. He was gone this morning. He ducked and ran from his own bed."

Freya's mouth twitched, something she did when she was thinking something over. "Maybe he didn't want to wake you. You might be reading it wrong."

No, I wasn't. I knew what waking up alone meant. I wasn't that naïve. It was best if we never did that ever again and pretended it never happened. I had gotten good at avoiding him and pretending I was a sleepy pregnant lady over the past month. I had no issue with keeping my distance. It was truly the best for everyone.

CHAPTER FIFTEEN

KILLIAN

I picked at the label on my beer as I sat in my parents' basement with my brothers, watching the Bulldogs game. I couldn't concentrate on the game since my mind was three thousand miles away. Or rather, on my night when I gave into temptation with my baby mama, and now the tension in my house was as thick as fog.

Ronan kicked my shin.

"Ow! What the fuck?"

"What's up your ass?" he asked.

"Yeah, you're moodier than Finn," Lachlan piped up.

Finn shoved Lachlan, a deep scowl across his freckled face. "Fuck off."

"You fuck off," Lachlan shot back.

Brian rolled his eyes. "Christ, youse are worse than my kids. And they're literal children."

"Fuck off, assholes," I muttered.

I took a swig of my beer and pretended I was watching the game, but my brothers knew better.

Tonight was a rare one when none of us had to work. Brian and I worked the weekends when the pub was the busiest, so a Monday night taking in a hockey game with my brothers was what I needed.

But it didn't help me forget how Siobhan seemed to run away at the sight of me. At the pub, she pretended to be busy, and we'd walk home in silence until she ran up to her room, slamming it shut before I could even ask her how her night went. And it was all my stupid dick's fault.

I never should have slept with her again for so many reasons, but now I couldn't stop thinking about that night. Of how her hair was wild as she tossed it back while she rode me to completion. Or the sounds she made when she came on top of me. I replayed every moment of that night in my mind, wondering when the awkwardness set in. Or when she decided it was better to avoid talking about the subject.

The next morning, I had woken up before her and discovered I was out of coffee and didn't have anything good for breakfast. I popped down to the coffee shop, asking her boss which bagels she liked the most—the French toast ones with strawberry cream cheese—but when I got home, she was gone. Without a note or anything. When I saw her later that day, she pretended nothing had happened, making an excuse to lock herself away in her bedroom.

"Is it Siobhan?" Ronan asked.

"No," I lied.

"BULLSHIT!" Finn called me on it.

Dick.

I crossed my arms over my chest.

"He needs to get laid," Ronan said with a shrug.

"I have," I muttered. I took another sip of my beer. When I looked up, Brian was seething.

"Killian..." he said in a warning tone. He always had to play dad, and that was my cue to leave. Besides, the Bulldogs were getting decimated anyway.

I set my beer on the coffee table and got up. My muscles were still aching from the work I did with Ronan yesterday. "I'm out."

Before any of those assholes could say anything, I was up the stairs. I almost snuck out unseen, but Mom called after me. That woman had an eagle eye.

"Killian, take leftovers for Siobhan."

I spun on my heel and walked into the kitchen. She opened the fridge and pulled out leftover containers, shoving them into my arms. You didn't say no to my mom when she handed you food; you let her do what she wanted. It was her way of showing love.

"Things good with you and Siobhan?" she asked.

"Fine. Why?"

"You know, Killian, she's a nice girl. You could really settle down with her."

I scrubbed a hand through my beard.

Not the first time Mom had said this. Probably the millionth time. Mom loved Siobhan and hated that she didn't have family in town anymore. She wanted to take her under her wing, but Siobhan was fiercely independent, and she didn't need my mom hovering.

"It's not like that," I tried to explain to her. Yet again.

"You sure?"

"Yes," I said through gritted teeth.

The thought of 'settling down' set my teeth on edge. A long time ago, I wanted to do that with Liz. Until I caught her red-handed. From then on, it was easier to not have feelings. Keeping things casual always kept me from that hurt. Not that I'd ever admit that. Not even to my brothers.

Mom gave me a small smile and squeezed my arm. "You should bring Siobhan for family dinner next weekend."

"Mom," I gave her another warning.

She put her hands up in the air. "I want her to know she's a part of this family. She only has her friend Freya here in town. Her parents are so far away."

I sighed but nodded. Mom had a point. That was exactly why Freya told me to cheer Siobhan up at Christmas. She talked to her mom a lot on the phone, and they seemed close. I had gathered she missed her family at this important point in her life. Must be different when you were an only child, and your family wasn't all up in your business twenty-four-seven.

"I know, Mom."

"Ask her over. For me."

"Fine. I'll ask, but she might have to work."

"Check her schedule. Or she can come on a Sunday when she doesn't have to work."

"I'll ask."

I was out the door as quickly as possible before she tried to trap me in a longer conversation. I got in my truck and drove the short distance to my house. Siobhan's car was in the driveway, so I parked on the street.

I got out of the truck and grabbed the food containers before heading inside. The lights were on in the foyer, and I heard the faint sound of the TV from my living room. I walked into the kitchen and put the leftovers in the fridge.

I paused at the ultrasound on my fridge. I pressed a finger against the image, thinking of how all the sleepless nights and aches in my body were for the baby. For Siobhan and the baby. To protect them always. I never thought I'd feel this way, but the moment I found out about Bean, all my paternal instincts kicked in.

I walked into the living room and found Siobhan on the couch with her knitting needles in hand. On the TV was one of those reality shows she loved.

I hefted myself into the armchair, and she jumped at the sound. "Oh! You scared me."

I gave her a weak smile. "Sorry, darling."

She frowned. "Stop calling me that."

"Why?"

Her fingers flew around the needles, and she wound the fabric around, creating something I couldn't quite see. "Because I'm not one of the women you take to your bed. Call me by my name."

Ah. That made sense. Little did she know no one else was darling. Baby, maybe. Sexy, even. But no, I couldn't explain why I called her that. It slipped out the first time I had her in my bed, and it locked in place in my mind.

The way she wouldn't meet my eyes proved she had been avoiding me.

"So, can you tell me what I did to piss you off?" I asked.

"No."

"No?"

She shook her head. "I'm not mad at you."

"Doesn't seem like it."

"I'm not."

I doubted that very much.

"You hungry?" I asked.

She nodded. "I can't decide what I want yet, though. My cravings are out of control."

"I have a plate from my mom."

She put her needles down and cocked her head. I tried to hide my grin at the cute expression she made when she was thinking. Though I'd noticed that everything she did was cute lately. Wasn't sure why I had never seen that before.

"I kinda want a cheesesteak," she said with a grin.

"Pub?"

She shook her head. "No. They'll see us and ask us to work."

I laughed. She wasn't wrong about that one. Especially if Miles was behind the bar tonight. He was a fine bartender, but he got flustered too easily. I let all the hustle of the bar roll off my back.

"Pizza shop?" I offered.

She stuck out her tongue. "I got food poisoning from them last year. Hard no."

"Brewery?"

Her eyes lit up. "Yes! I never go there."

"They have awesome beers."

She pointed to her pregnant belly. "Unfortunately, you did this, so I can't enjoy one right now."

"We don't have to go there. I'll go get whatever you want."

"No, let's go there. I need to get out of the house. My nerves are all over the place."

I was glad she agreed because the brewery was only a couple of blocks away. I'd drive into the city to get her a real Philly Cheesesteak if she really wanted it, but I didn't want to make that drive. The good news was the prospect of food made her mood improve.

She set her knitting needles down and put them away in the box she used next to the couch. She then went upstairs to get changed, and when she came downstairs, my heart climbed up my throat.

She wore one of those sweater dresses that showed off all her curves, displaying our growing child front and center. She wore red again, a color she wore often when not at either of her jobs. It looked great on her, even better than that slinky black dress she wore to Lila's wedding. Her legs were clad in tight black leggings, and on her feet were knee-high black boots. Protectiveness bubbled up to the surface, worrying about her slipping on the sidewalk outside with those heels.

She arched an eyebrow at me. "Did you just growl at me?"

Siobhan's fears about miscarrying had seeped into my brain. If I could wrap her in a bubble, I would, but she'd stab me with one of her knitting needles.

"Killian?"

I gestured to her boots. "Are you sure you should wear those?"

Her face set into a hard line. "Killian, these are tiny heeled boots. I'm not gonna plant on the sidewalk when we walk to the brewery. And if you're going to be annoying about it, I'm going by myself."

"Like hell you are!"

But she was already walking away. I followed her, finding her at the hall closet, wrapping a matching red scarf around her neck and pulling on her jacket. She took red gloves out of her pocket and slid them on. That had to be her favorite color.

I grabbed my coat out of the closet and shrugged it on. She walked out the front door without waiting for me. She was definitely still pissed at me.

I ran after her, locking up the house as quickly as I could and jogging down the street to find her. I grabbed her hand, only startling her slightly. "I told you I'd come with."

She didn't yank her hand away like I thought she

would. My heart beat fast at the connection, but I'd blame that on having to jog after her.

"Too slow," she teased. "This preggo wants a cheesesteak."

I laughed. "We're getting there!"

"Slowww!" she teased again.

The walk felt shorter than normal since Siobhan was practically racing to get there. I'd never stand in the way of a pregnant person and a food craving.

I held open the door for her, and we stepped inside. The petite brunette host seated us right away. For a Monday night, it wasn't that busy, but we likely just missed the dinner rush.

A tattooed bartender came over to grab our orders.

"Cheesesteak!" Siobhan cheered with a flourish of her fists against the table.

The bartender laughed. "A lady who knows what she likes, I dig it. What about you?"

"Old Man Sullivan, and I'll do a cheesesteak, too."

"You want a beer?" he asked Siobhan. His pierced eyebrow raised as he stared at her stomach, where she rested her hand.

"Nope. Just a water, thank you."

I grinned. Siobhan was extra kind to waitstaff. We knew the trials of his job better than anyone else.

A few minutes later, he was back with our drinks, and I sipped on the Irish Red as Siobhan surveyed the brewery.

A bunch of guys sitting at the bar distracted me with their cheers; I glanced up and saw the Bulldogs had gotten the lead back in the game. Siobhan was quiet when I took in more of the game. I was a pessimistic fan, and my team proved me wrong by getting the lead back.

"Why do you like hockey so much?" she asked.

I shrugged. "Fights, I guess?"

She wrinkled her nose. "Really?"

"Sometimes. They're fun. But it's a fast-paced game."

"Huh."

I grinned. "Trying to get into more hockey?"

She shook her head. "Nah. Trying to figure out the appeal. Freya's a hockey fiend."

I felt my eyebrow shoot up. "Really?"

She laughed. "I know she doesn't look it, but she loves hockey."

"That is unexpected."

"It always surprises people, and then dudes try to make her 'prove' she's a 'real fan.' They usually shut up when she shows them up. She's always trying to get me to watch with her."

"It doesn't have to be everyone's thing."

She gave me an appraising look, but then the bartender came back over with our order. I watched in amazement and pride at the way Siobhan destroyed that cheesesteak. Her cheeks grew pink when she realized what she had done.

She wiped grease from her face with a napkin. "This was a good cheesesteak."

I chuckled. "It's pretty good."

"I've been craving them so much lately that I felt like I might die if I didn't have one tonight."

I laughed. "Dramatic much?"

She shrugged, her eyes sparkling with a smile. "Okay... maybe I watch a bit too much reality TV."

"So, why do you like that?"

"The drama. But not for me. It's mostly to have something to quiet my brain while I knit."

I pointed at her scarf. "Did you make that?"

She nodded. "And the gloves that go with it. My mom taught me when I was little. When Doug and I were starting with IVF, it helped me relax. I..." she paused. "I started making a hat for the baby."

"Aw."

She looked down at the table. "I've been afraid to start it. I've made so many for babies that never came to be."

I reached across the table and grabbed her hand. "Make the hat, darling. Our baby will get the chance to wear it."

"You can't—"

"They will."

She squeezed my hand but didn't pull away. If I didn't know better, this outing could have been a date. I felt a pull to her, but before I could say anything, she severed our connection and pushed out of her chair.

"I gotta pee," she explained and disappeared like a gust of wind.

I sat back and drank my beer, casually glancing up at the hockey game again. Bulldogs still had the lead, but my mind was elsewhere. I sat wondering why this woman had such a magnetic pull. Was she a witch? Had she put me under some enchantment? Or was it simply my duty to the baby?

The bartender came by with the check, and I handed him my card, perfect timing because then Siobhan couldn't fight me if I already paid. He quickly returned with my card, and I gave him a generous tip.

"Hey, hot stuff. Haven't seen you in a while," a familiar but unwanted voice said from behind me.

I swore under my breath.

Molly.

Of all the places for her to catch up to me in Drakesville, it had to be when I was out having a good time with my baby mama. Christ, how did my life turn into one of the reality shows Siobhan loved so much?

"Hey, Mol," I greeted through a strained smile.

"Fancy seeing you here. You've been ghosting me."

"Been busy."

She pouted.

I looked her up and down. The leggy redhead was as smoking as ever, but something didn't kick off inside me to think about her that way. All I felt was annoyance.

"I thought you moved to New York?" I asked.

She sighed. "Hated the job and moved back home. I'm working for a firm in Center City now."

I nodded.

I hoped she would walk away before Siobhan came back from the bathroom.

Molly gave a sultry smile. "Well, since I'm back in town, we should hang out again."

Yeah, I knew exactly what she meant by that. I wasn't sure how to let her down easily. I was firm in telling her I wasn't interested in anything more. I couldn't have a stage five clinger when my focus had to be on my kid.

"Baby?" a familiar soft voice pulled me out of my thoughts.

I jerked my head up and saw Siobhan with both her hands on her belly. Molly looked between the two of us, and her eyes got wide when she noticed Siobhan.

"What's wrong?" I asked. The frown on Siobhan's face set the alarms off.

"Nothing. I'm fine," she said, giving me a look to say 'go with it.' Why was she calling me baby? She turned to Molly. "Hi, I'm Siobhan, Killian's fiancée."

Molly's eyes were saucers. "Fiancée?"

I blinked at Siobhan. What was she doing?

Siobhan slid into her seat, and she glared at me when she saw the paid bill on the table. "Baby, you didn't have to pay the bill."

"I got it—don't worry about it."

Molly was still standing there, her mouth agape.

Siobhan flicked an uninterested glance Molly's way. "Baby, aren't you gonna introduce us?"

"I, uhh... " My words were a jumble in my mouth. "This is Molly."

Siobhan gave her a smile. "Nice to meet you, Molly, but we gotta get going. Pregnancy makes me sleepy."

What was she playing at? I jumped up when Siobhan lifted out of her chair, and I helped her with her coat. She grabbed my hand, and we walked out of the brewery together with me, utterly confused.

CHAPTER SIXTEEN

SIOBHAN

*H*e was so cute when he was confused. When I came out of the bathroom and saw the way he leaned away from that chick, I knew he wasn't interested, and she wasn't taking a hint. Not sure what possessed me to pretend to be his fiancée. That was probably gonna bite me in the ass. But I didn't care because I was in a good mood after the delicious meal at the brewery. I should go there more often.

I didn't stop holding his hand once we had passed the brewery's windows. The pain in the ass was being weird about me wearing heeled boots, so he probably liked it that way. I didn't want to admit that I enjoyed the feeling of his hand in mine. Or the way he protected me and the baby, albeit in an annoying way.

"You wanna explain what that was back there?" he finally asked.

I belted out a laugh.

"Siobhan."

"You looked like you needed rescuing. Was that one of your conquests?"

He groaned. "Oh, my God. Don't call them that."

I grinned to myself. Totally was. "The one who couldn't take a hint?"

"Yes," he said through gritted teeth as we walked up the porch of his house.

He let go of my hand only to unlock the front door and hold it open for me.

I walked inside and wiped my feet on the mat before pulling off my coat. I unwrapped my scarf from around my neck and hung both in the closet. Killian locked the door behind us and did the same, pulling off his black wool coat and hanging it up. Tonight he was in a simple outfit of red flannel and jeans that looked painted on his perfect butt.

Okay, those were my hormones talking. Again.

Stupid hormones were the reason I was being so weird around him. I hoped he hadn't noticed, but instead, he thought I was mad at him. Not mad...just hurt. Even though I had no right to be.

It was still early, and I didn't work at the coffee shop tomorrow, so I took off my boots and sauntered into the living room. I wanted to work on the baby's hat and then start on the registry my mom and Killian's mom kept nagging me about. Those two ladies were already in cahoots about planning my baby shower.

I knelt to find my box of projects next to the couch and hefted myself into a sitting position. A smile painted across my lips when I realized the yarn was the same color as my dress. I loved red, so of course I was knitting stuff for the baby in my favorite color.

Killian found me in his living room, and instead of his

normal seat in the armchair, he plopped down next to me on the couch.

"Do you mind if I watch the rest of the hockey game?" he asked.

Oh. He was buttering me up.

I shook my head. "Nope."

He turned on the TV, and the sounds of the game filled the room. I worked at the new stitch, slowly making my way to shape the project into a hat. Right now, it didn't look like much of anything. Killian put an arm over the back of the couch behind me, but I flinched when his other hand rested carefully on my stomach.

He didn't say a single word, merely sat there in silence, watching the end of the game, while I knitted in peace beside him. It was nice. Everything about tonight had been that... nice. I tried to shake off how dinner felt like a date. The longer I lived here, the more I got to break down the hardened shell that was Killian. He still confused me with his insistence on being a commitment-phobe who wanted to be a present father our child needed. The man was truly a conundrum.

"So who was that?" I asked.

"Molly. Stage five clinger. Sweet girl, but..."

"Couldn't take a hint."

"My mom's gonna ask when we're getting married now."

I cringed. "Sorry. First thing I thought of to get her to leave."

"I'll explain to Mom. Thanks for the save."

"Mmmhmm."

His hand still splayed across my stomach. In this dress, the evidence of my pregnancy was way more noticeable. I couldn't wait until I felt the baby growing inside me. Maybe then I wouldn't still be afraid of losing this one, too.

Killian watched the screen in front of us, his eyes darting back and forth to find the puck. I couldn't keep up. How did anyone watch this game? Freya had tried to explain the rules to me countless times, but I could never keep it straight.

There was some call on the ice, and Killian swore.

"What's that mean?" I asked.

"Offsides."

"But there's no outside of the rink. I'm confused."

He let out a chuckle and then explained the rule. It sounded vaguely familiar, but it still made little sense to me. I asked him to explain something else a few minutes later, and he actually tried to make me understand. I didn't, but it was sweet he tried. If Freya couldn't make me understand the rules, no one could.

"Are you done being mad at me?" he asked during a commercial. There was only five minutes left in the third period, and our team was losing again.

"I wasn't mad," I admitted.

"You've been avoiding me all week."

I shook my head, ducking it down and paying attention to my project instead of his sexy face. If I looked at him again, I might pounce on him. "It's nothing."

"Tell me," he urged. He tilted my chin, forcing me to look into his beautiful blue orbs.

Damn this man for actually giving a shit about me. Why couldn't he have been an ass who wanted nothing to do with me and the baby? Why did he want to be my protector?

"Just moodiness," I lied.

Not a total lie. I was moody as hell. That was all the hormones, but it wasn't the truth either.

"Okay," he relented.

He was silent for a few minutes, and we sat together, watching the rest of the game. The Bulldogs ended up losing, and Killian grabbed another beer in solidarity. A grin spread across my face when he switched the channel to Real Housewives.

My phone beeped, and I rolled my eyes when I saw another annoying text about the baby registry, this time from Freya. My mother had gotten to her.

> FREYA: Make your registry! I want to buy you cute baby clothes!

> ME: Who's asking my best friend or my mother?

> FREYA: Guilty! Do it, so she stops bothering me.

I set my phone down with a groan. I loved my mom, and it was great that she and Mary Pat wanted to do my baby shower, but that was months away. They needed to calm down.

"What's wrong?" Killian asked.

"Can you tell your mom to cool her jets on the baby shower thing?"

His brow furrowed. "What baby shower thing?"

"Her and my mom are being annoying about the registry. I haven't made one yet."

"I'll talk to her."

"It's sweet, but I'm not ready."

Killian's hand smoothed down on my stomach. "I get it. I'll tell her to lay off. I should probably tell her you can't make family dinner, then?"

I turned to him with a raised eyebrow. "Huh?"

"She wants you at family dinner on Sunday."

"But I'm not—"

He put a finger on my lips. "You're family. Mom wants you there."

God, his mom was so welcoming, it made me want to cry. Scratch that—it did make me cry. I didn't tell Killian, but she came over the other night when I wasn't working and gave me a pregnancy pillow to sleep with. I literally bawled my eyes out while she hugged me and told me it was going to be okay.

"Oh-okayyy," I blubbered out, and I realized I was crying again.

Great.

Killian cupped my face and wiped the tears from my eyes. "What's with the tears?"

"Preggo," I muttered through the moisture falling down my face.

He laughed. "You were in such a good mood."

I wiped my face. "I was. But then you reminded me about how nice your mom is to me."

He nodded. "She can be a pain, but she means well. She wants you to know you're family no matter what. You and the baby will always have a seat at the Murphy table. Nothing will ever change that."

Why was he saying this sweet stuff to me? It made me want to kiss him again, but I couldn't do that. My feelings were already a swirling mass of confusion.

He pushed my hair behind my ears. "You and Bean are all that matter right now."

I couldn't look away from him, at the way he stared into my eyes, like he knew all the confusing thoughts in my head. It was better if I let him think I was mad at him.

God, I wanted to kiss him so badly. And run my fingers

through his beard and thread into his dark locks. And then be bent over the couch as he had his way with me.

Shit. I was so horny.

I needed to get away from him. But I didn't want to at the same time. There was a gravitational pull to him, and I didn't want to stop, but I had to put a wedge between us. I couldn't go there with him. Not again.

"Darling," he drawled out, his voice husky.

Oh no. There were big fat DANGER signs lighting up in my head.

I set my knitting down and stood up, putting up the block in front of me. "Well, I'm tired. I'm gonna head to bed. Tell your mom I can make dinner this weekend."

I didn't even wait for his reply. I darted up the steps toward my room, safety tucked away from Killian's seductive gaze.

I needed to get my act together and find an apartment. Then I'd be out of this house and away from my sexy, unavailable baby daddy.

CHAPTER SEVENTEEN

KILLIAN

*I*f I thought last week Siobhan was being weird, this week she was even weirder. It was like she couldn't stand being in the same room with me and couldn't wait to get away from me. I wasn't sure what I did wrong, but she was definitely still mad at me.

"Ready to go?" I called up to her.

"Gimme one more minute!" she yelled down from the bathroom.

I grabbed the apple bundt cake she insisted on making last night after our shift at the pub. I woke up dreaming of apple pie, and when I realized it wasn't a dream, I rushed down into the kitchen, thinking something was burning only to find my baby mama baking at four in the morning. Because she said her mom would kill her if she showed up at my parents' house empty-handed. She only did it that early because she worked at the coffee shop this morning.

We'd definitely talk about her working on no sleep

again. That schedule wasn't good for her and the baby, and I didn't like it.

The sound of her boots on my staircase caused me to look up, and my breath caught in my chest. She wore a red dress again, different from the one she wore the other night. This one flared out at the bottom, hiding her pregnant belly better. She had sheer tights on her legs and those heeled boots again.

What would it take to convince her to wear something else? The notion of her falling on the sidewalk made the daddy in me want to haul her upstairs and force her to change.

"Is this too much?" she asked.

I shook my head, drinking in her whole figure. "Perfect."

Not a lie. God, she was pretty. Her dark hair fell in loose waves, and her eyes shone bright tonight. It could make a lesser man crumble. If she kept looking at me like that, I might.

When I walked toward her, she skittered away and headed for the hall closet for her coat. She had been so jumpy lately.

"Let's go," she called, standing at the door waiting for me.

My parents lived on the other side of town near Brian, so we had to drive. I shrugged on my coat, but Siobhan was already out the door waiting by my truck. Locking the door behind me, I followed her, and she made a face when I tried to help her into the passenger seat. This woman was so stubborn, I swear to God.

I shut the door behind her, shaking my head as I climbed into the driver's seat on the other side. The drive to my parents was short; it didn't take that long to get anywhere in Drakesville.

Siobhan didn't wait for me to open her door. She hopped out before I turned off the engine. I turned off the car, got out, and tried to catch up to her. By the time I reached her, my mom had already opened the door and pulled Siobhan into a big hug.

Mom gave me a smile and ushered us inside. Before I could say a word, Siobhan followed Mom to the kitchen, and I took that as my cue to butt out of it.

My brothers crowded around in the living room with the hockey game on, except for Ronan, who was nowhere to be seen.

"About time you showed up," Brian teased.

"Siobhan was taking a while."

He narrowed his eyes. "Yeah, about that."

"Where's Ronan?" I asked, ignoring Brian's dig.

Ronan appeared at the top of the basement door, carrying a case of beer. "These assholes made me get more beer. "

I opened the top of the box, much to his annoyance, and grabbed a beer. Ronan rolled his eyes and then went around the room while my brothers all grabbed beers. He set one on the coffee table for himself and took the beer into the kitchen.

I slumped on the couch, stealing his seat. Lachlan passed me the beer opener, and I popped the top off my beer and took a long pull. My parents were big on local business, and Dad thought Old Man Sullivan was the funniest name ever. So, of course, he had a bunch.

"By the way, Mom's gonna grill you about your engagement," Lachlan piped up.

"What engagement?" I asked.

"The one Shev told Molly about, and now it's all over

town that you're engaged," Finn supplied with a smirk on his face.

Asshole.

"That was a misunderstanding."

Ronan re-entered the living room and shoved my shoulder. "There's no ring on Shev's finger, dick. What sort of asshole are you?"

I groaned.

My brothers gave me shit-eating-grins, letting me know they were messing with me because they all knew I didn't do commitment. Not anymore. Not after what Liz and Bobby put me through.

"Did you ask her about the paint colors?" Ronan asked me.

"Not yet."

Ronan was helping me turn my other guest room into the nursery for the baby. I had held off doing it for a while after Siobhan expressed her fears about miscarrying. She would've freaked out if she saw Ronan and me painting the nursery during the first trimester.

"Ask Siobhan so we can get started on it," Ronan said.

"Ask me what?" Siobhan's voice sounded from behind me.

I spun around, but Lachlan beat me to it by jumping to his feet and offering her his seat. She put a hand up, signaling she was fine.

"Kill and I are gonna start on the nursery," Ronan explained. "He wanted to check with you on the paint color."

She shook her head. "It's your house."

"Yeah, but it's our baby," I argued.

She shrugged. "Still your house. I'm not sticking around, so it doesn't matter."

Her nonchalant attitude about how she was only a guest in my home rubbed me the wrong way. I took another pull off my beer to prevent myself from saying something I shouldn't.

"Anyway, your mom said to tell youse all that dinner's ready. She said shouting usually led to mad dashes..." she trailed off as Finn and Lachlan bolted into the dining room.

Brian shook his head at them. Guess the babies of the family never changed.

Brian gave Siobhan a sympathetic smile. "You get used to those jerkoffs."

I stood up and led Siobhan to the big table in the dining room. We were always a sizable crowd, especially with all the spouses, but Mom made it work.

I gritted my teeth when I realized the only open chairs were next to each other. I had a feeling Mom orchestrated that one. Siobhan slid into one, and I dropped myself into the other.

My parents sat at the heads of the table while my brothers, Lachlan and Ronan, sat next to us. On the other side of the table, Kelsey and Brian sat directly across from us, and then Finn and Eilish were next to them. Sometimes, Mom set up a kids' table for my nieces and nephew, but they were nowhere in sight tonight.

"No kids tonight?" I asked.

"They're with my parents. We needed a break," Kelsey explained. She had dark rings under her eyes, and she looked like she wanted to puke.

Oh. Well, shit. I knew what that meant. Poor Kelsey. Good luck to my brother because she might actually kill him this time.

Mom made a roast with mixed veggies and her perfect mashed potatoes. It was a little more in-depth than our typical Sunday fare. Not that I minded, but she was trying to impress Siobhan.

Mom passed around the food, and we all hefted it onto our plates. I glared at my brothers when they took huge helpings before Siobhan could. Of course, she was too polite and took smaller portions.

"I have more," Mom said. "These boys have eaten me out of house and home all their lives. I'm prepared now."

Siobhan pushed a strand of hair behind her ear. "I'm good. Thank you."

We had a few minutes of comfortable silence as we all ate before Mom started in on me. "Killian."

"Yeah?"

I didn't bother to look up from my plate; I already knew what she was gonna ask.

"Why isn't there a ring on Siobhan's finger?"

My brothers hid their snickers behind fake coughs and drinks of their beers. Assholes.

Siobhan's cheeks pinkened. "Oh, Mary Pat, that's a complete misunderstanding. Killian and I aren't engaged."

Mom peered at us. "Well..."

"Dear," Dad warned her.

Mom held up her hands. But then Eilish saved us all by asking Mom how she prepared the roast. Good Ole Eilish. There was a reason we kept her around. It wasn't so Finn could make moon eyes at her when she wasn't looking. That was for sure.

Siobhan squeezed my hand under the table and mouthed, 'I'm sorry.' I gave a slow shake of my head. She had nothing to be sorry for. It wasn't her fault I didn't know how to get Molly to take a hint. I didn't let go of her hand, and she didn't pull away until she needed it to cut into her meat. A part of me felt cold when she did.

"Siobhan, we're so happy you're here with us tonight, honey," Dad told her with a wink.

Siobhan gave him a small smile. "Thank you. Can't remember the last time I had a home-cooked meal." She turned toward my mom. "Mary Pat, truly, you didn't have to go to all this trouble."

Mom waved her off. " I wanted you here. You're family now. Like Eilish."

"I'm not tied to one of these fools, but Mary Pat still invites me," Eilish piped up. "It means she likes you," she stage-whispered to Siobhan.

Siobhan tilted her head and looked between Eilish and Finn for a minute, likely seeing what every single one of us saw. "You and Finn aren't—"

"No," Finn cut her off sharply.

Finn was too far deep into his own head that he didn't see the dark look of hurt that crossed his best friend's face. God, I wanted to shake him so hard until he saw what was right in front of him. And then her too. Until they finally figured out what they had been searching for was there all along.

"By the way," Siobhan began, trying to cut the awkward tension in the room. "I sent you that registry link, but it's not everything yet. I haven't had a lot of time to think of everything we need."

"You did?" I asked. "You didn't tell me that."

She lifted one shoulder apathetically. "I didn't think you wanted it."

I shoveled another forkful of potatoes into my mouth before I said what I wanted to. I was sure annoyance was written across my face based on the glare and kick Brian gave me.

She didn't want to pick a color for the nursery in my house, yet she had a baby registry and didn't tell me.

"Send it to me," I urged.

"Okay," she relented but ignored me as my mom went on about the plans for the baby shower. The one several months away. Christ, my mom was going to drive her away with all this planning.

"Mom, it's months away. Take it down a notch."

"We're just excited," she insisted.

Siobhan grabbed my hand under the table again, a silent thank you that sent ripples of warmth down my chest.

"Well, I was going to give you some hand-me-downs, but we're gonna need it," Kelsey spoke up.

"What?" Dad asked, his brow furrowed, but Mom clapped her hands.

"Oh, honey, that's amazing news. Two new babies."

Lachlan went white as a ghost and turned toward Brian. "Didn't you just get a vasectomy? Did it not work?"

I laughed silently to myself. Despite all Mom's nagging about grandkids, my baby brother was firmly against it.

"Numb-nuts, they got pregnant before that," Finn explained.

Lachlan shivered. "That's my biggest nightmare."

Brian sighed. "Believe me, we weren't planning for another baby." He grabbed Kelsey's hand and kissed the back of it. "But we're excited nonetheless."

"See," Ronan cut in. "Lachs doesn't need to have kids. You have enough grandkids from Brian and Killian."

"I want more," Mom laughed.

I moved my hand out of Siobhan's and slid it on her stomach. It was too early to feel our baby yet, but I couldn't wait for that moment.

I bent my lips to her ear. "You okay?"

She stiffened beside me but didn't push me away. Instead, she tilted her head down in confirmation.

I pressed a chaste kiss to her temple. "See? I told you. You're part of the family now."

She pulled away and took a drink from her glass of water. The shift in her body language confused me.

I turned away only to meet Kelsey's gaze. She stared between the two of us, the gears in her brain working in overdrive. If I didn't know better, I wouldn't have thought anything of it. But that meant Kels was going to interrogate Siobhan later.

Sometimes, I really wished I was an only child.

CHAPTER EIGHTEEN

SIOBHAN

I needed to get away from him. The warmth of his thigh pressed up against mine throughout dinner had me in a bundle of nerves. Then, when I reached out to squeeze his hand, it was like fire licking across my skin. I was a mess of sexual frustration when he kissed my temple and asked me if I was okay after Kelsey and Brian's announcement. Like he sensed the jealousy coursing through me. Which was unfair because I was pregnant too. But after so many disappointments, I couldn't help but feel scared that I'd still lose our baby while Brian and Kelsey didn't even try for theirs. And that was such a mean thought to have.

The sleeves of Killian's flannel button-down were rolled up to reveal his forearms. God, were forearms sexy? They must be by the way my imagination was playing with thoughts of those arms pressing me against his bed and having his way with me.

What was wrong with me? I needed to simmer down

and fight my attraction to this man. That would only end in heartbreak, and I had to tell my heart he was just a good man who wanted to provide for his baby.

Dinner had been lovely, and Mary Pat was so kind to invite me and welcome me to the family. While I was a heathen sitting there pretending I didn't want to jump her son's bones. I needed to make an excuse to get out of here.

"Dinner was great, as always, Mary Pat," Eilish said after we all had finished our plates.

Mary Pat stood and started clearing the dishes. I took that as my chance to get some breathing room. "Let me help."

Kelsey and Eilish got to their feet as well.

"Mom, sit and relax," Kelsey told her. "Let us clean up."

"Thank you, girls. Siobhan brought an apple bundt cake. Will you bring that out when you're done?"

I nodded. "We got it."

Killian looked like he wanted to say something, but I grabbed our dishes and slipped away before he could.

I set the dirty dishes on the counter and sighed.

Kelsey let out a laugh. "Holy shit, you're sexually frustrated."

I spun round to face her and Eilish, who both gave me sly grins. "Huh?"

"You can cut the tension between you and Kill like a knife," Kelsey supplied.

"It's true," Eilish agreed.

Kelsey pinned her with an annoyed look. "You're one to talk."

Eilish's ears went as red as her hair.

Literally everyone in Drakesville knew Eilish had a crush on her best friend except for him. But tonight, I saw the way he looked at her with a sense of longing when she wasn't looking. Now that I thought about it, I saw him stare at her that way when they played at the pub. I always thought it was a musician's sense of pride, but seeing them today out of their element told me it was something so much more.

"Kels, he doesn't see me that way. Besides, I have a boyfriend," Eilish insisted. Even she seemed unconvinced.

Kelsey rolled her eyes. "You keep telling yourself that."

Kelsey opened the dishwasher, and I rinsed off the plates and handed them to her. Eilish took the cake out of the fridge and grabbed smaller plates from the cabinet.

"So you and Killian..." Kelsey started up again.

"What about us?" I asked.

Could she tell I wanted him to bend me over and take me? Were my horny thoughts that obvious? I was trying so hard to stay away from him in case I let my lust take over again. Our night together had been amazing, but my hot baby daddy needed to stay far away from me.

"Like I said, the sexual tension's sizzling."

I frowned. "I don't... we're not... well... ugh."

Eilish and Kelsey laughed at my fumbling for words.

"It's my pregnancy hormones," I explained. "Besides, Killian's not built for commitment. It's better to ignore it."

"Not always," Eilish whispered.

I snapped my head up and studied her. What was she talking about?

"Oh. I'm not sure we're allowed to talk about her," Kelsey said.

Eilish grimaced. "Probably not. Her name's like a curse. Poor Killian."

"What?" I asked.

Kelsey mimed zipping up her lips. "We've already said too much."

"But..." Eilish began and looked to Kelsey for approval, who nodded. "I've never seen Killian look at someone else the way he looks at you. Not since her."

"He's never brought someone to family dinner," Kelsey added.

I gave a slow shake of my head. "That was all Mary Pat."

"Killian wouldn't have had you come if he didn't want you to," Eilish said.

Kelsey pointed at her. "So true. And he's so sweet with you."

They didn't know what they were talking about. Killian only wanted to take care of the baby. He didn't have any lingering feelings for me.

I took the cake from Eilish and walked out of the kitchen, ending the conversation. I might have slept with Killian again, but he had been so firm in what this was. He just wanted to make sure the baby was taken care of, nothing else.

I set the cake down in the center of the table, and Eilish was behind me with the plates. Mary Pat shooed us back to our seats, and she cut the cake. She passed plates around the table, and I took a huge bite. I had to hold back the moan. This was probably the best cake I'd made in a while.

"Siobhan, this is great. Thanks for bringing it," Mary Pat told me.

I nodded in thanks.

The rest of the family murmured in agreement, and we all quietly ate.

After dinner, Killian went downstairs with Ronan, and I sat on the couch in the living room.

"You should give him a chance."

I opened my eyes, realizing I had let them drop, and found Brian next to me. "What?"

"My brother doesn't trust well. He guards his heart, but you're the first person I've ever seen him give a shit about since Liz."

Liz? Was that who Eilish and Kelsey were talking about? And why was his family so pressed about pushing us together? Just because I lived with him and we were having a baby together didn't mean we had to be a couple. Things didn't work like that.

I couldn't answer him because Killian walked up the steps. He smiled at me. "Tired?"

I nodded.

"That's what happens when you stay up all night."

I rolled my eyes.

After our shift last night, I tried to sleep. I really did, but I couldn't get comfortable. So I made that cake, waking him up, and then it was time for my shift at the coffee shop. I took a nap when I got home before dinner, but Killian didn't see it that way.

He held out a hand to me. "Come on, let's go home."

Home. He kept calling it our home, but it wasn't. It was his, not mine. I was merely a visitor.

That reminded me that Freya and I had some apartments to view next week. Killian was kind enough to let me live rent-free, but now that I wasn't feeling so sick, I had the time to look. If I got out of his house, then I wouldn't want to jump his bones so badly.

I took his hand, letting him help me up and into my coat at the front door. We said our goodbyes, and then I was climbing into his truck for the ride back to his house. Kelsey was right. The tension was thick between us, but I wasn't going to do anything to ease that. It was better with this wall up.

Killian helped me out of the car once we got to his house, and he unlocked the front door for me. I shed my coat, but before I could sprint off up the steps, he pulled my arm and spun me around.

"We need to talk."

His voice was firm and growly, which sent a delicious shiver down my spine.

"About what?"

I was being obtuse. I knew what he was mad about.

He stared me down. "Why are you so mad at me?"

I sighed. "I'm not."

He crossed his arms over his wide chest. God, those arms. "Really?"

"Yes," I lied.

"Siobhan..."

"I need to get a shower," I announced and sprinted up the steps. It was either that or my hormones were going to have me doing something foolish again.

After showering, I sat on my bed and brushed out my hair while I looked at the apartment listings Freya sent me. I wasn't looking forward to touring these places. My budget had me looking at some less-than-desirable places, and after reading reviews, I was even more discouraged.

I pulled out my phone and video-called Freya, propping my pregnancy pillow behind me so I could sit up on the bed.

Freya's face appeared as she answered. "Hey! How was dinner?"

"Good."

Not a lie. Dinner was great, and Mary Pat was an

outstanding cook. If you ignored the sexual tension between me and Killian.

"Can you do these apartment tours with me tomorrow?" I asked.

She frowned. "I can make it work, but would it be better to do it during the day?"

I held in my sigh. I didn't want to go alone, but Freya's life differed from mine with her teaching job. She was swamped with more kids than usual this year in addition to being on the event planning committee. Not to mention her dad enlisting her to help with fundraising for the volunteer fire company. She might be stretched even more thin than I was.

"You should take Killian with you. I'm sure he'll be a big help."

I ground my teeth. What was with everyone trying to push us together?

"He'll be annoying."

She laughed. "But... he'll be able to see the things you don't notice, right?"

"I guess..." I grumbled.

"You're grumpy tonight."

"Sorry. Pregnancy's making me cranky. Tell me how your date was last night."

I laughed as Freya told me about another awful date with one of her dad's firefighters, where she spilled a drink on him on purpose because he was that douchey. We chatted for a few more minutes until she needed to get ready for bed. Sometimes, it was hard when we kept such different hours.

I hung up with her and turned on the TV in the guest room. I flipped to a syndicated block of old CSI episodes while I browsed more apartments.

I lifted my head at the knock on the door and saw Killian standing in the doorway. "Can you send me the baby registry?"

"Come here and see."

He crossed the room and slid onto the bed beside me. I opened a tab on my laptop for the registry. I barely put anything on here yet, but enough that his mom and mine would stop pestering me about it.

"You don't need a crib."

"Yes, I do."

"Ronan's already making one."

That was sweet of Ronan, but he meant for Killian's house. I wouldn't ask Ronan to make one for me, too.

"Well, I need one for when I move out."

Killian's jaw ticked, but he said nothing in rebuttal. I passed my laptop to him, letting him look at the other items while I tried to get comfortable. If I was uncomfortable now, I couldn't imagine what the third trimester would be like.

"You have a lot of foxes on here."

I laughed. "Oh. I loved Fantastic Mr. Fox as a kid. Plus, I don't want anything too gendered. Woodland creatures are a safe bet."

"Really?"

I turned back to him. "Really, what?"

"That's my favorite book."

"Oh. That's funny. I love Roald Dahl."

Killian frowned. "What's this?"

"What?"

He spun my screen around and pointed at the crappy apartment I was last looking at. "You can't move into this dump."

I rolled my eyes. "I don't have a big budget, Kill."

"We're not going to that one."

"Excuse me?"

He pinned with an annoyed look. "My baby's not gonna live there. If you're so stubborn about doing this all on your own, I'm going with you to find a suitable place."

"Killian..."

"Don't even start with me. Not happening. No kid of mine's living in a place like that."

The urge to punch this man in the face was back instead of the one where I wanted to fuck his brains out. I wasn't sure which impulse made me more conflicted.

"If I agree with you, will you shut up and stop badgering me about this?"

"When's the first showing?"

I sighed. "Trying to get in this week."

"I'm going with."

His words had an edge of finality, and I was too tired to argue. This was probably what Freya had in mind when she said Killian should go with me. While I agreed these places weren't ideal, I was being realistic about my finances. Freya even offered me to move in with her because she had the room, but I didn't want to put her out. The same way I felt like a burden living with Killian rent-free. Plus, I think she was just being nice with the offer. She had to have an actual reason for pushing me to take up Killian on his offer instead of hers.

"Fine," I huffed out. "Can you go away now?"

He leaned back on the bed next to me. "Nope. This is a good episode."

At least we could agree on one thing.

The silence between us engulfed the room. I tried to pretend this was normal for us. Sitting up in bed watching reruns of CSI together. But it wasn't. When Killian rested a hand on my belly, Brian's revelation came reeling back to me.

I should have stopped myself, but I had to know Killian's secrets.

"Killian?" I whispered.

"Hmm?"

"Who's Liz?"

I felt him stiffen beside me, and I instantly regretted my question. Especially as he recoiled from me like my pregnant belly was on fire.

"Nobody," he muttered.

His voice was full of venom, but something else too. A deep hurt he tried to hide.

I blew out a breath. I should have left it at that, but I wanted to know more about this man who had dropped everything for me yet was known as the town commitment-phobe.

"Doug was gonna divorce me," I admitted.

I hadn't said the words out loud before. Hadn't even told Freya. I shredded the divorce papers the moment I found them after Doug died. They were blank, but the fact he printed out the forms and shoved them in the back of his desk told me everything.

Killian turned to face me. "What?"

I brushed the tears from my eyes. "I found divorce papers after he died. Not filled out."

"Because of the miscarriages?"

"Probably."

"Shev, I'm so sorry."

I shrugged.

"I don't want to talk about her," he whispered, clued in on what I was trying to do.

"Okay."

I let more silence linger between us as we watched reruns of our favorite police procedure TV show without another word.

I only told him that to get him to open up, but it felt like a burden off my shoulders. Everyone made the dead out to be saints, but Doug had his moments. I knew our marriage was over when he asked me what I did to cause the last miscarriage. It didn't mean finding those papers hurt any less. Or how much I hurt after his death. I had lost my baby and my husband all within a few weeks of each other. The pain of it had nearly broken me.

Killian's hand returned to rest on my belly, and a warm sensation spread through me at his gentle touch. Maybe one day, this man would open up to me. Then I'd understand the complexities of Killian Murphy. But tonight wasn't that night.

CHAPTER NINETEEN

KILLIAN

I woke to the sun hitting me in the face and a mouth full of pillow. I breathed in the scent of Siobhan's body wash and sleepily pretended this was normal while hoping she didn't wake up.

Her nosy questions from last night came roaring back at me, reminding me why I needed to keep my distance. It also made me curious which one of my brothers told my secrets and needed a good sock to the face. All of them, if I had to guess.

I couldn't think about any of that because my doorbell chimed, and Siobhan jolted up beside me.

I placed a hand on her stomach, easing her back down on the bed. "Easy. It's just Ronan."

I found my phone buried in my pocket and pulled it out, squinting at the numbers on the display. Why was Ronan here so early?

RONAN: Open up, time to work!

ME: We work NIGHT shift!

RONAN: TOO BAD!

Siobhan settled back down into the bed, and I felt the chill from her moving out of my arms. That shouldn't have disappointed me.

"What's he doing here?" she asked. She rubbed the sleep from her eyes and scanned the room. "Why are you in my bed?"

"We fell asleep watching CSI again."

She laughed.

Not the first time that had happened, but usually, we were downstairs on the couch, and I'd wake her up and tuck her into her bed. I had no intention of sleeping in here last night when I came in. I didn't even intend on hanging in here with her, but we must have been so tired, we both passed out.

"Go back to sleep. I'll deal with Ro."

I hefted myself out of bed and groaned at sleeping in my clothes last night. The doorbell rang again, and I cursed my brother out in my head. I stomped down the steps and flung open the front door.

Behind it, my brother stood tapping his foot and glaring at me. He had his toolbox in his hand and a bag from the coffee shop in the other. Ronan was nothing if not the guy that got shit done.

"Sorry—didn't set an alarm," I explained and gestured for him to come inside.

He set his toolbox down and shed his winter coat. I walked into my kitchen, rubbing the sleep from my eyes, and made a pot of coffee.

"Hey, Siobhan," Ronan greeted.

"Morning," she said back to him.

I hadn't even heard her come in. She dressed casually, wearing a pair of leggings that clung to her thighs and a big sweatshirt.

"How are you feeling?" Ronan asked. "Family dinner too much for you?"

She laughed. "No. Everyone's great."

"Well, Kill and I are gonna get working on the nursery today. Are you sure you don't have a color preference?"

She shook her head. "Maybe neutral? But it's not my house. I won't be here for much longer."

I gnashed my teeth at her sentence and stared at the coffee dripping down into the pot. Why did that bother me so much? That was always the plan for her to live here until she got back on her feet and found a new place to live. But the idea of not finding her hair ties on my bathroom floor or the lingering scent of her perfume in my house made me want to convince her to stay.

Why did I care? I should want her out of my house as soon as possible.

Ronan set down the bag of food. "Well, I got bagels for us. Kill told me what you like."

She cocked her head at me. "You don't know what I like."

The coffee finished, and I poured myself and my brother a cup. I spun around and handed a cup to Ronan. I glanced over at Siobhan. "I asked Willow for your order."

"Oh. Thank you," she said.

Ronan grabbed paper plates from my cabinet and took out the bagels, handing Siobhan hers and practically throwing mine at me. Dick.

Siobhan didn't stick around, floating back upstairs as

quick as she had appeared. I couldn't help but stare at her swaying hips retreating.

Ronan shoved my shoulder. "Brian's right."

I took a sip of my coffee and then bit into my bagel sandwich. "About what?"

Ronan stared me down. "You haven't looked at someone like that since Liz."

I clenched my hand around my mug. "It's not like that."

"You sure about that?"

I nodded.

Siobhan was just having my baby. Sure, we had some fun in the sack, but the day I found my girlfriend fucking my best friend in the house I'd just bought us was the day I buried my heart. Having casual hookups made my life so much easier. I was only taking care of Siobhan and our baby like anyone would in my position. As soon as she moved out, all these confusing thoughts would go away.

"It's okay to move on," Ronan pressed on.

I rolled my eyes at him. "Have you?"

"That's not the same thing."

"Sure it is. We're both chumps that got cheated on. That's not happening ever again. You could learn a lot from me."

"Yeah. I have," he said, his eyes flaring. "I learned not to let a bad relationship color my worldview."

I was tired of having this conversation with him. Ronan blamed himself for his marriage deteriorating, but Chrissy was the one who cheated. Same with Liz and Bobby. They were the ones who betrayed me. I was never letting that be a possibility again. I'd be there for Siobhan in every other way, but not that. Never again.

"Are you here to work or gossip?" I snarled at him.

He muttered under his breath, and I didn't even care

what he said. He needed to drop this argument once and for all.

"Fine. Eat up, and then we'll get to work."

"Lift with your knees!" Ronan yelled at me.

"You fucking lift with your knees!" I retorted.

I loved my brother, but after cleaning out my office together, I wanted to throttle him. Currently, we were attempting to move my desk into my bedroom, but the narrow doorway was proving difficult.

Ronan pivoted on his end slightly, and I walked backward into my bedroom, finally getting the desk through. We placed it in the corner of the room, tucked out of the way. When Siobhan moved out, I'd move it into the guest room.

I rubbed the sweat off my brow. "This is taking longer than I expected."

Ronan laughed. "Yeah, that's because you didn't clean a damn thing. Come on, let's review what we wanna do."

I shuffled behind him into what was once my office but was now a barren room.

"Siobhan really doesn't care what color?" Ronan asked.

"No."

He raised an eyebrow at me. "Okay...what about you?"

I rubbed my beard as I thought. After looking at what she had on the registry, I had an idea.

"Who did the mural for Bri and Kels in Callum's room?"

Ronan nodded, understanding where my head was at. He walked around the room, surveying the space. He pointed to the one wall. "It was actually wallpaper. We could make this wall the accent wall and then do the others with a neutral color. What are you thinking?"

"Foxes."

"Foxes?"

I shrugged. "Or woodland creatures. She has all that shit on the registry."

Ronan nodded. "Mom showed that to me last night. Let's paint these other walls, then we can wait for the wallpaper."

"Sounds good."

"When's Siobhan moving out?"

That was a good question. "I don't know. We're going to look at apartments this week."

Ronan raised an eyebrow. "She's letting you go with her?"

"No," came the woman in question's answer. Siobhan stepped into the room wearing her Sullivan's Irish Pub t-shirt and a pair of leggings instead of her normal work pants. "You think he gave me a choice?"

Ronan laughed, and I shot him a glare.

Siobhan turned to me. "I have to head to the pub. Do you think Bri will give me crap for wearing yoga pants?"

"Why are you wearing them?" I asked, the gruffness in my voice unmistakable.

Siobhan slid a hand down her growing belly. "I can't fit into my pants anymore."

Oh. Well, now I felt like a dick. But good God, did she look amazing in those. Leggings, yoga pants—I didn't know the difference, only that both made her ass look amazing. Which meant every sleazeball in town would ogle her at the pub tonight. That got my hackles raised.

"Bri won't care," Ronan answered for me, sending me a glare as if he knew where my mind had gone.

"Cool. Gotta go."

She whirled out of the room faster than she had come in, not giving me a second to walk her to the pub.

Did I watch her walk away with my mouth hanging open? Yes. I was a horny man, after all. And her ass was fantastic.

"BRO!" Ronan yelled at me.

I snapped out of it and turned back to him. "Huh?"

He shook his head. "You got it bad."

"Fuck you, man. No, I don't."

He crossed his arms over his chest but let the argument drop. "Come on, we're getting primer and starting on this shit today. You at the pub tonight?"

I shook my head. It surprised me that Siobhan was going in tonight. I swore she didn't put her hours on the calendar for today. Monday's were a shitty night to work, and I got away with not having to go in on them. That was the benefit of being one of the best bartenders there.

I tried not to think about it as Ronan and I made our way downstairs to make a trip to the hardware store. On my way out, I double-backed into the kitchen. Siobhan and I had gotten in the habit of putting our work hours on the calendar on my fridge. It made it easier to coordinate our schedules with doctor's appointments. It annoyed her to no end.

I sighed when there wasn't anything listed for today for either of us. We weren't supposed to work. Why the hell did she go in tonight?

"What's wrong?" my brother asked.

"Nothing. Let's get this over with."

We walked out of my house and climbed into Ronan's pickup. On the way over, he gave me his update on the progress with the crib.

When Brian and Kelsey got pregnant with our niece Cora, Ronan handcrafted a crib for them. They used it for all their kids, and after I told my family about Siobhan being pregnant, he started working on one for us. He needed a project to keep his mind off his failed marriage. I loved that he wanted to do something nice like that, and the quality would be better than any cheap manufactured one we'd buy.

While in the passenger's seat, I pulled out my phone and texted Siobhan because I couldn't help myself.

ME: Your hours aren't on the calendar.

SIOBHAN: I picked up a shift. Sorry, I didn't run it by you, DAD!

Oof, she was annoyed with me.

SIOBHAN: I need the money. Stop micromanaging me.

I didn't argue with her and instead shoved my phone back into my pocket. I didn't like this one bit, but I wasn't trying to piss her off any more than I already had.

CHAPTER TWENTY

SIOBHAN

I held in my sigh as Killian walked around the apartment, inspecting every square inch. I wished I hadn't been so tired when he asked to come with me. I regretted it the minute we walked into this place.

This was my number one apartment, but it wasn't without issues. The biggest plus was the location. It was above the tattoo shop within walking distance of both the pub and the coffee shop. It also had central A/C, which was a must in the heat of a humid Pennsylvanian summer. The downside was that it was only one bedroom, and it was pricier than I wanted. That's why I picked up that extra shift last night. It would be perfect if I could make the numbers work.

Killian frowned. "How many bedrooms?"

The landlord pointed to the closed door on the other side of the living room. "Just the one through here."

I brushed Killian off and strode over to the door, flinging it open and stepping inside the bedroom. It was a decent size. The last tenant had already vacated the place, so it was hard to tell what could fit. I might need to consolidate more of my things when I move. I got rid of a lot when I put the house on the market, but there were still a ton of boxes stored in Freya's basement.

I imagined putting the crib in here for now, but not having a room for my child once they got older wasn't ideal. If I moved here, this would only be temporary. I needed something more permanent.

I could tell by the look on Killian's face that he wasn't happy about the idea of this place. "Where would you put the baby?"

I gestured to the space in front of me. "Crib in the bedroom with me for a while."

"You can't move into a one-bedroom, Shev."

"I don't see how it's your business."

He was right, but I wouldn't admit that. This was a possibility, but not one I was going to jump on. I had another appointment in Green Willow. It was bigger and cheaper, but I wasn't sure about safety.

"Shev..."

"I want to check out the other place first. Then I can decide."

I walked back over to the landlord and shook his hand, thanking him for his time and letting him know I'd be in touch. The place was nice if I was single, not for raising a child in.

We walked down the steps and out onto the streets of Drakesville again. I didn't want to move to Green Willow. I'd miss the accessibility of living in town too much.

"Where's the next one?" Killian asked, walking in-step beside me.

"Green Willow."

"Where?"

"In Green Willow," I repeated.

"No. I mean, what neighborhood? Do you know if it's a good area?"

I had no f-ing clue—that was why I was doing these tours. All I knew was that the apartment had two bedrooms, and it was within my budget. Which probably meant it wasn't in that great of an area. I had to weigh these options as I really honed in my search.

"Not sure," I admitted.

When we got back to the house, we climbed into his truck and headed out for the next town over. Green Willow was a little bigger than Drakesville. There were some good areas and some bad. The mall was there, and the major grocery stores, but I didn't really know the area. I never thought I'd have to move out of the town I grew up in.

I stared out the window as we drove, my mind racing to all I needed to do to get my life together. A baby had not been in the mix after I sold the house, and it wasn't ideal to be raising a child with a man who'd never love me. But I would do whatever I needed to for my child. I'd work double or triple shifts if I had to.

"You don't have to move out," Killian spoke up after we had been driving for a few minutes.

"I know."

"I'm not kicking you out. My offer was to help you through your pregnancy. It's not like as soon as the baby comes, I'm putting you out in the cold."

I sighed.

Killian had made that abundantly clear. He really stepped up these past couple of months. I was so grateful for that, but I had to get out of his house. The longer I stayed, the harder it would be to resist him. It was better to get out as soon as I could and quit cramping his style. Then things could go back to normal for both of us. Save for co-parenting a child together.

Killian pulled into the apartment complex and cut the engine. "I don't want added stress for you. You worry about keeping the baby healthy."

I turned back to him and unbuckled my seatbelt. "I need to go my own way."

"No, you don't. I'm here to help you through this. Why are you being so stubborn?"

"Because I need my own life. And I'm sure you want to go back to your old life without having to worry about a pregnant lady making you sacrifice your freedom."

"Darling—"

I didn't let him finish his thought and hopped out of the truck, ending the argument.

I stared up at the two-story brick building in front of me. Kinda old, but not bad from the outside. I had to see inside first.

Killian slammed the car door and joined me outside. He had a frown on his face, even worse than at the last place. He surveyed the building and the surrounding area. "I don't know about this place."

Was I going to tell him I agreed with him? Nope.

Instead, I held my head high and walked toward the entrance. A blonde woman stood at the front, obviously waiting for me. She held out her hand to me. "You must be Siobhan. I'm Debra."

I took her hand. "Hi. Is the unit still available to view?"

"Come upstairs."

We followed her inside and up the steps to the second floor. I was out of breath from one flight. Not good if I had to do this while my pregnancy continued. Maybe I could see if there were any ground units available soon.

Debra led us down the hall and opened a door on the left. We stepped inside the apartment, and the smell of bleach whipped me in the face. Like someone had scrubbed the place from top to bottom. It made me want to hurl.

The living room was tiny, and there was a white carpet on the floor that looked permanently stained. I stepped further inside, finding a tiny kitchen off to the side. I noted the small counter space and the lack of a dishwasher.

Killian didn't say anything, but I could press into that crease in his brow if I wanted to. I walked into the bigger bedroom, surveying where I'd put my furniture. It was small but doable. But the second bedroom was even smaller. How this closet could even be considered a bedroom was beyond me. What concerned me was the big stain on the carpet.

Was that blood?

Killian frowned, and we both stared at it and then back at each other. I knew what his raised eyebrow meant. There was no way in hell he was going to let me raise our baby here.

"So, what do you think?" Debra asked.

"I have some things to think about," I told her coyly.

Not a lie. I had to think about if I wanted out of Killian's so badly that I'd take either of these places or continue looking. This place wasn't too terrible, but I wasn't sure if that sour feeling in my stomach was the smell affecting my hormones or my gut instinct telling me this wasn't a good choice.

Debra nodded.

Killian tipped his head toward the radiator. I had barely noticed that, and now it worried me. It was rusted out like it wasn't taken care of very well. I had assumed the chill was because there wasn't a current tenant.

"Is this working?" he asked.

Debra nodded. "Oh, the utilities aren't on right now. It will work for sure when you move in."

Killian made a noise of discontent.

"Thank you so much for showing us," I told Debra. "But we have another appointment. I'll let you know if I want to take it."

She led us back out and down the steps again.

Killian didn't say another word until we got into the car. "Absolutely not."

I sighed. "I can't be choosy."

"The fuck you can't. You have time to find the right place. This isn't it."

He turned on the engine and pulled out of the parking lot, getting us back on the road toward Drakesville.

"I don't want to move out of Drakesville," I admitted.

"You don't have to."

"My budget says I do."

I gazed out the window again, watching the streets pass us by. I should text Brian and see if there were more shifts tonight. I could really use the money.

My stomach rumbled, and Killian belted out a laugh. "You wanna get lunch?"

"No," I muttered.

"Not at the pub. We'll go somewhere else. How about Old York Grille?"

I wrinkled my nose.

"You don't like it there?"

"It's okay. But bougie."

"But they have great sandwiches."

My stomach made itself known again.

Killian reached a hand out and put it on my stomach. "I think Bean's telling you we're going there. Come on, I'll treat you."

"Okay."

He pulled his hand away, and I felt the weight of his absence. I shouldn't feel this way about him. This was why I needed to find an apartment—and fast.

We drove in silence for the rest of the way back to town. Killian found a spot on Main Street, and we walked over to the diner together. It was the middle of the day, late for lunch, so it wasn't terribly busy. It didn't take long for us to be seated.

Killian ordered a coffee while I asked for water, and we browsed the menu.

"So, can we talk about that obvious blood stain?" he asked.

I cringed. "That might not have been what it was."

He looked up from his menu. "Are you serious?"

I shrugged and closed my menu, deciding on some sugary French toast. This baby had a sweet tooth.

The server dropped off our drinks, and we ordered. Killian went with a Reuben, which made me want to barf just thinking about it.

"Can I tell you my opinion now?" he asked.

"You already have," I said with a sigh.

"Okay. First place was decent, close to town, but what are you going to do when the baby gets older?"

He'd already voiced these opinions, so I wasn't sure why he felt the need to badger me about it. But I let him say what he wanted.

"Second place... Hell fucking no. Not a good neighborhood. Too small. Pretty sure the utilities didn't work."

"Okay, okay. I get it."

"I'm just looking out for you."

"Being an annoying asshat more like," I muttered under my breath.

Was he being annoying, or was I irritated by pregnancy hormones? Probably both. He didn't get to ask me what I said because our server brought our food over. Thank God.

I shoveled it in, trying to contain myself from moaning at the sweet taste of the syrupy goodness. Killian tried hard to not make it known that he was laughing at me. The French toast was so good that I let him.

"Siobhan?" someone called my name.

I paused at that voice. The shrill, high-pitched, harpy voice of my former mother-in-law, Margaret.

Of course she was here. She was retired and had nothing better to do than sit at the diner and harass the nice people who worked here. I hadn't seen her since the day after Doug's funeral, where she demanded I give her my husband's ashes. When that wasn't insulting enough, she asked for my engagement and wedding ring. Neither of which were family heirlooms. Margaret was just a vindictive bitch.

I swallowed my food and tried to center myself. I couldn't let my blood pressure rise around her.

"Margaret, hi," I greeted, giving her my fake customer service smile.

Her perfect blonde hair was pulled back into a tight bun, and she had a sour look on her face. "I'm surprised to see you here."

"I still work nights," I explained.

"Hmm." Her gaze went to my stomach. "I've heard rumors about you."

"Gossip's not polite."

"Well, is that my grandchild or not?" she asked, pointedly looking at my stomach.

What the hell? Margaret hadn't been kind throughout our fertility issues. She blamed it on me. A lot was my fault. When Doug died and I realized the financial situation, I asked for help, and she told me it was my bed and I had to lie in it. Also, she needed to re-do her math.

"There's no way this baby is Doug's. As much as you blamed me, it's clear I wasn't the problem," I snapped at her, surprising even myself.

"Can I help you?" Killian asked.

A chill went down my spine at the rage in his voice. The last time I heard his voice have that icy edge was when he told those guys at the bar to kindly go fuck themselves.

Margaret bristled. "Well. I guess the rumors are true, then. It seems like you moved on quickly. You're the kind of woman to do that."

"Lady, what the fuck is your problem?" Killian snapped.

Margaret ignored him. "I told Doug you were no good for him. I'm glad I was right. As always."

"Well, he's fucking dead!" I screeched. "So it doesn't matter!"

I pressed a hand against my stomach, trying to calm myself down. Couldn't wait to hear the rumors about me after this.

"Do you mind?" Killian asked. "We're trying to have lunch, and you're harassing us."

"Well, we'll see what your mother has to say about that," Margaret huffed and stormed off.

"Mom hates that lady," Killian admitted.

I felt the weight of eyes on us. I loved living here, but sometimes the gossip mill of Drakesville made it harder to live in peace. I was sure today would be twisted into something more, and I'd get a call from my mother about it.

A sob bubbled up inside me, and I tried to keep it in, but the tears rolled down my face.

"No, oh, Siobhan..." Killian said softly.

"I'm sorry," I sobbed.

Our server rushed over to our table. She handed me a pack of travel tissues. "I'm so sorry," she said. "If it makes you feel better, we pick straws to wait on that lady."

I laughed through the tears. "From one server to another, it does."

She laughed. "You work at Sullivan's, right?"

I nodded.

"Thought you looked familiar. What sort of bitch makes a pregnant person cry like that? My manager said to comp your meal."

Killian waved her off. "You don't need to do that."

"You deserve it. Congrats on the baby."

Then the tears flowed again because what a kind thing for a complete stranger to do for me. The girl hurried away, but I felt the eyes of the fellow diners still on us.

I dried my tears after a while, and Killian silently ate his sandwich. I felt his brain turning with his silence. He dropped a stack of bills for our server, and we quietly left.

When we were buckled into his truck, he asked the question on his mind. "Who was that?"

"My mother-in-law. Ex-mother-in-law."

"She..."

"Hates me," I answered. "Always has. I was never good enough for her 'baby boy.' It was kinda gross, actually."

Killian nodded and started the engine of his truck. I wanted to know what he was thinking, but he didn't ask any more questions.

It occurred to me as we drove that Killian's mother was the type of mother-in-law I wanted. We weren't even together, and Mary Pat had welcomed me into the family with open arms. All of his brothers, too. They made me feel like family, even though Killian was merely some guy I had an accidental pregnancy with. That made me cry even harder. Damn hormones.

Killian pulled into his driveway, and he reached over into his glove box and handed me tissues. He waited with me as I wiped my tears.

"You didn't deserve that," he whispered. "My family will never ever treat you that way, okay? You're family."

"I know," I sobbed out.

He rested his hand on my stomach. "You don't have to rush out of my house. You'll always have a place in my home. You and the baby. I'm always gonna take care of you. But you're not fucking moving into either of those places."

"O-okayyy," I blubbered out. The tears kept on coming, and I couldn't stop them. "I set up some more appointments next week. Will you come with me?"

"Absolutely."

I wasn't even sure why I asked him. Maybe it was because he was patient while I cried out all the emotions swirling inside me. Or maybe it was because this man who played off that he didn't have a heart had the biggest one of all.

CHAPTER TWENTY-ONE

KILLIAN

*C*hrist, where was she finding these God awful apartments? I scanned the room, pretending I didn't notice the dead cockroach in the corner. I couldn't help but glare at the sleazeball landlord staring at Siobhan's breasts.

I didn't blame him since Siobhan's always had a great rack, and her pregnancy had done wonders for her. Her body had changed as she grew our child inside her, and I couldn't help but stare in wonder every time she wasn't looking. But this jerkoff didn't need to be doing that.

I shook my head, hoping to literally shake the dirty thoughts from my mind. Siobhan surveyed the kitchen of the tiny studio apartment in Green Willow, a frown on her face as she noticed all the terrible things I saw. No exhaust fan in the kitchen or smoke alarms, and there was a huge wet spot above the drop ceiling. This place had major issues. Like I didn't see the bars on the window before we walked inside.

I met Siobhan's gaze, and she gave a sad shake of her head.

She turned to the landlord and put on a fake smile. "Thank you so much for showing it to us today. I have a couple more places to tour, so I'll be in touch."

I held in my laugh at her sugary-sweet tone. Siobhan was good at that. That was why she was a beloved server at the pub.

She turned to go, and I followed behind her, walking out of the rundown apartment building and back into my truck. I helped her into the passenger seat and ran around the other side into the driver's seat.

I started the engine and drove off, not saying a word while she was quiet beside me. The disappointment radiated off her. The apartments we toured today were worse than the ones from last week. I hoped today didn't end in tears again.

I got an earful from my mother about our interaction with Margaret. But Mom said she hated that bitch. It was probably the first time she ever swore in front of me, so it had to be bad. Mom loved everyone. For her to cuss meant the woman was akin to the devil.

Siobhan still hadn't said anything by the time I pulled into my driveway. Instead, she got out of the truck silently.

I sighed, cut the engine, and followed her inside. She disappeared into her room, and I found Ronan in the nursery, finishing up the second coat of paint on the walls.

"How'd it go?" he asked.

"A bust," I muttered. "I could have helped here."

He shrugged. "Not much to do. Need to decide on the accent wall."

"Right. I gotta order that, and then we can install it."

He gave me a sarcastic grin. "That's three you owe me."

"Get the fuck outta here."

He cackled on his way out. I loved my brothers, but I also wanted to punch them most days.

I walked out into the hall and saw the door to Siobhan's bedroom still closed tight. We both worked at the pub later tonight, and she was probably taking a nap.

I headed into my room and sat at my desk in the corner. It made the room crammed, but I'd deal with it. One day, I'd finish the basement and move all my stuff there.

I opened my laptop and browsed the site Brian sent me. There were a lot of different options, but I scrolled until I found one that fit the theme of Siobhan's registry. My lips twitched at the thought of surprising her and seeing the look on her face when we finished the registry. She would love it. A twinge in my gut reminded me she wouldn't be here long enough to care, but I ignored it.

I ordered the wallpaper and did my bills. With all the expenses of the baby on the way, I was more worried about money than ever before. I didn't like that Siobhan was so desperate to move out of my house, she was looking at any and every apartment available. I wasn't sure how to make it clearer to her that I'd always take care of her and Bean. We hadn't talked about child support yet, but she had to know that I'd make sure they'd never want for anything.

Footsteps sounded out in the hall, and I lifted my head at Siobhan's light knock at my open door. Her Sullivan's Irish Pub t-shirt fit snug across her growing belly. I couldn't help but stare.

"Are you working tonight?" she asked. "I'm about to walk over for my shift."

I checked the time on my computer. I hadn't realized how busy I got. "Yeah. Lost track of time."

I didn't warn her as I pulled my t-shirt over my head

and walked over to the dresser, searching for a uniform shirt.

Her eyes bulged out of her head. "Killian!"

I rummaged in my drawer. "What's wrong?"

"You could wait for me to leave the room."

I shrugged. I finally found the shirt and pulled it over my head. I rubbed a hand through my hair and smoothed down my beard. She stood there frozen but not in fear. She swallowed hard but never took her eyes off me.

Almost like...

Holy shit, had she been so weird around me the past couple of weeks because of lust? Was she resisting me as hard as I was resisting her?

"Darling..." I breathed out.

She spun on her heel. "Come on. Let's go before Brian gets on us for being tardy."

If she had been in the room for three more seconds, I might have done something that made us really late.

Christ. This woman was such a temptation. She'd made it clear she had no desire to be back in my bed again. As much as I wanted that, I had to respect her boundaries. I needed to take another woman to my bed. Then I'd be out of the spell she had cast on me. I tried not to think too hard about it as I rushed to catch up to her.

My brother's band played in the corner while I poured beer after beer all night long. For a Tuesday night, the pub was hopping. Maybe it was the $2 Tuesday special Lila was testing out because we didn't have this many people come out last week. She might be good at this pub-owning business, after all.

I was working my ass off tonight because Miles called out sick. Brian tried to pitch in, but he was swamped with other work, so it was just me behind the bar. Not like I couldn't handle it. I won over all the ladies with my smile and a head nod to the guys in understanding.

I made another rum and coke and set it down on Sarah's tray, making drinks as fast as I could. She walked off, giving me a moment of reprieve. But I ended up spending it by staring across the bar at the beautiful brunette with her service smile on. God, she was so pretty when she smiled, even when it was a fake one.

"Hey, stranger," a voice pulled me away from my horny thoughts about the woman carrying my child.

I recoiled at the sound. I knew *that* voice.

It belonged to someone I never wanted to see again. Someone who hadn't shown their face in this place in years. All the blood in my body froze as I stared into the chocolate-brown eyes of my ex. She had a lot of nerve showing up here with that sultry smile and flirty voice.

"What do you want?" I barked out.

Liz pushed her dark hair behind her ear. Her hair was short now but stylish as ever. Nothing was ever out of place when it came to Liz. Not a hair nor her make-up. And you'd be hard-pressed to find a wrinkle on her clothes. I didn't care how hot she was. She was still the woman who took my heart and smashed it with a hammer. Her and Bobby.

"A drink, Kill," she said with a devilish smile.

I used to love that smile. Now it felt condescending.

What was she doing here? She and Bobby still lived in town. Pretty sure they had kids now, but I avoided them like the plague, and they'd never stepped foot in here. They knew better than that.

"Find it somewhere else," I snarled at her.

Her smile never faltered, like she was enjoying how her appearance made my blood pressure go to the roof. "Come on, Kill. Everyone knows you make the best long islands. Make me a special."

I pointed to the door. "There's the door. Get some other bartender to make it for you."

"Don't you miss me, baby?"

I blinked at her. I hadn't seen her in five years. Five years since I walked into our house and found her in bed with my best friend.

I curled my hands against the bar, my knuckles going white. "Are you fucking for real? Get the fuck out."

"Kill, make me one of your famous drinks, and maybe we can have some more fun later?" she teased, giving me that sultry smile.

WHAT. THE. FUCK.

"Baby?" a soft voice called out to me, and I felt a familiar touch on my arm. Siobhan's angelic voice pulled me from the raging storm inside.

I turned, finding her peering up at me with worried eyes. Alarm immediately coursed through me. "What's wrong?"

She shook her head and slid her hand up my chest, sending a shock through me. "Nothing. Just missed you."

Huh?

She gave Liz a sideways glance but then shifted back to me and cupped my jaw. My eyebrows rose to my hairline when she lifted on her tiptoes and pressed a kiss to my mouth. My instincts took over, and I slid my hands down her sides, pulling her toward me while she deepened the kiss. She wasn't tender or sweet but rather laying a claim to me with her mouth. Aggressive in a way that turned me on and reminded me of the last time her mouth was on mine.

My head spun when she pulled back and let go of me. She turned to Liz. "Hi. I'm Siobhan. And you are?"

Liz frowned. "Liz. You must have heard of me."

Siobhan shrugged. "Gossip only happens in this town if it's about someone who matters. Besides, Kill would have told me about you if you ever meant anything to him."

Holy shit.

Siobhan never spoke like that to anyone. Not even the douchebags she waited on here at the pub. She put a hand on her hip as if daring Liz to say the wrong thing. Because who was gonna argue with a pregnant person?

Liz's mouth hung open, but Siobhan ignored her, turning back toward me again. "Can you get me three Drakesville Lagers ASAP? I had a pregnancy brain moment, and they asked like twenty minutes ago."

"Okay..."

I grabbed the drinks, and by the time I placed them on a tray, Liz had disappeared. Siobhan had a satisfied smirk on her face while she sauntered away.

"What the fuck..." I whispered.

"Bobby cheated on her," Brian explained, sneaking up behind me and taking the empties off the bar.

"What?"

"Word on the street's he cheated with the nanny and ran off."

"So she thought she could come crawling back to me? Fuck that."

Brian shrugged. "Seems like you're spoken for, anyway."

I furrowed my brow at him. "Siobhan and I aren't together. How many fucking times do I have to tell you that?"

He gave me a knowing look. "That kiss said otherwise."

I gazed across the bar, spying Siobhan flitting from table to table, her positivity radiating off her. I should have considered what my brother told me, but my dick was in charge, and all he was thinking about was the taste of her lip gloss lingering on my lips. Reminding me of how much I wanted to taste something else of hers.

Brian shoved me. "Get back to work."

I did as he asked, but not without my impure thoughts about my baby mama swirling in my head.

CHAPTER TWENTY-TWO

SIOBHAN

I cringed at the front door slamming behind us. Rolling home after closing the pub was draining, but instead of being tired, I was bouncing off the walls. After a shower, I could use some time to wind down, watching TV and knitting to help me sleep again. But I had a feeling Killian and I were going to have it out about my little stunt tonight.

I shed my coat and hung it up in the closet. I tried to dart away, but Killian caught my arm. "Oh, no you don't. We have to talk."

I peered up into those ocean-blue eyes, getting lost in them. My thoughts were such a horny mess. I shouldn't have kissed him again tonight, especially with an audience. I only did that to get that woman to leave him alone, but I knew it threatened his playboy status to have all the town gossip about us being together. But I wouldn't apologize for it. It had been a damn good kiss, and I wanted to do it again.

Until we were writhing horizontally once more. Because I wanted this man so bad, and I'd do anything to be beneath him again. To chase that relief I'd find in him because holy hell, fighting my attraction to him had been hell on earth.

"Darling," he whispered. No, he more like purred it. His eyes were dark, which confused me because I thought he was mad at me.

"What do we need to talk about? I was trying to help you again. It's not my fault you're the town bicycle and don't know how to let them down easily."

I slapped a hand over my mouth. That was so rude and unlike me. I wasn't sure what had gotten into me tonight.

He raised an eyebrow. "Explain that one to me."

"What?"

"Town bicycle."

"Everyone's gotten a ride," I muttered under my breath and looked down at my feet.

He lifted my chin with his finger. "Including you, huh?"

"Yes..." I breathed, remembering our last night together. He let me take the reins and gave me the pleasure I wanted.

He gave me a cocky grin. "Uh-huh. So that's why you kissed me again? Because you're looking for another ride?"

"What? No," I balked, stepping back from him.

If I put some distance between us, I wouldn't give in again. I'd have the wall up to protect myself. If only to make me forget how good his mouth felt on mine.

He stepped forward, leading me into his kitchen until my back connected with the center island. "So why'd you do that?"

"Because..."

He framed my face, brushing my messy hair behind my ear. "Huh, darling? Why do you keep coming to my rescue and marking your territory?"

Was that what I was doing? Did these raging pregnancy hormones make me possessive over the man? When that redheaded girl came onto him at the brewery, I sensed his unease and wanted to end it. Tonight, I practically saw the steam coming out of his ears, and I wanted to calm him. That brunette tonight looked at him like she already possessed him, and when she told me her name, my blood boiled. I wanted to slap that stupid, smug look off her face.

"Darling..."

"I didn't like the way she looked at you."

"How's that?"

I pressed my hand against his chest like I had done at the pub. The connection immediately sent a shudder down my spine. A mere touch on this man and my libido was in overdrive, screaming at me to kiss him again. This was why I wanted to get out of his house as soon as possible. I was wearing down my resolve, and soon, I'd give into those carnal desires again.

"Like you belonged to her," I whispered.

He angled my head, forcing me to stare up into his darkening eyes again. "And that's why you kissed me like that? Because I belong to you?"

"N noo..." I stuttered.

"Then tell me why, Siobhan. Explain it to me."

"Because I wanted to, okay? Because I spend every day avoiding you so I don't kiss you again. Okay?"

His mouth twitched on one side. "Tell me what else you're resisting."

His voice was like honey, thick and low and so damn sexy. He was putting me under his spell again, and it pulled out all my secrets.

I reached a hand up and stroked his beard. "Every day, I pretend I don't imagine this between my thighs. Or sinking onto my knees and showing you what you've been missing. Some days, I picture you bending me over the couch and having your way with me."

There was that satisfied grin again. "You can have me any day, any way you want, darling. Just say please."

I bit my lip. This was such a bad idea. The last time we had sex, he was gone in the morning. All he was offering tonight was the comfort of his body. I wanted a relationship. I wanted a partner. But my body wanted relief more than any of that, and I couldn't resist any longer.

Maybe I should listen to Freya and let it be casual. Let Killian take care of all my needs, but not let my heart get in the way.

"Fuck it," I muttered.

I leaned up, and he bent his head just in time as our lips touched. It was soft at first, a light, tentative touch of his lips against mine. As the kiss lingered, he moved urgently, darting his tongue across the seam of my lips, and I opened to him.

He lifted me onto the kitchen island, spreading my thighs and pressing into me. He deepened the kiss, taking charge by pressing his hand on the back of my neck and guiding me where he wanted. I fought back, biting his bottom lip and squeezing my legs around his waist.

He wrenched his lips from mine, and I gasped for air at the disconnect. His lips marked a trail down my neck until he was at my ear. "Tell me to stop."

"No."

He nipped at my ear. "No?"

"Please, Killian."

"What do you want, darling?"

"You. I want you. Please."

"Atta girl."

Before I could stop him and tell him this was a bad idea, he had me off the counter and in his arms, bridal-style. I clung to his neck, holding on while he sprinted us up to his bedroom. He gently set me down at the foot of his bed, and then he knelt on the floor in front of me.

"What are you doing?" I asked.

He fingered the hem of my yoga pants. "Giving you what you want. Can we get you out of these clothes?"

He didn't need to ask me twice. I pulled my Sullivan's Irish Pub t-shirt over my head and flung it across the room. I reached behind me, unhooking my constricting bra, and threw it in the other direction. Insecurity wrapped around me as I sat topless on Killian's bed, but he had a deep-seated hunger in his eyes.

He fingered the waistband of my leggings, and I nodded at his unasked question. He peeled them off me, taking my underwear with them. Thank God, because I was wearing some seriously unsexy underwear. Thongs while pregnant, hell no. I didn't like them normally, but definitely not while my stomach grew larger each day.

"Lay back, darling," he ordered.

I didn't like being ordered around in the bedroom. I was usually the one on top, taking what I needed, but his growly tone of voice gave me pause. I kinda wanted to see what he'd do if I disobeyed.

He dropped his head down between my thighs and parted me before I could object.

"Oh my God," I moaned out.

His hand gently ran up my stomach, and he guided me on my back, being careful so I didn't hurt the baby.

He lit my body aflame, and I didn't want him to stop, but then he lifted his head, ceasing his actions for a moment. "Let me take care of you."

I didn't object, and he dipped his head back down and made circles on my clit. He knew the pressure and speed I needed to make my orgasm press up against me. When his mouth was on me, I lost all thought. I forgot that sleeping with my baby daddy was a terrible idea. All I could focus on was the way he played my body with finesse and expertise. Like it was his favorite thing to do in the universe.

He pulled back for a second, leaving me panting for more. "Mmm. You taste good."

"Don't stop," I breathed out and tried to press his head back down.

"Look at me," he ordered.

Oh God, he could have asked me anything, and I would have done it. I looked down at him through heavy-lidded eyes. "Killian...please."

"Watch me as I make you come all over my beard," he purred.

"I—"

"Darling."

I did as he commanded. I watched his tongue flick out and go in for the kill again. My body was electric as he pressed on, taking his time to learn every contour of my core. The soft brush of his beard against my thighs made me grind up against him. I forgot what I was doing, only wanting to coat his beard with the evidence of what he did to me.

When he wrapped his lips around my clit, everything froze. Then I felt the orgasm wrench through my body. I arched my back and cried out his name.

When I came back from the out-of-body experience, Killian was wiping off his beard. God, could that be sexier?

"Killian?"

I still needed to catch my breath. But I wanted more. I

wanted him to give me another orgasm and another until I begged him to stop.

"Get up here," I demanded.

He gave me a playful smirk. "Yeah? What for?"

"If you don't get in the bed and fuck me like the animal we both know you are, I'll find someone else who can."

"Bossy," he teased.

I smirked back at him. "You like it."

"Hell yeah, I do."

"Now, Killian," I ordered, my voice low and demanding.

He climbed into the bed with me, and our lips fused together again before I had another moment to think. He threaded his hands through my hair, deepening the kiss. And I let him. Giving him the lead as we writhed together side-by-side. He brought one of my legs over his thigh and ran the head of his cock over my clit. He was toying with me, not giving me the release I needed yet.

"Please," I moaned in a desperate plea for relief.

"You want this, huh?"

I nodded.

"Hold on, darling."

I whined in annoyance as he turned around to find something in his bedside drawer.

"We don't need a condom," I protested.

He turned back around and had a bottle of lube in his hand. Oh. Damn, he thought of everything. He uncapped the bottle and spread a liberal amount on his cock. Then he reached down and speared me with his fingers. He threw the bottle aside, not caring where it went, and hitched my leg over his hip again. We groaned in unison as he slid inside me, filling me in the best way possible.

I bent my head to his neck, kissing him softly. "Yes."

He moved in shallow thrusts, and I gripped onto him as if for dear life. "Easy. I got you. Let me get you there."

I thrust back at him. "No. I like being in control."

He didn't stop his motions but cupped my face. "Let go, Siobhan."

"No..." I fought him with every arch of my hips, meeting his movements as if our joining was a battle.

But I was letting him win. The way our bodies moved so perfectly together had my emotions spinning out of control. I wanted him to take me until I couldn't think anymore. Until I was a weightless cloud of pleasure.

"Yes, darling. I got you. Come one more time for me," he urged.

He lifted my leg higher on his hip, opening me up for a better angle, and then he stroked me through another orgasm. I clung to him as I cried out. The bed creaked as his movements got faster, more urgent, until he groaned out his own release into my neck.

It was hot when men moaned, and Killian had no issues making his pleasure known. I loved every minute of it. Of the way our bodies joined and how he made me relax until I lost myself.

He dropped his head onto my neck and nosed across it. "You got what you need, darling?"

"No," I admitted.

I wanted more. To come again and again and again. Until I was spent and couldn't take it anymore.

He lifted his head, his mouth crooked into that wicked grin yet again. "No?"

I severed our connection, only to push him onto his back. I climbed on top of him. "I'm not done with *you* yet."

There was that naughty smirk again. He gave it as good

as he got it, and he loved when I took charge as much as when I let him take the reins.

"Oh, darling, don't you worry. I'll give you what you want tonight. Everything you ask for."

I should have been concerned about that, but I wasn't. I'd worry about that tomorrow. Instead, I bent to kiss him once more.

CHAPTER TWENTY-THREE

KILLIAN

*T*wirled her hair around my finger as we lay entwined during the early dawn. Working nights, we were used to being awake in that weird twilight place when it was too late for night owls yet too early for early birds. We basked in it, catching our breath after having given in to temptation for a couple more rounds.

Her brain was spinning beside me, but I let her stew in her thoughts as I lay beside her. She likely regretted what we had done, but I didn't. The moment she kissed me at the pub, making a show of possessiveness to anyone watching, I knew we'd end up in this position tonight. I didn't regret giving my baby mama everything she needed, even if those multiple orgasms made my tongue tired.

"So... did you like that bike ride?" I teased.

She belted out a laugh. "You ass!"

"You started it." She shook her head with a grin, and I pulled her closer. "Like I said, you can ride me any day, any time."

"Men," she muttered under her breath like she didn't want me to hear but did at the same time.

"You love me," I teased.

"Can I ask you something?"

"Sure."

"That was her tonight, right?"

I blew out a breath.

Siobhan lifted her head from my chest. "Killian?"

"She's the reason I'm the way I am," I whispered so quietly even I barely heard it.

I never admitted that out loud to anyone. Didn't have to because my brothers knew, but saying the words was like a punch to the gut.

"Oh."

I glanced down at her. "Oh? That's all you have to say?"

She shifted off my chest and lay on her side, propping her head on her elbow. "I know you don't want to talk about her. It's okay. I don't need to know."

I nodded. But it was like something else possessed me as the words tumbled from my mouth. "She was my fiancée. Or was going to be."

"What do you mean?"

I gestured to the room. "I had just bought the house and asked her to move in with me. I had the ring in my pocket, ready to propose, but..."

Siobhan put a gentle hand on my arm. "What happened?"

"I was supposed to close the pub but had switched hours with someone else so I could surprise her. But then I found her with *him*."

"Who?"

"My best fucking friend," I seethed. The venom seeped into my voice like I had found them yesterday.

Memories of the worst night of my life flashed before my eyes. Of the ring burning a hole in my pocket and the spring in my step at the prospect of finally asking Liz to be my wife. I heard the moans when I reached the first step. Finding them in my bed made me see red. Liz had screamed, but Bobby laughed. As if it was all a funny joke. Until I dragged him from the bed and wailed on him until Liz begged me to stop. All her shit was on the front lawn the next morning. I didn't need friends after that; my brothers were more than enough.

They deserved each other. I didn't care if he did her dirty now. I'd call that karma for the pain they put me through.

"Just because she hurt you doesn't mean you have to shut yourself off from love. If you want that," Siobhan reassured me.

"It's better this way."

My brothers had tried to convince me of the same thing, but they didn't get it. They didn't understand the way my heart shattered at the betrayal of the two people I loved most in my life. It was easier to live my life with no attachments. Better to never feel the way I did that night.

"I'm sorry," she said.

"Nothing for you to be sorry for."

She frowned and shifted onto her back, putting a hand on her belly. The protectiveness crawled up inside me each time I saw the evidence of the life we created. I joined my hand with hers without a second thought.

We lay there in silence for a couple of moments. I never admitted that to anyone before. I wasn't sure what it was about this woman that made me say the things I kept locked inside.

She shifted again, pulling away from me and sliding out of the bed.

"Where do you think you're going?"

"I need a shower."

"Me too. How about we save some water?"

She grinned. "Oh, I'm game for that."

She yelped when I lifted her into my arms and carried her into the bathroom.

"You're gonna hurt yourself by doing that," she said after I gently lowered her down to the floor in the bathroom.

I flexed my biceps. "No way. Working with Ronan's giving me these guns."

She turned on the water and stepped into the shower. "Cocky, much?"

I followed her in, and as soon as I closed the curtain, I had her pressed against the tile wall. "You know it, darling."

"Behave," she warned.

I gave her a cocky grin and took her mouth again.

I didn't behave myself in the shower, not one bit, and she didn't care. Not when I went down on her and then lifted her in my arms and took her until the water was icicles on our skin. We laughed as we rushed to wash off in the freezing water.

I got out first and handed her a towel, wrapping my own around my waist. She lingered in the bathroom while I got dressed and changed the sheets on my bed. I lay on the bed, waiting for her to come back in. When she did, her hair was still damp, and she was dressed in her cute flannel jammies.

She bent to pick up her clothes.

I patted the bed beside me. "C'mere."

Her nose wrinkled, like she was thinking too hard about the request. But then she finally moved across the room and sat on the bed beside me.

"Stay."

"What?"

I stood up and pulled the covers back. I switched off the light, plugged my phone into the charger, and slid into the bed. She didn't move at first, but when she walked out of the room, I thought she was telling me our fun was over. But then she came back with that weird U-shaped pillow.

She lay on the bed and positioned the pillow to her liking. "It's to help me get comfy. Your mom brought it over for me."

Oh. Brian talked about getting one of those for Kelsey when she was pregnant with Cora.

I lifted the covers over us and placed my hand on her belly.

"Killian?" she whispered.

"Hmm?"

"Thank you."

"For what, darling?"

"Everything."

Before I could ask her to explain, her eyes fluttered closed, and I was plunged into silence. I pressed a kiss to her temple and let myself drift off to sleep.

The coffee shop had a line out the door when I walked up to it. I cringed and checked my phone, hoping Siobhan hadn't woken up yet. I was out of coffee again, and I needed carbs before I helped Ronan with a job later. I waited in line, and when I got to the front, a frazzled-looking Willow explained why.

"Killian, hey. What can I get ya?"

I eyed her. "Are you alone today?"

She shrugged. "Part of being in business. Now what will it be?"

"Latte for me and hot chocolate for Siobhan. Bacon, egg, and cheese on an everything bagel, and she likes... I know you told me..."

"French toast bagel with strawberry cream cheese," Willow supplied.

She rang me up, and I handed over my card. In a flash, she had darted over to the machines, starting on my latte with lightning reflexes. I shoved a twenty in the tip jar and stepped out of line for the next customer.

Poor Willow. I had noticed the Help Wanted sign in the window, but I didn't realize it was this bad. I got now why Siobhan didn't want to cut down her hours.

I waited for the food and drinks and gave Willow a sympathetic smile before walking out of the shop and back to my house. I sipped on my latte on the short walk until I crept into my home, hoping I didn't wake Siobhan.

I set down the bag of bagels and the to-go cups on the kitchen counter and walked upstairs. I carefully opened my bedroom door and stopped in my tracks at the sight of Siobhan peacefully asleep in my bed. She was curled on her side but with her hand outstretched toward my half of the bed. The sight of her felt so natural, like this was our normal life. As if it was perfectly normal for me to grab us breakfast while she slept soundly.

The déjà vu hit me like a ton of bricks. I used to do this for Liz.

Every Sunday morning, I'd go out for bagels and coffee, and we'd have them in bed. Until the night she betrayed me.

I shouldn't want Siobhan in my bed, let alone my house. I should be glad she wanted out as quickly as she did. But the thought of her moving into any of those apartments set my teeth on edge.

She stirred in the bed, her eyes fluttering open before I could let those thoughts linger. "Killian, how late is it?"

I checked my watch. "About ten. You need the sleep."

She rubbed her eyes. "What are you doing? Come back to bed."

I grinned. "Why?"

"Because I'm sleepy, and you're warm."

I laughed. "I brought breakfast. Are you hungry?"

She reluctantly sat up in bed, groaning as she stood up.

She followed me downstairs into the kitchen. She shook her head when I handed her the hot chocolate. "No coffee."

"Hot chocolate," I explained. I took plates out of my cabinet and pulled the bagel sandwiches out of the bag.

Siobhan unwrapped hers, and her face lit up. "My favorite!"

"I know."

She took a seat at the island, and I sat next to her, sipping on my coffee and eating my sandwich.

"How did you know my order?" she asked. "You said the other day when Ronan came over that you asked Willow, but when did you do that?"

"The last time we had sex, I went and got us breakfast, but then you ghosted me."

She set down her bagel. "No, I didn't. You left me alone in your bed."

"To get us bagels. When I came back, you were gone, and then you pretended nothing had happened."

"Oh."

I eyed her suspiciously. "Were you mad at me?"

She dipped her head down and avoided eye contact. "A little."

"Is that why you've been weird the past couple of weeks?"

"Yeah..."

I wasn't sure what to say to that. I didn't get why she was mad at me when she knew what type of guy I was. Now she knew exactly why. It was so much better to keep feelings out of it, so I never went through that again.

We sat eating our breakfast in silence for a couple of minutes. Last night had been fun, but I felt the tension wrapping around us tight again. Where did we go from here? I didn't want her to get the wrong idea. I still wasn't the guy you married, but I didn't like the awkwardness between us.

"How was the coffee shop?" she asked, changing the subject.

"Fine," I lied.

If I told her the truth, she would have scrambled to put on her uniform and go over to help. I wouldn't blame her, but I didn't want extra stress on her. For all the talk about her worries about losing our baby, working herself too much could be a deciding factor. Besides, she didn't need to worry about money. I had it handled.

We finished breakfast, and I told her to go sit in the living room while I cleaned up. She didn't like that, and I heard her stomp upstairs.

I unloaded the dishwasher and put dirty dishes into it. Walking into the living room, I found her in her spot on my couch with her knitting needles in hand. She was dressed now but comfy in a pair of yoga pants and a soft-looking red sweater. There was a hat beside her while she worked on something new.

I sat down beside her and picked up the red hat. "Did you make this red because it's your favorite color?"

She tipped her head to the side. "How did you know that?"

I gestured to her sweater and tucked her hair behind her ear, revealing the red gemstone earrings she always wore. "You wear red when out of uniform."

"You noticed that?"

"Yeah?"

"Huh."

She went back to her knitting, and I watched her start a new row, intrigued by how her hands finessed the needles and fabric together. She was good with her hands.

My blood ran cold when she dropped the needles in her lap, her eyes going wide, and her hand went to her belly.

"What? What's wrong?" I asked, my voice rising as panic coursed through me.

But Siobhan shook her head, her eyes shiny as she placed both hands on her belly.

"Darling, what is it?"

"I think I felt the baby," she whispered, like if she said it too loud, it wouldn't be true.

"Really? Are you sure?"

She rubbed her hands down her belly, searching for the motion again. "It's like... You know when you want to kiss someone? And you have butterflies in your stomach? It's like that. I think—oh my God!"

I cupped her face. "Really?"

She nodded, happy tears streaming down her face. "Kill...I can feel the baby."

I brushed away her tears with my thumbs. "That's amazing."

"I..." But she didn't finish her thought; instead, she leaned up and met me in a gentle kiss.

She was tentative at first until I deepened it, angling her

head the way I liked. I took her mouth again, possessing her with my lips until we were a mess of lips and hands desperate for friction.

"Killian," she moaned against my mouth. Her breath was ragged and coming in pants.

I groaned at the sound of my phone buzzing in my pocket. "Fuck. I gotta go."

Her face fell. "Oh."

I put a hand on her stomach. "I'm sorry. I'd love nothing more for you to ride this bicycle again, but I have to do a job with Ronan."

She pulled away, her face tinted pink, but she nodded. "That's okay. I got caught up in the emotions. I can feel the baby. I've never felt any of my babies before. This is..."

"This is great news. I told you everything would be okay, and it will. Soon, we'll be holding Bean in our arms. I promise you that."

I bent to give her a goodbye kiss. I really shouldn't have, but I couldn't help myself. Maybe it was the fact my kid was in there making their presence known. Yeah, that had to be. It wasn't because the woman invading my home was making me feel anything but lust.

CHAPTER TWENTY-FOUR

SIOBHAN

I felt the baby. I finally felt that little movement of life inside my body for the first time. That had to explain why I kissed Killian again. My emotions were out of sorts.

But it didn't explain why he kissed me goodbye when he had to rush out. Like we were a couple when we most definitely were not.

I tried to shake it off as I shot off a text to Freya.

> ME: I know you're in class but... I FELT THE BABY!

She was busy with a room full of thirty kindergartners and wouldn't respond for a while, so I dialed my mom next.

She answered on the second ring. "Hi, honey, what's wrong?"

"Nothing wrong. I felt the baby."

"Oh, wow."

"Mom..." I whispered. "I've never felt one of them before. It's exciting, and I had to tell you."

"That's great."

"Maybe this one will last," I whispered.

"They will—I promise you, honey," Mom reassured me. "By the way...I heard from Margaret the other day."

I scoffed. Did freaking Margaret tattle to my mother because I was rude to her? Whatever, she was the one who made me cry.

"What did she have to say?" I asked, even though I didn't want to know.

"That she was so glad her baby boy didn't have kids with such a rude and disrespectful woman. And that I should have raised you better."

I groaned. "God. She's such a... witch."

Mom laughed. "Witch with a B. She's an unpleasant person and I know you only lashed out over whatever rude thing I can imagine she said to you."

There was no love lost between the two of them. Mom knew the nightmare of a mother-in-law I dealt with. She was always diplomatic, and Dad usually chugged his beer to keep his mouth shut when dealing with Margaret.

I changed the subject, asking how she and Dad were doing. We chatted for a little longer, and she was already making plans to come visit closer to when the baby came. I told her not to book any flights. There was still that little voice in the back of my mind that whispered all my fears to me. After so much loss, it was hard not to listen to that voice.

I checked if Freya responded after I hung up with my mom, but nothing yet. I fingered the quartz crystal I had been superstitiously wearing, even though I didn't think it worked. It had been sweet of Willow to give it to me.

> ME: I think the crystal from your friend worked. I felt the baby today.

I grinned as I saw her text me right back.

> WILLOW: YAY! I'm so happy for you.

> ME: How's the shop doing?

> WILLOW: BUSY! On my own today.

> ME: WHAT?!? OMW!

I ran up the steps and quickly changed into my Drakesville Drip uniform. I had a shift at the pub at five, but I could help Willow for at least a couple of hours. Besides, I still very much needed the money. I had a sneaking suspicion Killian wasn't being truthful earlier when I asked how Willow was doing.

I grabbed my coat from the hall closet and left, locking the door behind me. I shoved my hands in my pockets and walked the short distance to the coffee shop. Having to move away was going to suck because Killian's house was in such a prime location. I'd love to at least stay in town even if I had to drive instead of walk. Moving the next town over or even farther wasn't ideal. But after looking at a couple of hideous apartments, I might have to widen my search.

There were three customers in line at the shop when I got there. Not too busy, but overwhelming when you were the only one on staff. I waved to Willow as I went into the back to put my coat away.

I came around the counter and clocked in. "What do you need?"

"God, you're a lifesaver." She breathed a sigh of relief,

and the tension in her shoulders dropped slightly at my presence. "Make me some lattes?"

"On it."

I worked behind the counter making the drinks while Willow rang up the customers. It was a breeze, even if the smell of coffee still made me want to throw up. The lull afterward gave us the time to clean off the espresso machine and wipe down the counters.

"How long can you stay?" Willow asked.

"Until four."

"An angel! You didn't have to come in."

I shrugged. "I need the money."

"I need to make calls to interview new baristas."

I shooed her away, pushing her toward the office. "Go on then. Do the boss lady things while I have a handle on the front."

She squeezed me into a hug. "Thank you. And big congrats on the baby. That's so exciting."

Instinctively, I placed my hands on my growing belly. I was getting bigger every day, but watching my child grow filled me with a joy I couldn't describe.

"Go on. I can hold down the fort," I told her.

She skipped off toward the back to do work in the office while I manned the front. Customers milled in and out for the next hour, but nothing I couldn't handle. Some black coffee regulars and college-aged kids wanting the latest drink special Willow had concocted. She was ready for spring and already planning the new seasonal offerings.

Working was good, and being busy kept my mind off the fear that anything could go wrong with this pregnancy. It made me forget all the uncertainty between Killian and me.

I didn't want to dissect that we yet again succumbed to

my hormones. Although I had to admit it was probably why I was in such a good mood. He gave into my desires last night, every last one of them, and it was amazing.

The bell on the door rang, and I lifted my head to see who it was. For a split second, I thought it was Killian, and my mouth worked itself into a small smile, but then I noticed the man's height and lack of a full beard.

"Lachlan, hey," I greeted Killian's youngest brother.

"Hey, Siobhan."

"What can I get you?"

"Small black coffee."

Knew it. Artists were so easy to guess.

I rang him up, ran his card through the machine, and handed it back to him. Spinning around, I found the drip coffee behind me and filled a to-go cup to the brim with the dark liquid. Then I handed it over to the man in question. His lips twitched, and I couldn't help but notice the family resemblance. But Killian, with that beard and naughty smirk, was so much hotter.

Wait a second. What was wrong with me? Why was I thinking about Killian right now?

"Can I ask you something?" Lachlan cut through my thoughts. I hadn't even noticed he was still standing there.

"Um. Sure?" I answered, perplexed by what he wanted.

I didn't know Lachlan all that well. He was still commuting from the city while he got his studio up and running next door. We said little to each other besides polite greetings.

"Maternity photos," he blurted out.

"Huh?"

"Yeah. Do you want me to take some?"

I inclined my head at his question. Where had that come from?

He rubbed a hand across his scruffy jaw. "Truthfully? I need a favor."

"Okay?"

"I need to build up a better portfolio for the studio. Kelsey's not far along enough, so she suggested asking you. Free of charge, of course."

"Um. Sure."

"If you want them. I even have a model friend who would stand in. Unless?" he let his question stand in the air.

Unless Killian wanted to be in them. That's what he wanted to ask.

"He might. It's his baby too. I'll ask."

He gave me a quizzical look. "Have you met my brother?"

"Yeah?"

"He hates photos. That's why I suggested an alternative."

"Lemme ask him. He might surprise you."

He studied me for a second, his gaze reminiscent of his brother's. But Lachlan's gaze wasn't so heated it made me want to jump out of my skin. His glance didn't make my heart skip a beat when I stared into those crystal blue orbs. His was a look of admiration, not the look of a man who wanted to feast on me.

"I heard a rumor about you," he said.

I pointed to my stomach. "What? That I'm pregnant with your brother's baby?"

He laughed. "No. That someone finally locked down the town hoe."

I cringed and shook my head. "That was all for show so Liz would leave him alone."

His eyes widened. "He told you about Liz?"

"She showed up at the pub, and he told me everything."

"Damn," Lachlan breathed out, disbelief marring his face. "He never talks about her. We have to refer to her as 'that woman.' I'm surprised he even told you her name."

I wiped down the spotless counter, avoiding his gaze. The hurt in Killian's voice last night told me he didn't open up about what happened. He shoved his feelings down into meaningless sex so he didn't get hurt again. My heart ached for him, but also made me wonder what else he bottled up.

Willow saved me from a response by emerging from the back office. Her face lit up at the sight of Lachlan standing in front of the counter. He looked like a deer in headlights as he fiddled with his leather jacket.

"Oh, hey, Lachs," she greeted.

"Hi, uh...Willa... I mean, Willow...hey, um..." He stumbled with his words and looked down at the ground.

I stared at him, noticing the pink tinge creeping up the back of his neck. Was he blushing? Lachlan was the quiet one of the Murphys, but it never occurred to me that he was shy.

"We'll work out the details later," he said to me, and I swore he ran out of the coffee shop.

Willow groaned in his wake and pretended to bang her head against the wall.

"What was that about?" I asked.

"God, I don't know," she wailed. "He's so hot, but every time I talk to him, he can't wait to literally run away from me."

I eyed her. "Maybe he's shy. He's the quiet one, you know."

"I like the quiet ones. They're always the kinkiest ones and are amazing in bed."

I couldn't help the laugh that erupted out of me. I was

not expecting that response at all. Was that true? I didn't want to think about it too hard.

"Gah! Why doesn't he like me?" she cried.

"I'm sure he does."

She gave her head a slow shake in disagreement. "Anyway, thank you so much for coming in today. How much longer do I have you?"

I eyed the clock. "I can hang for another couple of hours. I'm at the pub at five."

Her eyes widened. "If I'd known you were doing double duty, I wouldn't have let you work."

I waved her off. "I need the money. Any good interviews?"

She pressed her fingers against her temples and rubbed at the tension trapped there. "Nah. A bunch of college kids that couldn't bother to answer their phones. I have a teenager I'm gonna talk to later. She's a friend's kid and has a good head on her shoulders, so she could be promising. Her first job, though."

"Gotta start somewhere."

"True."

We restocked the coffee bar until we had an onslaught of more customers. I went as fast as I could, loving how the time passed so quickly when we got busy. I felt bad leaving when I had to as the evening crowd rolled in. Willow waved me off while I dashed off toward Killian's house. I needed a quick change into my Sullivan's Irish Pub t-shirt, and then I'd be good. I was glad I wore my maternity black slacks to the coffee shop, so I didn't have to change those.

There was still a chill in the cold late February air, but as it edged toward spring, it was heating up. PA didn't tend to see a real spring until later. Even then, sometimes we got plunged straight into the humid summers. I was not looking forward to being super pregnant when we hit those days.

A smile tugged at my lips, and I put a hand on my stomach, reminding me I finally felt my baby for the first time. Bean was finally making their presence known, and I couldn't be happier.

CHAPTER TWENTY-FIVE

KILLIAN

I smirked to myself as Siobhan literally skipped ahead of me on our walk home after closing down the pub. I regretted rushing out after she told me she felt the baby earlier, especially after that kiss. It didn't look like that halted her cheerful mood. Even watching her at the pub tonight, she flitted from table to table with that giddy smile on her face. It wasn't her fake customer service smile, either.

I wished I had her energy because I was beat from helping Ronan with another project. In a couple of weeks, he'd have more things lined up if I was interested. Mid-March was when things ramped up for him again. I needed the money but was unsure I could handle these double shifts. When I saw the look on Siobhan's face light up at the feeling of our baby inside her, I knew I'd suck it up and take those long hours. She and the baby deserved to be taken care of.

"Wait up," I called after her.

She stopped on the street to wait, but not without giving me an exaggerated roll of her eyes. "Why do I need to wait? We both know where we're going."

I grabbed her hand. "Because it's late."

"Again, we live in a super safe small town. Only people out here are us."

She wasn't wrong about that last part, and even though Drakesville was a pretty safe town, that didn't mean anything bad couldn't happen. She didn't yank her hand away as we finished the walk to my house. I opened the front door for her, letting her step inside first before shutting it behind me and locking it up for the night.

After hanging up my coat, I found her in the kitchen, her hand on her stomach again, with that permanent smile on her face.

I crossed over to her and tilted her chin up toward me. "Now where were we?"

"Huh?"

I didn't let her form another sentence. I cupped her face and slanted my mouth on hers. This time, she let me. She didn't fight for dominance like normal; instead, she leaned in and let me take the lead.

I'd been thinking about kissing her since the moment I left this morning, my thoughts dominated by these soft, plump lips. Of her velvety tongue grazing across mine and imagining her doing other things with that tongue. The kind that made my jeans tighter.

Tentatively, I darted my tongue out, and she opened to me again, letting me take control as I branded her mouth as mine. The kiss lingered on until her hands were in my hair, and I lifted her up onto the kitchen island again. Our breaths came in pants, and I dragged my mouth away from hers to trail down her neck.

"Mmm," she let out a soft moan.

"Whatcha need?" I grunted out, licking and sucking at the flesh below her ear.

"You."

"Yeah?"

She lifted my head to peer into my eyes, and all I saw was heat behind hers. "Yes. Killian. Give me what I want."

"What's that, huh?" I teased.

"I want another bicycle ride." Her voice was teasing and light, but oh so sexy.

"Oh, really?"

"Mmmhmm. I'd really like to hop on there right now if you don't mind."

"Well... what if I say you have to wait?"

"Killian," she groaned.

I laughed. "You never have to wait, darling. You can hop on this bike any time you want."

I lifted her into my arms and carried her upstairs to my bedroom. All the work I'd been doing with Ronan had been paying off. Her body in my arms didn't make my muscles scream nearly as much as all the digging I did today.

I stepped inside my bedroom and gently placed her down at the foot of my bed. She nodded at my t-shirt. "Strip, Killian." Her voice was demanding and her gaze heated. It was sexy as hell.

"You first, darling."

She gripped the edges of her Sullivan's Irish Pub t-shirt and pulled it over her head. I tried to keep my tongue in my mouth at the sight of her breasts spilling out of her bra. I probably looked like a cartoon character with my eyes bulging out of my head. She was so gorgeous. From her groaning chest to the curves our child gave her. Something protective and carnal crawled up inside me at her body on display for me.

"Killian..." she whined, making her impatience known.

I ripped my t-shirt off, the pants and boxers next, not wanting to wait any longer. She had lost her pants too and lay naked, waiting for me in my bed. My brain froze at the image. I wanted to remember her waiting in my bed. Right where she belonged.

I knelt on the bed, but before I could descend on her, she pounced on me first. Siobhan needed to be in control tonight, and I'd grant her that. I'd give this woman everything she wanted.

I was on my back in a flash, her lips meeting mine in a hungry kiss. I couldn't help myself by running my fingers down her body until I was between her thighs. She was slick with her desire already, a discovery that made me growl into the kiss. That didn't stop her from biting my lip and dominating my tongue with hers. It also didn't stop me from swiftly finding her entrance and pumping my fingers inside. The heat of our kiss increased until she was gasping for breath and moaning into my ear.

"Fuck," I ground out beneath her.

"Killian, I need control tonight."

"Then take it. Take what you need. I'm yours."

I tried not to think about the implications of my sentence. It was just dirty talk, nothing more.

I pressed my fingers deeper, pumping my digits in a slow rhythm just how she liked. Her face contorted, and then I snickered, pleased with myself, when she cried out my name.

"You're a horny little thing tonight," I purred.

"Mmm," was all she squeaked out as she recovered.

After a breath, the vixen was back. She crawled on top

of me, pressing her hands against my chest, and then we groaned together as we joined once more. I leaned back and let her take what she needed, watching her ride to her heart's content.

She was so beautiful when she took her pleasure in my body. I slid my hands down her chest and rested it on her stomach. My heart beat loudly as I watched her writhe above me. I pretended the sensation was due to the release of endorphins.

"Come with me," she begged. She leaned down and met me in a soft kiss, and I rocked back against her movements.

I slid my hands through her hair and kissed her deeply. We moved in sync together, taking what we needed from each other.

I tried not to imagine this every night. I pushed down the nagging at my heartstrings and instead gave my baby mama what she so desperately needed. That was all I could ever give her. For my heart would never belong to anyone ever again.

"I feel like I jumped you."

I belted out a laugh. "I wasn't complaining."

She curled around me, laying her head against my naked chest. "This baby's making me a horny mess. Every time I see you, I imagine..."

"What?"

She shoved her head down into my chest further, but I spotted the redness of her ears.

I lifted her chin to look me in the eye. "What, darling?"

"My imagination's filled with the horniest images of us."

A naughty grin tugged at my mouth. "Like what?"

"Imagining you taking me on my couch. Or pressing into me from behind. In the shower. On the kitchen island. Fuck, I even had a sexy dream of you fucking me on the bar at the pub."

I made a face. That bar was dirty as shit. But I didn't hate the idea of taking her from behind.

"Dirty girl."

"Shut up."

I waggled my eyebrows at her. "You're the one with such a dirty mind."

She shoved me in the shoulder, pulling away from me and laying on her back. "This is your fault. I was never like this before you put this baby in me."

I pulled her back toward me, loving the feel of her body pressed against mine. "I don't mind."

"Of course not," she scoffed. "You love the no-strings sex."

I did. But something struck me in the chest at the way she said that. With venom and a little hurt. I tried to shake it away, but it killed the moment. She must have sensed it, too, because she hefted herself out of the bed and padded across the hall.

I ran my hand through my hair, thinking she was done with me for the night, but then she walked across the hall dressed in her pajamas and holding her pregnancy pillow. She took her place beside me in my bed, just like last night.

I should kick her out. Tell her I'd only give her my body and not these quiet moments. But I couldn't because I wanted her beside me.

She adjusted her pillow the way she wanted and lay back down. "You wanna stay up?"

I nodded.

I was beat after working a double shift today between

the two jobs, but we were night people and needed time to wind down after a shift at the pub. I grabbed the remote on my nightstand and turned on the TV, clicking onto a random episode of CSI on my streaming app.

"Oh!" she exclaimed.

I jerked my head toward her, fear immediately filling my psyche. "What's wrong? Did you feel the baby again?"

She waved me off. "Just remembered I promised Lachlan I'd talk to you."

I studied her for a second. Had Lachs stopped by when I was out working with Ronan today? That was odd. He usually texted if he wanted to talk, and I hadn't heard from him much since he opened his studio. My brothers and I had been asking him when he needed help moving, but he kept waving us off.

"He wants to take maternity photos for us," she explained. "For his portfolio. I said I'd be glad to help him out. You don't have to—"

"I'll do it. It's my baby too."

"You don't have to, but I told him I'd talk to you about it."

"When did he stop by?"

She shook her head. "When I picked up some hours at the coffee shop today."

Wait a second. When I got home, she wasn't here, but I didn't think anything of it. She kept taking extra shifts at the pub and not putting it on the calendar. But she wasn't supposed to pull doubles anymore.

I gritted my teeth. "Siobhan."

She rolled her eyes. "What part of 'I need the money' do you not understand?"

"The part that I don't want you to lose the baby!"

She reared back at my outburst. "What does me picking up shifts have to do with that?"

I rubbed the back of my neck. My blood pressure was through the roof. "The stress isn't good for you. Your doctor even said so."

"I need money for rent."

"And I'm going to help you. I'm not kicking you out the moment you go into labor."

"Killian, I'm not stupid. I know you'd much rather go back to your bachelor ways. The quicker I make more money, the quicker I'm out of your hair."

She was right. Of course, she was right.

But picturing her raising the baby in one of those rundown apartments away from me didn't sit right with me. Only seeing the baby every other weekend didn't either. But it wasn't like I was looking for a relationship. That shit went south the moment Liz betrayed me. The fact Siobhan wanted to run away as soon as she could proved she felt the same way.

"Don't do doubles again, okay?"

She rolled her eyes again. "I'm an adult. I can make my own choices."

"Please."

"Fine. No more doubles, but I'm fine." She put my hand against her stomach. "I can feel them again. So cool it with the overbearing baby daddy shit. At least for tonight."

Instead of starting another argument, I kissed her once more. Then we tumbled down into desire once again.

CHAPTER TWENTY-SIX

SIOBHAN

"*A*re you ready?" The ultrasound tech asked us as she held the wand over my exposed belly.

I cast a glance at Killian, who squeezed my hand harder. I nodded at the tech.

She put the wand on my stomach and rolled it around slowly while we watched the monitor. The seconds felt like agony as she searched for the little life inside me. Anxiety reared its ugly head as I wondered if this was where they told me my baby was gone.

Then the tech smiled. "Aw, there she is."

I breathed out a slow, shaky breath. We knew that today meant we'd find out the sex of our baby, but that hadn't been my main concern. That she was still thriving and alive inside me mattered more than anything.

Killian squeezed my hand. "I told you everything would be fine."

"You want the printouts?" The tech asked us.

"Yes, please," I told her. "Everything else looks good, though?"

She nodded. "Your bloodwork last week was good. Your doctor says you and baby are looking healthy."

She wiped off the jelly on my stomach and put the machine away. She walked out of the room and came back to hand us the ultrasound of our baby.

"Darling, no tears," Killian said, his voice soft and calming. I wiped my eyes, but then he cupped my face and kissed me.

I should have pulled away. But I didn't. Like I hadn't been pulling away these past couple of weeks. Since Liz came crawling back, I marked Killian as mine. At least as far as the women in Drakesville knew.

It didn't help that each night we crawled into bed together. Or how sometimes, if he was in a good mood, he'd catch me in a kiss in the service aisle. Sarah would give me that look and ask me to spill later, but there was nothing to tell. Asking Killian what was going on between us would only bring up all the things we didn't want to discuss. So we didn't.

I was still looking for an apartment, but a part of me didn't want to rush any longer. Not when this man filled my needs and was the perfect birthing partner. I truly didn't know what to expect when Killian Murphy, of all people, knocked me up. But it definitely wasn't this.

Killian pulled away. "Buy you lunch?"

I was so hungry, and my cravings had been so weird lately. "Can we go to the brewery again?"

"Whatever you want."

"I'm gonna eat a big soft pretzel all by myself."

His eyes sparkled as he laughed. "Okay, Mama, let's go."

My chest fluttered at the nickname. He had taken to calling me that lately, and even though it was cheesy, I loved it. Soon, a tiny being would be screaming that at me, and I couldn't wait.

Killian offered his hand and helped me off the exam table. We left together, hand-in-hand, another thing I had stopped questioning, and headed back home to Drakesville. We went home first, and Killian proudly pinned the ultrasound on our fridge.

His fridge. It was his house. Not mine. I had been living here so long, playing house with him, I kept forgetting none of this was mine.

We walked over to the brewery, and I did, in fact, eat a whole Bavarian pretzel without his help. Except the cheese sauce since it was beer cheese sauce, and I wasn't taking any chances.

Killian tried so hard not to laugh behind his beer while I took a huge bite of my cheesesteak.

"Have you come up for air yet?" he teased.

"Shut up."

I placed my hands on my ever-growing stomach. I woke up yesterday, and I felt so much larger, but it had been a gradual change. As I edged closer to the third trimester, I noticed the changes in my body more. I loved seeing it because I never thought I'd ever see a baby growing strong in my body.

"Let's talk names," he said.

"Okay..." I trailed off and thought back to all the names I had on my mental list. I hadn't shared them with him yet out of fear we'd never get this far. "What if I want something traditional Irish?"

He made a face. "Like what?"

"I really like Aoife or Saoirse."

"Hell no!"

I balked at him. "What? They're so pretty."

He scowled. "My brother's best friend is named Eilish, and everyone pronounces it wrong. I'm sure people struggle with your name, too."

Okay, fair. Eilish's name was tough—that was why half of us called her 'Lish' instead. I understood her plight because the number of people who tried to mispronounce my name to 'Sib-be-han' or something even worse was astounding.

"Okay, fair point. I like Fiona, too."

He shook his head. "Too close to Finn, and he'll get a gigantic head about it."

I sighed. "Why do you hate your brother so much?"

He picked up a fry and popped it into his mouth. "Don't hate him. He's an idiot who needs to see what's right in front of him."

"With Eilish?"

He nodded. "I want to slap the shit out of him. Every time she gets into a new relationship, he's a grouchy asshole. Yet when he's dating someone, he doesn't notice how she stops coming to Sunday dinners or looks at him with those puppy dog eyes."

I felt the crinkle of a smile on my lips. Killian loved his family but in his own weird way. I've seen him locked into heated arguments with Finn, but what he said was a confession of his love. It was adorable.

"So you want him to be happy?" I asked.

Killian shrugged. "Nah. Just want him to pull that enormous head out of his ass."

"Speaking of your brother..."

"Which one now?"

"What's up with Lachlan?"

"He's bisexual." He crossed his arms over his chest like he was ready for a fight. This man truly didn't see how he pulled up arms for his brothers.

I waved him off. "Not that. Is he really shy? I saw him stumble over his words in front of Willow the day he asked about the maternity shoot."

Killian rolled his eyes. "Painfully so. He has no game."

"Really?" I asked.

Killian nodded. "Lachlan's...complicated. I worry he planned this move back home not because he wants to, but because his ex Henry fucked him up too much."

I raised my eyebrow. That was interesting.

"Truthfully? I think they got back together, and he doesn't want to tell us."

Interesting, indeed.

"Why do you think that?"

"Because every time I ask him when he's moving here, he waves me off. Why would he want to keep doing the commute? He should have opened a studio in the city if he was still living there. Something's up."

God, couldn't he see how much he loved his family? He was worried about his baby brother, and it was so endearing.

He picked at the label of his beer. "He's a romantic, but he gets into partnerships with people who don't care about him. Lachs isn't like me. He couldn't stomach it."

I nodded and went back to my cheesesteak. That was the elephant in the room we didn't speak about.

We ate in silence for a couple of minutes, both lost in our own thoughts. He sipped on his beer and stared off at something behind my head. There was probably a game on.

Killian paid for lunch, and we walked back to his house. A jolt of shock went through me when he grabbed my hand on the street, and we walked back hand-in-hand again. I didn't want him to let go once inside, but I slipped my hand through his grasp and pulled off my coat.

"I'm gonna take a nap," I announced.

"Okay."

I walked upstairs and stopped for a moment in front of Killian's bedroom door. My pregnancy pillow lay on his bed. I entered his room and grabbed it off the bed.

"What are you doing?" Killian asked.

I spun around and was met with his naked chest. He tossed his shirt on the floor and slid his jeans off.

My tongue felt thick in my mouth. I had to admit since he started working more with Ronan, his muscles were more defined. He didn't look like the guys with six packs on the cover of my romance novels, but his body was stronger.

A nap. I wanted a nap, not sex. Definitely not.

"Siobhan?"

"Huh?"

He tipped my head up. "My eyes are up here."

I ran my hands up his chest. "It's not my fault you're so hot."

He gave me a wolfish grin. "I thought you wanted a nap."

"We can do that later," I whispered. I didn't have to ask him twice before his lips descended on mine again.

"Are you working tonight?" Killian asked.

I curled in his arms and shook my head. After succumbing to our desires again, we took an afternoon nap together. It had been nice waking up beside him.

"No, but I'm going to Freya's, so you get a night free of me."

"Oh."

His voice was laced with disappointment, which confused me. Isn't that what he wanted?

I stretched my arms above my head and rolled out of the bed. Killian stared into a space on the wall, not saying a word. He was being really weird today.

I collected my clothes and walked across the hall to the guest room. I set out new clothes and then took a shower. After I was scrubbed clean, I brushed out my hair and found comfy clothes to change into.

I tossed clean clothes into an overnight bag and walked downstairs. Killian sat on the couch with the sports network blaring on, but he wasn't paying attention to it. He stared at it mindlessly, but he played with the ends of the baby hat I made, lost in thought.

"Killian."

His head snapped up at the sound of my voice.

"I'm heading over to Freya's."

His eyes hardened as he spied my bag. "Oh, for the night?"

"Yup. Freya said she needs a girl's night. I've been a shitty friend lately. But, hey, like I said, it's a taste of your freedom. As soon as I find an apartment, I'll be out of your hair."

He nodded. "Right."

I frowned. What was with him tonight?

"Okay. Well, I'm off."

"Have fun."

I tried not to think too hard about his strange mood. I put my coat on and walked down to his front porch. Killian insisted I park in his driveway instead of the street, so I walked over and got in my car.

I stared up at his house, imagining the day I'd leave his

place for good. If I didn't find an apartment soon, I might convince myself to stay as long as I could. With a sigh, I pushed the button on my car's engine and sped off to the other side of town.

It wasn't a lie that I'd been a poor friend. I had been so sick in my first trimester that Freya had been understanding of my absence, but now my only excuse was that I was spending too much time with my baby daddy. I hadn't been forthcoming with Freya about that. For fear, she'd think it was something more than it was.

I parked in front of her house. My bestie lived in an old stone colonial home across the street from the elementary school where she taught. The house was gorgeous, and she never would have been able to buy it on her teacher's salary had her grandmother not left it to her in her will.

I got out of my car, slung my bag over my shoulder, and walked up the steps. I forgot about Poppy and rang the doorbell. The excitable dog barked her head off, and I heard Freya yelling at her to calm down from behind the door.

Freya answered the door, holding Poppy back by her collar. She had her hair up in a messy bun and wore leggings and her college sweatshirt. "You should have called when you were at the door."

I cringed. "Pregnancy brain."

"Come in."

Once I was inside and gave Poppy lots of love, she calmed down. Freya led me into the living room, and once we were seated on her couch, she handed me a drink.

"Here's your sparkling water," she said. She tucked her legs underneath her and took a sip of her wine. "I haven't seen you in ages."

"Sorry. I'm a rotten friend."

She eyed me. "No. Probably too busy sleeping with Killian Murphy all over the place, huh?"

I gulped. Was that written all over my face?

"Umm..."

She cackled. "Oh my God, you know we live in a gossipy small town, right? I've heard so many rumors about you lately, but you've been screening my calls."

"Sorry, but it's not what you think."

She waggled her eyebrows. "What, you using your baby daddy for sex? Nah, I'm shocked."

I blew out a breath.

She tilted her head at me. "Unless..."

"No. Just sex. Killian's firm about not being one for commitment. What about you? What's been going on with you?"

She glared. "Nuh-uh, we're not done talking about this."

I pulled out my purse and dug around in it for the piece of paper from earlier. I shoved it at her.

She squinted at me, but then her mouth dropped open when she saw the image on the paper. "Aw! Does it feel real now?"

"So much so."

She set down her wine and squeezed me into a hug. "I cannot wait to spoil your kid. How's Killian feeling about it?"

I frowned. "He's been weird lately. Anytime I mention getting out of his hair soon, he gets all broody."

She pet Poppy's head in her lap. "Interesting..."

"What?"

"Maybe he doesn't want you to get out of his hair."

I shook my head.

That was definitely not the case. Killian had been so

firm about who he was, even after he bared his soul to me about why he was that way.

She didn't look convinced. "Do you want to move out?"

"Yes."

If I didn't get out of his house, these feelings that were growing inside me were going to sprout. I had to guard my heart around Killian. I wasn't even sure if these were my own feelings. Or the hormones from the baby.

Freya took another sip of her wine. "Okay. So I found more apartments that could be great options for you if you want to look this weekend."

"Sure."

She glanced around her living room. "Or my offer still stands."

I couldn't take her up on the offer to move in with her. My bestie loved me, and she'd love my baby, but she was a single, carefree woman. She didn't want to deal with midnight feedings or a baby who doesn't sleep through the night. Especially someone who didn't want kids. Freya would be my kid's fun aunt, but I didn't need her to bear the burden of childcare with me. That would be too much pressure.

An image of doing that all on my own in a rundown apartment came to mind. I never wanted to be a single mom, but I had to remind my heart that was my future. I had to physically shake the image away.

"Tell me about your latest date," I urged her. "Catch me up on everything."

"I slept with one of my dad's firefighters," she said with a grimace.

"Wait, for real? I thought you said never again."

She wrinkled her nose. "Firefighters are such douches. This guy sucked in bed, too. I had to fake it."

"No!"

I never had to fake it with Killian. Ever. I couldn't always say the same about Doug.

Damn, that made me sound like a bitch. Doug had been my husband. I loved him with all my heart, and his death had devastated me. I couldn't keep comparing him to Killian. We had a good relationship, despite those divorce papers I found or the mother-in-law from hell. It had been good... until it wasn't.

Freya frowned. "I'm gonna go on a hiatus."

I crossed my arms over my chest and narrowed my eyes at her. I did not, for a single second, believe that sentence. "Do you hear the words out of your mouth?"

She laughed. "I'm serious, Shevy."

We burst into laughter together. Poppy howled at the noise, and Freya threw her favorite toy. Poppy jumped from the couch and tossed her rope back to Freya.

I rubbed a hand down my stomach. I jumped at the sudden movement below my hand.

Freya sat up straight, ignoring her dog for a moment. "Are you okay?"

"The baby's moving around a lot now. She's really in there, Frey."

My bestie pulled me into a big hug. "I cannot wait to meet her. Auntie Frey-Frey's gonna spoil her rotten."

I hugged Freya back. "I can't wait."

She pulled away. "I bet you I can hold out until your baby's born."

I chuckled. When pigs fly.

"I'm serious. No more men for me until you have the baby."

"I don't believe you."

"Believe in me, Shevy."

"You're so full of crap," I teased.

She grinned. "I'm glad you came over. I missed these nights."

"Me too. Sorry for being an awful friend."

"You have an excuse." She knocked back the rest of her glass of wine. "Okay, can we talk about the baby shower again? Your mom and Mary Pat have been non-stop about it."

I groaned, and Freya melted into laughter. It was going to be a long couple of months before I had this baby. Thank God for my bestie keeping me sane in this all.

CHAPTER TWENTY-SEVEN

KILLIAN

I flicked through the TV channels, trying to find something to keep my attention. The house was quiet without Siobhan here. I used to welcome that, but tonight, the absence of sound echoed off my walls.

I landed on the hockey network. The Bulldogs weren't playing, but I settled on a national game between the Carolina Thrashers and the New York Gladiators. God, I hated both teams. Try as I might, I quickly lost focus in the game.

I could go to the pub, except Brian would pull me behind the bar. Although I needed the money, so that wasn't a bad idea. I could try to pick up someone at the Brewery or the Drakesville Tavern.

Scratch that. The Tavern sucked. I worked there before Brian got me the job at Sullivan's. The owner was a piece of shit who barely paid his staff. Fuck that.

This was what my nights were like before I got Siobhan pregnant and moved her into my home. I got to do what I wanted when I wanted, and I didn't have to answer to anyone. If this was a taste of life without her, I wasn't sure I wanted it.

I scrubbed my hands over my face. What was I saying? Of course, I wanted my freedom. That was why I never got involved with anyone. It was too much after what Liz had done.

I scrolled through my phone. None of the names in there wanted anything to do with me. I opened one of the hookup apps and swiped over a couple of profiles before I realized they all bore a striking resemblance to the woman who had been sleeping in my bed for the past couple of weeks.

I missed her.

Goddamnit. I wasn't supposed to feel that way. I should relish this time alone.

I flicked off the TV and stormed out of the house. I needed to get out of here. All this house did was remind me of the things I couldn't have.

I got in my car and drove over to my parents' house. Maybe Ronan could distract me with a home improvement project. I swear he hadn't moved out of Mom and Dad's because Mom kept giving him more shit to do.

I entered the house and greeted my parents, who sat in the living room watching TV.

Mom gave me a big smile. "Hi, honey."

Dad nodded at me in greeting.

"Hey."

Mom tilted her head. "What's going on?"

"Nothing. Ronan around?"

"Shed," Dad explained.

I nodded and walked out the back door before Mom could interrogate me. I entered the shed and found my brother putting the finishing touches on the crib. Seeing the beautiful stained wood handcrafted with Celtic knots and our name MURPHY in the center squeezed my heart.

"Whoa," I breathed out.

Ronan looked up at my voice. "Hey man, perfect timing. I was about to call you and see if I could bring it over."

"Wow."

I walked around the crib, admiring my brother's craftsmanship. Ronan was the handyman in the family. He worked hard to build up his landscaping business, but he also was a jack-of-all-trades. He was the brother you called when you wanted to rip up carpets or put in a new bathroom.

I ran my hand over the wood. This crib was so much better made than the cheap shit at the big department stores. Siobhan would love it.

"What do you think?" Ronan asked.

"It's awesome. She's gonna love it."

He wiped the sweat off his brow. "Well, I made it for you. Since she's moving out."

I tightened my grip around the crib's handrail. "Right."

"Do you want to take it over?"

I nodded. "Yeah. I still gotta put the wallpaper up. You wanna help? I don't have shit to do tonight, anyway."

He crossed his arms over his chest. "Okay. What's going on?"

"Nothing," I lied.

Thankfully, Ronan didn't poke at me. He either knew I didn't want to talk about it, or he couldn't tell I was lying. Probably the former.

I helped him carry the crib into his work truck. We laid

a tarp down and secured it, even though it wasn't that far of a drive to my house.

I waved to him and got into my truck. Back at my house, I helped Ronan bring the crib inside.

"Where do you want it?" he asked.

"Let's put it in the hall for now while we work on the wallpaper."

We left it in the hall and stepped into the nursery. Ronan put a hand on the walls we had painted earlier. We had painted them a soft pale yellow that brightened up my previous grey and dull office. We left off the accent wall since we planned on covering it with wallpaper.

"This came out good," he said.

"You think we need another coat?" I asked.

He shook his head. "Nah. But lemme do the trim. We missed some spots."

Ronan got to work on fixing the trim so it looked even. I went downstairs and grabbed us beers. I pulled two bottles of 611 Ale out of my fridge and joined Ronan back in the nursery.

I needed a project tonight. It had been too quiet in here earlier without Siobhan, but doing this kept my mind at ease. It quieted the raging storm in my heart.

I handed Ronan a beer, and I sipped on mine while I watched him finish his work.

"You gonna tell what's really bothering you?" he asked.

"No," I grumbled.

"No?"

"Nothing's wrong," I lied.

Ronan set his paintbrush down on the paint tray and examined the wall.

He stood and turned toward me with his hands on his

hips. "We both know you're a terrible liar. Is Siobhan at the pub tonight? Is that what's wrong with you?"

I gritted my teeth. No. That wasn't what was wrong with me. "Man. If you're not gonna help me with the wallpaper, you can fuck off."

He let out a light laugh. "Damn, you miss her."

"She went to Freya's for the night."

His eyes widened. "What did you do?"

"Nothing," I protested. "Girl's night."

"Ah."

I pushed him. "What asshole?"

His lip upturned into a smug grin. "You miss her."

"No, I don't. Can we get back to work?"

He shook his head but picked up the package that the wallpaper was in, reading off the directions on the back. He took out the provided squeegee and unrolled the first panel. He held it up against the edge of the wall and gently laid it on the surface. I stood back and gave him direction, but my brother was meticulous and got the first panel on perfectly. He used the squeegee to get the air bubbles out, and then I helped him with the next panel.

We worked together, getting the rest of the wallpaper up in no time. I stood up and examined our work while Ronan went around using his knife to trim the excess material.

We retrieved the crib from the hall and put it against the woodland creature-themed wall. There was still some decorating I wanted to do on the blank walls. We also needed a changing table and a rocker for when Siobhan nursed.

Dammit. She wasn't staying put. She made that so clear to me. I didn't need that shit if she wasn't sticking around.

Ronan nudged my arm. "Okay. You gotta talk now."

"Man, I don't gotta do shit."

He glared at me. "What's up your ass tonight?"

I rubbed the back of my neck. "What if I don't want her to leave?"

Ronan groaned. "Then you gotta use your words, dumbass."

"But what if..."

"Christ. Killian, I need you to answer something for me."

"Yeah?"

He poked me in the chest. "Do you love Siobhan?"

I stepped back at the thought of that. No. I didn't love her. That wasn't what this was.

But she had only been gone for a couple of hours, and I already missed her something fierce. And my heart ached at the idea of her moving out of my house. I couldn't love her and risk she'd yank it all away like Liz had.

"No," I told my brother firmly, hoping he wouldn't catch me in a blatant lie.

Ronan stepped back and took a large drink of his beer. "You wanna watch the end of the Thrashers game?"

He knew when to change the subject.

I nodded.

He stood back and took a picture of the room. "It looks great, Kill."

We went downstairs and flopped down on the couch. I found the remote and turned on the game. The third period only had a little left, and the Thrashers were up 2-0.

My phone buzzed, and I grinned at a message from Siobhan.

> SIOBHAN: Freya would like to put in her
> name as an option.

ME: She wishes!

SIOBHAN: Maeve?

ME: That's a fairy.

SIOBHAN: Niamh?

ME: Again with the Irish names! Ruby?

SIOBHAN: Ew.

Ronan nudged me. "So, how was the appointment?"

"Good. Baby's all good. But Siobhan's driving me up a wall with the Irish names."

He laughed. "Your name's basically Irish McIrish."

"I didn't pick it!"

The announcer on the TV screamed out, and we lifted our heads to the screen as the Thrashers sank an empty-netter to end the game. It was a good game, but I didn't care because it wasn't my team.

"Nice!" Ronan cheered.

We watched the post-game interviews, waiting to finish our beers.

"Lachs says he asked Siobhan to help with maternity photos for his portfolio."

I nodded. "Yeah, I think we're gonna go into the studio next month to get some shots for him. Siobhan will be further along then."

"That's cool."

I shrugged. "He needs our help."

"And Siobhan will love having those."

"Sure."

He kicked my foot. "Are you going to be straight with me now?"

I kicked him back. Not sure why he was on my ass right now. "About what?"

"Did you lie to me earlier?"

I drained the rest of my beer.

"Killian..."

"Yes," I muttered.

"Then maybe you should tell her."

I set my beer on the coffee table. No, I couldn't. Siobhan was ready to get out of my house and away from me. She might enjoy her time in my bed, but she didn't have any feelings for me. And that was fine because I was a good baby daddy, but I'd never be boyfriend material. Not ever again.

Ronan left a little while later, leaving me to stew in my thoughts. I shut the TV off and walked upstairs. I took a shower and crawled into bed. Siobhan's pregnancy pillow still lay in the bed from our nap earlier. I breathed in the scent of her shampoo on it.

I never felt like my bed was empty before. Not until this woman came into my life and stole my heart.

But opening my heart again risked it getting torn to shreds again. I couldn't have another Liz on my hands. Once Siobhan found her new apartment, everything would go back to normal. We'd co-parent, sure, but I could go back to my bachelor life, and this melancholy would disappear. I'd forget about how she made my heart feel again. This was just a passing phase.

CHAPTER TWENTY-EIGHT

SIOBHAN

"Would it be wrong if we just named the baby Bean?" Killian asked with an exaggerated sigh as we walked hand-in-hand over to Lachlan's studio.

I laughed.

I honestly didn't hate that idea. We had been locked in a battle of wills over the last month about potential baby names that I wanted to wring his neck. We always seemed to work out those arguments between the sheets. Had to admit I didn't hate that. Although we had to adjust so I wasn't uncomfortable now that the baby was growing more.

"Maybe a nickname?" I suggested.

He rubbed his beard, a habit I learned he did when he was mulling something over. I loved running my fingers through the soft hair on his face. Or when he rubbed it against my thighs.

Geez. These pregnancy hormones were making me a puddle of libido. What had gotten into me?

"Admit you don't hate it," he said. I didn't have to look at him to know he had that annoying, smug look on his face.

"I like it."

"What about that, then?"

"Let me think about it."

He hung his head and groaned.

"We'll figure it out," I reassured him.

We walked past the coffee shop, and I waved at Willow from inside. She excitedly waved back while ringing up customers.

A pang of guilt spread through me at seeing her alone behind the cash register with a line of people waiting. If I tried to pick up hours, Killian might lose it. I didn't need to stress myself out, and since the baby was healthy, I hated to admit that cutting my hours had been the best course of action.

Killian pulled open the door to Lachlan's studio. The name was painted on the front door, reading Lachlan Murphy Photography. It was simple and to the point.

Inside, the studio was bright and cheery. On the left was the desk where Lachlan sat waiting for us. Behind him, he had blown up big canvases of his photography. There was a photo of two brides as they kissed as a married couple for the first time, one of a straight couple getting engaged, and a fierce-looking photo of Eilish belting out a song for Celtic Kiss. The last photo was a self-portrait of Lachlan in a commanding pose with the bisexual flag wrapped around his shoulders. I loved that he was so unabashedly himself.

I scanned around the room. He had a soft-looking couch on the right where his clients could wait, and in front of it, further into the space, was a backdrop prepared for today.

Lachlan gave me a big smile. "Hey, you two. Cute dress."

I beamed and removed my hand from Killian's and dramatically shoved it into the pocket. "Thanks. It has pockets."

I did a little twirl, showing off the new maternity dress Freya and I had found last weekend. It was a cute red one with little white flowers and had been the pick-me-up I had needed after the apartments we looked at had been such duds. We had a couple more we wanted to view, but I wasn't exactly wowed by even the pictures.

The corner of Killian's mouth twitched like he was trying not to smile. We perfectly matched today with him wearing a red plaid flannel that made him look like a lumbersnack. His beard was freshly trimmed, and he got his hair cut yesterday in preparation. Freya came over and put my hair in loose beach waves and did my make-up before she had to be at school. She made me look so glamorous. She was a wizard at the make-up table.

"You look like a lumberjack," Lachlan said to his brother.

"He looks hot," I blurted out.

Lachlan gave a sideways glance to Killian, who just shrugged. "Let's get this over with."

Lachlan shook his head and led us over to the backdrop. He positioned Killian behind me. Instinctively, Killian wrapped his arms around me, putting his hands on my belly while I placed my hands above his.

Lachlan ran in front of us and grabbed his camera. "Okay, that's perfect. We'll do a couple of shots in the studio, and then we'll go over to the gazebo in the square."

"That's fine," I told Lachlan, sensing Killian's rebuttal. "Shots in the square will look awesome."

Lachlan clicked away at his camera, taking as many

shots as possible in the studio. He repositioned us a few times, much to Killian's annoyance.

Lachlan set down his camera and walked over to a box. He pulled some props out and handed me a sign with a rainbow.

"Did you bring the ultrasound picture?" he asked.

Killian pulled it out of his back pocket. "Yeah, why?"

I knitted my eyebrows together as I stared at the sign.

"I know this is your rainbow baby," Lachlan explained.

Oh.

Oh wow, this family.

I blinked back the tears at the thoughtfulness.

Panic struck across Lachlan's face. "Oh no. Was it something I said?"

"Asshole, you can't make Siobhan cry," Killian seethed.

I carefully wiped the tears from my eyes so as not to smudge my make-up. "It's okay. Thank you. I prayed for this baby for so long."

Lachlan sprinted over to the counter, where he grabbed a box of tissues. He handed it to me. "Take a minute."

I took the offered tissues and ran off to find the bathroom. Inside the bathroom, I fixed my make-up. I hadn't expected to cry during this photo session. Lachlan was a gentle soul and so empathic. From the anguished expression on his face, he felt terrible about making me cry.

I never thought I'd be at the end of my second trimester and getting maternity photos with anyone other than my husband. Guilt swirled around in my chest for almost forgetting about Doug. The longer I stayed with Killian, the more I forgot why he was a bad idea. My heart was getting big feelings that it had no right to feel.

I dabbed at my eyes once more and took a deep breath.

We were doing this for Lachlan's sake. I had to remember that.

I tossed my tissues in the trash and left the bathroom, my tears now cleared away.

"Okay?" Killian asked.

I gave him a reassuring smile. "Sorry. Pregnant tears. I'm ready."

Lachlan brought his camera up to his face again as we got back into position. He clicked away, taking shots of me holding up the rainbow sign. He directed us into different positions. While I held the rainbow sign, Killian held up the ultrasound. Then Lachlan had us change, so I was holding up the ultrasound, and Killian's hands were splayed across my belly protectively.

The baby was really active today. Maybe Bean sensed my torrent of emotions because she was kicking all over the place. Killian had yet to feel her, and I knew that bothered him, but she made her presence known to me.

After some more shots in the studio, Lachlan led us outside, and we walked over to the town square. He took a couple of photos of us in front of the gazebo.

While he was positioning Killian in front of me so we were in profile, Killian's eyebrows shot up, and he pulled his hands away from my belly. "What was that?"

The panic made his voice crack.

I pulled his hand back and placed it on the spot where I'd felt the movement. "That's the baby. Can you feel that?"

He nodded, a mix of emotions swimming across his face.

I put my hand on top of his. All the while, Lachlan's camera clicked away. "That's Daddy, Bean."

"Wow..." Killian breathed out.

I nodded.

His eyes were shiny as he felt around my belly. That made my heart lurch. This strong, stubborn man looked like he was about to cry at feeling his baby inside me for the first time.

I gasped when he bent and took my mouth, his emotions coming out in the kiss. He was so wrapped up in me, he didn't stop to think about what he was doing. I let him kiss me until I was out of breath, all the while knowing that Lachlan was taking pictures of us.

He pulled away and knelt down to kiss my stomach. He whispered soft words I couldn't hear to the baby. Lachlan was getting awesome shots for his portfolio, but I didn't dare remind Killian of that.

He stood and pressed his forehead against mine in a sweet embrace. I leaned up and kissed him, giving in to the moment. I had imagined this so many times with Doug. I never imagined Killian would be the man I created life with.

Pregnancy hormones. Just pregnancy hormones. I didn't love Killian. Loving him was a recipe for a broken heart.

Lachlan cleared his throat. "You know...I offer boudoir photos, too, but I'm not sure we can do those in public."

I pulled away, realizing I had been gripping the lapels of Killian's flannel. He also somehow had hiked me up into his arms, my thigh-high boots wrapped around his waist.

Oh shit. We got carried away.

Lachlan gave us a grin. "I'm serious. If you guys want to do that, too, I could use more shots. Makes sense how you two got in this situation. I've done a couple of maternity boudoir shoots."

I felt my face flush with heat while Killian gently

lowered me to my feet. "I thought you were supposed to be the shy one."

Killian laughed at his brother's bold statement. "He's not wrong, darling. I had fun making the baby."

"Killian," I said in a warning tone.

He ignored me and turned back to his brother. "Are we done now?"

Lachlan rolled his eyes. "Yes, grumpy. I got what I needed. Probably more than necessary."

"Thank you, Lachs," I told him.

He waved me off. "No, thank you, this will be great. I want to build up my business in Drakesville, and I need all the help I can get."

"We appreciate it," I told him.

Lachlan's ears went pink, and he dipped his head down. He was so modest. I had looked at his portfolio on his website, and he was very talented. I hadn't realized he had done all the new photography of the pub, too. I could see him doing well here in town for years to come.

We said goodbye to Lachlan and headed back to Killian's house. I couldn't wait to see how the photos turned out. Lachlan said he'd bring some preliminaries to family dinner.

Tonight, Killian and I were closing down the pub again. We quickly changed into our work clothes, but before we were out the door, Killian bent to my belly again. "Hey, Bean. I love you so much. Don't give your mama too much grief, okay? We can't wait to meet you, baby."

I choked back the tears at his kind words.

He stood, and before I could stop him, he kissed me again. It was the kind of kiss you gave to someone you loved. Not the woman you'd never commit to.

I had to find an apartment and get out of here. My heart

was already trying to convince me that falling in love with Killian was a good idea. Spending every waking hour together was doing a number on me. He didn't love me and never would. The sooner I put distance between us, the better.

Tomorrow, I'd call those other apartments and gain my independence again. Once there was distance and we were co-parents, everything would go back to normal. Even if it broke my heart in the process.

CHAPTER TWENTY-NINE

KILLIAN

"*D*arling, let's go!" I yelled up to Siobhan.

I stood pacing in my kitchen, waiting for her to be ready to go over to my parents' house. I wasn't sure what was taking her so long. It was just family dinner, like we had every Sunday. Or at least every one we could attend. The only time she didn't come was if she was working, and even then, Mom got upset about that because Siobhan was part of the family, and she wanted us all there.

"Gimme one second!" she yelled down.

A few minutes later, she descended the steps. She wore a deep red dress that clung to her every curve, her now bigger pregnant belly on display. She wore black flats after complaining that her boots didn't fit on her swollen feet anymore. Her dark hair was in those pretty curls again, and I wanted to sink my hands into her long locks. I probably would later.

She wore a ruby drop-shaped pendant around her neck

that I only noticed because it set against her breasts, making me stare.

"Killian," she snapped.

I lifted my head. "Huh?"

"My eyes are up here."

"Then stop looking so sexy."

She rolled her eyes and fiddled with her earrings that matched her necklace. "I couldn't find these. They're my favorites."

"You love rubies?"

She nodded. "My favorite color and my birthstone."

I calculated something in my head. "Bean will have the same stone."

"If she comes by her due date."

I held out my hand toward her and she took it, walking with me outside hand-in-hand. She didn't fight me when I helped her into the passenger seat of my truck. As the baby grew, her stubborn resolve was slipping.

I drove over to my parents' house and helped her out of my truck once there. She threaded her fingers through mine, not letting go even when I walked inside.

"Hey, Mom!" I called out. "We're here."

"Kitchen!" Mom yelled back.

Siobhan slipped away toward Mom, and I frowned at the loss of her presence beside me. I found my brothers in the living room, drinking beers and watching the hockey game.

"There he is," Brian said and handed me a beer.

I nodded in thanks and popped the top off the bottle.

Lachlan jumped up and searched for his messenger bag. "I want to show Siobhan, too, but I have some of the photos done."

Finn moved, letting Lachlan sit beside me. He opened a

folder, and an image of Siobhan and me appeared. I was behind her and had both hands on her belly. I held the ultrasound against her while she held the rainbow sign below it. She would love this one.

Lachlan flipped to the next page, showing me kneeling in front of Siobhan and kissing her belly. That was right after I felt my child for the first time. A hand squeezed my heart at the memory.

He was showing me the photos out of order. In the next one, I was kissing Siobhan and had my hands on her belly.

Lachlan turned to me. "This last one is a bit much, so I'm not using it, but I figured you'd want it."

Of course, all my brothers leaned over to see.

In the photo, Siobhan was in my arms, her legs wrapped around my waist. We were kissing as if the photo wasn't being taken. Like we forgot Lachlan was there...because we kinda did. She gripped my shirt like she wanted to get as close to me as possible, and my hands were firmly on her ass.

Lachlan closed the folder and handed it to me. "You should tell her you love her already."

My other brothers nodded in agreement.

Ronan got up and grabbed a box behind him. "I made some frames that match the crib. They'd look great in the nursery."

I took the box and peered inside at the handcrafted wooden picture frames. I loved them.

"You don't want her to leave, do you?" Brian asked.

"No," I whispered so quietly, I hoped they hadn't heard me.

Anytime she brought up going to look at apartments, I changed the subject. I knew she was still looking, and she made comments about me getting my life back all the time.

But I didn't want the life I had before her and the baby dropped into my life.

"Because you love her," Ronan said.

"Of course he does, you ding-dongs!" Finn cut in. "Everyone can see except for them."

I raised an eyebrow at him. That was certainly the pot calling the kettle black.

Brian shook his head, sensing what I wanted to say. "Oh, we'll deal with him and Eilish later. This is about you and Siobhan. Why don't you tell her?"

I scratched the label of my beer. "She doesn't feel the same."

Lachlan leaned over and opened the folder on my lap. "Look at this photo."

I stared down at it, of the two of us in that passionate embrace. We looked like the cover of one of her romance novels. It was kinda ridiculous.

"Show her what I saw behind my camera," Lachlan urged.

"Before it's too late," Ronan warned.

I couldn't argue with them because then Mom yelled for us that dinner was ready. I put the folder in the box Ronan gave me and followed my brothers into the kitchen.

Mom had made shepherd's pie again because Siobhan loved it and had been craving it. She had even been waxing poetic about how much she loved Mom's home-cooked meals.

"Where's Eilish tonight?" Siobhan asked and nodded at her empty chair.

"Not here," Finn said dryly.

"Finnegan Murphy," Mom scolded. "Don't be rude."

"She's busy," he answered but stabbed at his food.

Siobhan shot me a concerned look. I mouthed 'later' to her, and she nodded.

Mom knew it was time to change the subject and turned back to Siobhan. "So...can we have the baby shower now?"

"Mom, give it a rest," I groaned.

Siobhan was more tactful. "I talked to my mom this morning, and I'm so happy you both want to help, but can it wait until I reach the third trimester?"

Mom understood what she meant and nodded. "Of course, honey."

"My parents want to come in for it. They haven't seen me since before I found out about the baby."

"Are they going to move back?" Dad asked.

Siobhan put a finger on her lip. "I'm not sure. They love Florida. I don't think my dad can handle winters in PA anymore."

"We're family now, so anything you need, honey, we can help," Mom reassured her.

"Thank you," Siobhan whispered and dipped her head down. Her voice was shaky, a sign she was holding back tears. Last night, she cried at a car commercial. Her tears were coming on suddenly and for no reason lately.

"So anyway, do you want to see the photos I took of them?" Lachlan cut in, trying to relieve the tension.

"Yes!" Kelsey and Mom cheered in unison.

I nodded at my brother in thanks, and he gave me a sympathetic smile. My brothers were a pain in my ass, but they could be good for something. Sometimes.

I lay awake, staring up at my ceiling, while Siobhan snored soundly beside me. She didn't believe me about the snoring, but it was so cute I couldn't be mad about it.

After dinner with my parents, I took the box Ronan had handed me and shoved it into the back of my truck. Siobhan didn't even ask what it was. We spent the rest of the night on the couch. She started a new knitting project while we watched old CSI episodes.

I couldn't imagine what my routine was going to be like when she finally left. That scared me so much that I couldn't sleep.

I carefully pulled the comforter off my body and crept out of bed. I shut the door behind me as quietly as I could and padded into the nursery. I pulled out the box of photo frames and took three out. Opening up the folder Lachlan gave me, I flipped through all the images and made quick work of putting them in the frames.

I sat on the floor of my baby's nursery and stared at the three photos in front of me. While I studied the photos of Siobhan and me sharing our love for our baby, I knew the truth. The truth that I had been trying so desperately to hide.

I was in love with Siobhan O'Connor.

I loved her with all my heart, even more than I had ever loved Liz.

It wasn't because she was carrying my unborn child. It was because I loved *her*. It happened slowly and then all at once. I had resisted it at every turn, reminding her every chance I got that I was the guy you took to bed but never the one you kept. I was the town bicycle, and that was never gonna change.

Until it did. When I brought this woman into my home. I was in love with the stubborn woman who would rather stay in and knit in front of the TV instead of going out. With the woman who fit in with my family better than Liz ever had. Who came to my rescue and showed all the women in Drakesville that I was decidedly off the market, even when I didn't want to be.

Because the thought of her leaving made me want to fall down onto my knees and beg her to stay. My heart squeezed inside my chest at the idea of us raising our baby in different homes.

I ran a finger down the photo of me kissing Siobhan's belly.

It was there at two in the morning, sitting in my baby's room, that I realized I had to do something to win Siobhan's heart. Before it broke my own.

CHAPTER THIRTY

SIOBHAN

*F*reya gave me a thumbs-up as I peered around the apartment. I was so tired of looking at apartments. But this one was perfect. Like I found the golden egg and had to jump on it.

The place was in an apartment complex just on the line between Drakesville and Green Willow. It was within my budget and had a second bedroom so the baby could have their own room. It was small but livable, and it even had a washer and dryer unit in the kitchen.

So why was I so apprehensive?

I rubbed my belly, hoping Bean would help me decide, but my heart told me not to leave Killian.

I had gotten so used to waking up beside him. To kissing him good morning or afternoon, based on our schedules. To spending my night next to him on the couch. Leaving him behind made me want to break down in tears, but I had no right to feel this way. I wasn't supposed to fall in love with the most unavailable man in town. We were just supposed to be co-parents.

"What's wrong?" Freya asked.

I shook my head. "I don't want to decide right now."

She frowned at me. "Okay..."

I said goodbye to the landlord, telling him I needed to think it over. He reminded me it wouldn't last, but I had to talk to Killian about this. It was his baby, too. He deserved to have a say in where she was raised.

Freya didn't say a word until we were back in her car. "Okay, what's going on?"

I burst into tears, and her face fell.

She dove into her glove compartment and thrust a handful of tissues at me.

She stared at me as I blubbered through the tears, trying to tell her what was going through my head.

She handed me another tissue. "Wipe your eyes. Then talk."

I dabbed at my eyes and took a deep breath. "I'm in love with Killian."

She gave me a 'well, duh' look and rolled her eyes. "Yeah, everyone knows that."

"What?"

"Why do you think I pushed you so hard to move in with him?"

I glared at her. "I didn't love him then."

"Maybe not, but I saw the potential. This guy who was known as the town hoe wanted to step up and be there for you. It seemed more honorable than the man you married. Plus, he's so hot, and I knew you'd be cute together."

"That didn't mean I'd fall so hard for him. This is such a bad thing. He doesn't love me."

She squinted at me. "Are you sure?"

"Yes."

"Are you really sure, Shevy? The man who dropped everything and comes at your beck and call doesn't love you?"

I shook my head. "He's been so clear about his intentions."

She gave a disappointed shake of her head and started her car. "You two need to talk because if you can't see what literally everyone else can, then you have a bigger problem than I thought."

What was she even talking about?

I didn't argue with her, and she pulled her car out of the parking lot. I stared out the window while we drove back to Killian's house, reflecting on her words.

Freya pulled up in front of Killian's house but didn't turn off her car. She gave me a big hug. "Shevy, I love you, but you need to tell Killian how you feel."

"I can't," I protested.

"Then don't complain when it's too late."

I got out of her car, her words still rattling around in my head, and walked inside.

I found Killian in the living room, sitting in his armchair. "Hey. How did the apartment hunting go?"

"Okay..."

Worry worked its way across his face. "What's wrong?"

"Nothing. I found an apartment."

A flash of hurt crossed his face but then immediately disappeared. Had he always reacted that way and I'd just never noticed before? Could Freya be right?

"Don't go," he whispered so quietly I thought he hadn't said anything.

"What?"

He reached out and grabbed my hand. "Please... don't go."

I tried to pull my hand away, but he held tight, squeezing my hand like he needed to be tethered to me, or I'd float away. "Killian, what are you saying?"

"I don't want you to go. Please, darling."

I stepped back from him, my thoughts scattered inside my mind. "I—"

He stood, stopping me in my train of thought. "I want to show you something."

I let him take me by my hand and lead me upstairs. He stopped at the door to the nursery. I hadn't gone in there since the day Ronan was here to help get it ready. I didn't care how Killian decorated his nursery for the baby. It was always going to be *his* nursery, and my opinion didn't matter.

He opened the door and gestured for me to walk inside first. I entered the room and gasped at what I saw.

The walls were painted a pale yellow except for the one wall that had a wallpaper of cutesy foxes, bunnies, deers, and bears in a woodland setting. Against it stood a wooden crib. I walked over to it and ran my hand over the well-crafted bars, noticing the little Celtic symbols carved into it. My heart was in my throat when I saw MURPHY etched into the center.

I spun around, noticing a changing table on the adjacent wall and a rocking chair in a similar style to the crib in the corner. I turned to say something to Killian, but then I saw the three photos hanging on the wall opposite the crib. They were in wooden frames that matched the details of the crib. If Ronan made these, he should stop the landscaping business and go into woodworking. The craftsmanship was impeccable.

That wasn't what made my mouth drop open. It was the images in those frames.

On the far left was the image of Killian kneeling in front of me and kissing my belly with the gazebo behind us. The middle photo was of us kissing after Killian felt the baby for the first time. The last image was when he had hiked me up into his arms, the two of us captured in a warm embrace.

Why would he put these up in the nursery when we both knew I was always leaving?

I turned toward him, and for the first time, Killian looked nervous. He took my hand and put it against his heart. "Siobhan..."

I knitted my eyebrows at him. "What's going on?"

"Please don't go."

"Why? That was always the plan. I'd find my own place, and you'd get to go back to your bachelor life. We'd still co-parent—"

He cut me off with a kiss, slanting his lips on mine. I melted into it, sighing into him.

He pulled away and cupped my face. "I love you, and I want you to stay. Forever." My face must have displayed my confusion because he tilted my head up to look into his eyes. "I love you more than you could ever know. With all my body and all my soul."

"That's because of the baby!" I blurted out.

Bean seemed to take that moment to be active, like she had something to say about it, too.

He shook his head and put his hand on my stomach. His eyes lit up when he felt the baby. "Hey, baby Bean. I know Mommy's confused, but I love her, and I'm trying to get it through her stubborn head. I hope you don't inherit that."

"Killian," I sighed.

He couldn't be serious right now. He couldn't love me

the way I loved him. He made it so clear that was never on the table.

"I love our baby, and I can't wait to meet her, but that's not why I love you," he continued. "The thought of not waking up beside you tears my heart to shreds."

"But all those things you said about Liz. That you'd never risk that again."

A smile played on his lip. "You're worth the risk."

"Killian. I don't know what to say."

This was not what I had been expecting at all. My emotions were swirling around, trying to get a grip on what he was saying to me. Could he really love me?

"Siobhan, please. I couldn't bear it if you left. Tell me you feel the same way."

"Of course I fucking do, you dumbass!"

He pulled back in shock. "What?"

"Why do you think I've been trying so desperately to get out of your house? I'm in love with you. And not because you're my baby daddy." I pressed my hand against his chest. "I fell in love with this heart. The one you hide from the world. Because I love the way you love your family, even if you want to literally knock sense into your little brothers."

He chuckled at that.

"You may annoy me sometimes, but the moment we found out about the baby, all you've done is take care of me. To give me the life I deserve. I love that you'll do anything to protect me and Bean. To keep us safe. And I love that you don't care that I'd rather stay home watching old CSI reruns and knitting instead of going out."

His lips twitched at that. "I want to be with you. What-ever that means."

"I love the way you give me what I need. And fight me

when I'm stubborn. I love every part you've shown me these past couple of months."

A frown morphed across his face. "Then what are we still arguing about?"

"I don't know!"

He didn't let me get another word in and slanted his lips on mine again. This kiss was one to last, the kind that told you just how much you were loved.

I pulled away from the kiss and cupped his face. "I want you to be honest with me."

"Of course."

"Are you sure?"

He frowned. "About what?"

"About us. Are you sure this is what you want? I never wanted to change who you are. It was why I had to keep away from you for so long. I don't want you to regret changing yourself because of me and the baby."

His face fell. "Siobhan, you did change me. You allowed me to unlock my heavily guarded heart. You wormed your way inside and made me see I could have love without getting hurt again."

"But is that what you really want?"

"Do you know what I did that night you slept at Freya's?"

I wrinkled my nose, trying to remember which night he was talking about. There had been a few times I went over for girl's night with Freya to spend much-needed time with her.

Oh... He was talking about when we started arguing about names.

Killian pulled my hands from his face and held them against his heart again. "I burned a hole in the hardwood, pacing the floors. I had to go see Ronan because I was clawing the walls without you."

"I was only gone for a few hours at that point."

He gave me a sheepish grin. "I know. But you got into my head about moving out soon, and I realized the thought of you leaving crushed me. I didn't want you raising Bean across town without me. I didn't want to wake up without you by my side stealing all the blankets."

I gave him a light shove on the shoulder. "I don't steal the blankets!"

He grinned. "Darling, you know you do. And I don't care. I love waking up to that pretty face and knowing I get to spend my days and nights with you."

Tears pricked my eyes, but I didn't let them fall. "That's exactly why I didn't sign the apartment lease today. I couldn't imagine waking up each morning without you. But you've been so firm on never wanting to be tied down."

He gave me a cocky grin. "Well, if you want to tie me down, I don't have a problem with that."

His smug, self-assured look had me tipping back my head in laughter.

"I've never been more sure of anything than how much I love you. I'm not letting you go so easily. So I'm asking again... Siobhan, please stay?"

I nodded. "You're not getting rid of me that quickly. Not ever."

He bridged the gap between us until our lips were almost touching. "Promise, stubborn woman?"

"Promise."

Our lips met in a searing kiss, sealing our promise to each other. It was urgent and desperate, but it was exactly what we needed.

I wrenched my lips away from his, trying to catch my

breath. "Bedroom," I panted out before I lost all sense and got down on all fours here in the nursery.

He gave me a wolfish grin. "Oh. What for?"

"You know what for. Show me how much you love me right now."

"Yes, ma'am!"

And then he did. Again and again, until the energy was sucked out of us both.

Afterward, I lay beside him in his bed—our bed—trying to catch my breath and wrap my head around this whirlwind of a day.

Killian loved me. He really loved me, and it wasn't just because I was carrying his child.

I nuzzled my head against the crook of his neck. "I love you. Did I tell you that yet?"

"You moaned it a lot, but tell me again," he said and brought my hand up to kiss the back of it.

I grinned. "I love you, Killian Murphy. More than you could ever know."

He wrapped a protective hand around my pregnant belly. "I love you too, Siobhan O'Connor. More than I ever thought possible."

Then he kissed me once more and showed me again how much. I didn't complain one bit. Killian Murphy was not the man I thought he was. He was something so much more, and I couldn't wait to keep peeling back the layers and fall more in love with him each day.

EPILOGUE

KILLIAN

END OF JULY

"Squeeze my hand," I told Siobhan. My gut wrenched at the look of pure anguish across her face. "I know, darling. I'm so sorry."

She squeezed my hand harder, shutting her eyes and wrenching out the worst sound I had ever heard. No way I was putting her through this again. Holy shit. How had my mom done this five times?

"You're doing great," the nurse encouraged her.

"I can't do this," she moaned. "Killian, make it stop."

That was like a punch to the dick. I hated that there was nothing I could do to make the pain of childbirth stop for my girlfriend.

The last few months of Siobhan's pregnancy had flown by. Her parents came in for her baby shower in May, and I finally got to meet them. Her dad and I bonded over loving hockey, which she never told me he liked. He was a good guy, and my mom and hers got on great. They were so glad Siobhan had my family in PA to help her.

We got along so well, her parents came to stay with us right before the birth. We had all been sitting down to dinner at my parents' house when Siobhan's water broke. It surprised all of us because everyone said your first baby was usually late. But not my daughter; she was punctual.

"I know, darling. I know it hurts," I reassured Siobhan again.

"You did this to me!" she screeched.

I wiped her forehead. Her hair was in a messy bun, and she was make-up less, but she had never been more beautiful to me.

"Almost there," Dr. Lee said. "One more push, Siobhan."

The most animalistic groan came out of her as she gave it her all, and then the sound of a loud cry broke out in the room.

I kissed Siobhan's forehead. "You did so good."

"I love you," she said.

"I love you more."

The doctor had me cut the umbilical cord, and they cleaned Bean up, taking her away for a couple of minutes to get her height and weight, setting Siobhan into a panic. I kissed her and reassured her until they brought our baby back.

The medical staff wrapped the baby up and placed her in Siobhan's arms. She wailed her little head off, but Siobhan kissed her. "Hi, Bean. I prayed so long for you. Mommy loves you so much."

"Are we going to keep calling her Bean?" I asked.

"Beatrix," Siobhan said suddenly. "Beatrix! We can call her Bean as her nickname."

"Yes! It's perfect."

Siobhan handed her off to me, and I got to hold my daughter for the first time. I cradled her in my arms, rocking her so she'd stop crying.

"I know, baby. The big world outside is so scary. I'll give you back to Mommy soon. I love you more than you could ever know."

"She's probably hungry," Siobhan said. She lay back in the hospital bed, exhausted. She was my little trooper. Both of my girls were.

I handed my daughter back and helped Siobhan unbutton her hospital gown. She held our daughter against her chest, guiding her through feeding. She sighed in relief when Bean finally fed.

I stroked my daughter's head while she ate. "She's just as gorgeous as her mama."

Siobhan laughed. "Baby, I look like I rolled in garbage."

"Cute garbage," I joked.

"Our family's champing at the bit to come see her, aren't they?"

I held back my groan. My phone had been buzzing throughout the whole labor, but my focus had been on Siobhan and our baby. They were the two people who mattered more than anything else. They were my focus and always would be.

Once we got home from the hospital, I'd prove that to Siobhan when I finally asked her the question I wanted to ask since I figured out how much I loved her.

Siobhan pulled the baby off her chest and burped her. I cheered at her loud belch.

"There's Daddy's girl," I joked.

"You can let Lachlan in, but no one else right now," Siobhan said.

"Why Lachs?"

"He's gonna take photos of us and the baby. I look like hell, but I want them."

I grinned and pressed a kiss to her temple. The baby squawked at me. "Oh, I'm sorry, my apologies." I bent to kiss the top of her head, too.

"Daddy's girl already," Siobhan teased.

"She already has me wrapped around her little finger. Just like her mama."

She smiled up at me, her eyes shiny with tears. "Thanks for forgetting a condom all those months ago."

I laughed. "I'm glad I forgot too. I wouldn't have gotten you and Bean out of it. Or have ever opened my heart again."

"I'm glad you did. You give me everything I've always wanted."

I beamed at that and kissed her again.

I jolted awake to the sound of my daughter's cries from the nursery.

Siobhan groaned. "I nursed her like an hour ago."

"I got her."

We'd been home from the hospital for about a week, and already, Bean was keeping us on our toes. I was taking a couple of weeks of paternity leave to be with Siobhan while she was on a longer maternity leave. Her parents were still here but found a hotel after a couple of sleepless nights. I didn't blame them.

I padded across the room and went out into the hall. I entered the nursery and found my daughter screaming her little head off. She had a pair of lungs on her and wanted us to know.

I picked her up. "Okay, baby, it's okay."

I bounced her in my arms, but she wasn't stopping. I took her over to the changing station and discovered that wasn't the problem. She might still be hungry.

"What do you think, Beanie? Is it time to ask Mommy that question?"

She cried some more.

I changed her into the onesie I had sneakily bought that read, 'Mommy, will you marry Daddy?'

She looked so stinking cute.

I stopped by the guest room, holding my daughter against me. She liked to be walked around a lot, so her cries had already subsided. I opened the top drawer and pulled out the ring box. I opened it, looking at the round ruby engagement ring I picked out for Siobhan.

"What will Mommy think? Will she say yes?"

Bean gurgled at me.

I shut the ring box and walked over to my bedroom. Siobhan sat up against the headboard but looked puzzled at the calm baby in my arms. "She's not hungry?"

"Nope. But Bean wanted to ask you a question."

Siobhan cocked her head, trying to read the words on the onesie. "Who bought that?"

"Bean did," I lied.

She squinted at me suspiciously. "Killian, what's going on?"

I handed off our daughter, and Siobhan stood her up to read the letters across her chest.

While she did, I knelt on the floor and held out the ring box so Siobhan could see what was inside.

"Oh my God," she gasped, it finally clicking. "Killian..."

"What? Our daughter's very demanding. She wants Mommy and Daddy to get married."

She bounced Bean in her arms. "Is that so, baby? Do you want Mommy to marry Daddy?"

"What do you say, darling?"

"I would have said yes months ago. If you had asked that night you confessed your feelings, I would have said yes then, too. I was that deep in love with you."

She held out her hand, and I slid the ring onto her finger. One day, we'd have matching wedding bands.

She wiggled her fingers as she admired the gemstone. "Although I'm glad you gave this to me now because my fingers were really swollen before." She stared at the ruby on her finger, and then tears leaked from her eyes. "It's my birthstone."

"Yes. I paid attention. You don't want a diamond?"

She shook her head. "Absolutely not. This is so thoughtful."

I got in bed beside her, and Bean launched at me. I grabbed her in my arms, and she immediately grabbed my beard. "Such a little stinker."

Siobhan smiled. "You're stuck with us now, Kill."

"I wouldn't trade it for anything."

She raised an eyebrow at me. "You wouldn't want your bachelor life back?"

I shook my head. "Nope. I've got everything I need right here."

ACKNOWLEDGMENTS

When I finished the MacGregory Brothers Brewing Company series, I said it wouldn't be the last you'd hear of my small town of Drakesville, PA. So technically this new series is a spin-off! But I hope new readers come to love Drakesville too.

Now onto those I want to thank! As always my editor Charlie Knight for championing this book and helping me with the trouble spots. My critique group for helping fine tune and listening to me work through plot issues. And of course to my beta readers Becky and Chris for their help as well.

I can't wait to bring you more of this series soon! Next up is Lachlan Murphy and I'm so excited for you to read his and Willow's story. It's a lot about Queer joy and I loved writing that.

ALSO BY DANICA FLYNN

PHILADELPHIA BULLDOGS

Take The Shot

Score Her Heart

Against The Boards

The Chase

The Fake Out

Game On

Risky Play

MACGREGOR BROTHERS BREWING COMPANY

Accidentally In Love

Trapped In Love

Temporarily In Love

ABOUT THE AUTHOR

Danica Flynn is a marketer by day, and a writer by nights and weekends. AKA she doesn't sleep! She is a rabid hockey fan of the Philadelphia Flyers. When not writing, she can be found hanging with her partner, playing video games, and reading a ton of books.